JUST SAY THE WORD

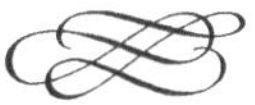

TIFFANY PATTERSON

PROLOGUE

*S*andra

Ten years ago ...

I can't have this baby. That was the mantra that'd been rolling through my mind all morning since my eyes first popped open. There was absolutely no way I could have the baby that had just been confirmed was growing in my womb. Not only was I unemployed, but I was just getting ready to enter my freshman year at Williamsport University on a full academic scholarship—a goal I'd worked long and hard for. Becoming valedictorian of my high school class hadn't been an easy feat, but I'd made it and earned the opportunity to study at such an exclusive university as a result.

There's no way I can have this baby.

Besides all of that, there was the matter of how this child was conceived. How could I look him or her in the eye? Surely, I couldn't love it the way a mother is supposed to love their child.

"Now that we have confirmed your pregnancy, let's discuss your options ..." the nurse practitioner at the local Planned Parenthood clinic I'd gone to began saying.

"O-options?" I questioned, looking up through watery eyes. My mind was reeling, and processing simple words was just too difficult to manage.

"Yes, Sandra." The petite woman with greying roots nodded and sat down in the chair opposite from me, granting me a sympathetic look. "Of course, your first option is to keep your baby. We offer prenatal services here, and I can give you a list of low-cost OB-GYNs in the city. There is also the option of giving your child up for adoption. If you go this route, we could still take care of your prenatal needs while also referring you to a few different agencies who work with parents looking to adopt an infant. Lastly," she paused, and I swallowed the lump in my throat, "there is the option of terminating your pregnancy. That is something we do here at this facility as well." Her voice was soothing, calm—as if she'd given this speech many times before but hadn't lost the empathy with which she gave it.

Termination.

She meant abortion. My hands instantly went to my still flat abdomen, clutching it. That had been my original intent in coming to this clinic. I'd had the pregnancy confirmed by the pregnancy test I'd purchased with the money I saved up from my grandmother. Each week she gave me an allowance to go out to eat or to the movies since she absolutely refused to let me get a job. Instead of food, for the past few days I'd skipped lunch and traveled on a bus across town to purchase the test where hopefully no one would know who I was. Two days prior I shed real tears when I found myself staring at two lines, confirming my greatest fear.

The next day I made an appointment with the clinic, hoping beyond hope that somehow, I'd just gotten a false positive. But deep down I knew. Me, the girl who actually *enjoyed* studying into the wee hours of the morning over going out to party with friends. Not like I had very many friends anyway, but still. And me, the girl who vowed to herself that she'd remain a virgin until marriage was now sitting in a clinic listening to a health care practitioner deliver my options on how to handle an unexpected pregnancy.

"H-how would it work?" I forced the questions from my lips.

"Which option, Sandra?"

"A-abortion." My answer was barely audible even to my own ears.

"Since it looks like you are very early in your first trimester, we can make your appointment for next week. By law, we are obligated to give you the details on your baby's gestational growth." Her voice seemed to carry a hint of annoyance on that last sentence.

I understood. So many laws were being pushed through at the federal and state level to reduce access to abortions. It placed health care workers and vulnerable women in a precarious position. One I'd never thought I'd be in myself.

I lowered my gaze to my hands that were placed in my lap. I thought about all of those conversations I'd heard my grandmother go on and on about how irresponsible women didn't need access to places like the one I was currently sitting in. They just needed to *close their legs and keep their heads in the books!* She'd rail on and on about the importance of abstinence-only programs in high schools. And because my grandmother was one of the smartest people I knew and the woman who raised me, I'd gone along with everything she'd taught me.

My hands went to my stomach again. *A baby.* Not a fetus, a baby. That was what I was carrying. That thought alone had me sitting up a little straighter. But could I love it? Like really love him or her? What if every time I looked into its eyes I only saw the way in which its presence came to be?

My eyelids fluttered closed and a warm feeling moved through me. I couldn't describe it aside from saying that it felt comforting. I let the feeling wash over me before re-opening my eyes.

I shook my head. "I can't abort this baby." I was unsure but my voice was steady, as if the words were coming from a place much deeper than my conscious mind.

"I understand if you don't want to have to walk through those protestors again when you come back. We can arrange for someone to escort you—"

I held up my hand, shaking my head again. "It's not that." The protestors holding up those horrific signs were extremely difficult to pass through the first time around, but I would've done it again *if* that's what I wanted. But it wasn't. "I'm going to keep my baby," I stated with an assurance that stunned even me. "And love her."

The nurse raised an eyebrow. "Her? Sandra, you're very early on in your pregnancy. Gender hasn't been determined—"

"I'm aware. I just have a feeling." Again, I had no idea where it came from, but just as sure I was of my next breath, I was sure that I was carrying a little girl.

"In that case, I'd like to provide you with some information on prenatal care and recommend vitamins you should be taking."

Feeling overwhelmed, I pushed out a deep breath. "Okay."

Fifteen minutes later, I chose to go out the back door of the clinic, hoping to avoid the protestors. In my bag was a list of prenatal vitamins and supplements recommended for expectant mothers, as well as a list of foods to make sure I ate enough of and foods to avoid while pregnant. I also had a list of doctors around the city who took either insurance, Medicare, or sliding scale forms of payment.

I sighed and hiked the backpack I'd stuffed all of the papers into on my back and raised the hood that was attached to my dark blue sweatshirt over my head. It was drizzling a bit, but the main reason I covered my head was to do my best to disguise myself from anyone who may notice me. The last thing I wanted was for the news getting back to my grandmother before I had a chance to tell her myself. I assured myself with the belief that though she'd be disappointed, she would eventually embrace me and this baby.

* * *

"Grandma!" I called as soon as I shut the wooden framed door behind me. We lived in a three-level brownstone in one of Williamsport's oldest neighborhoods.

"Sandra! What have I told you about yelling through the house?" my grandmother scolded as she rounded the corner, holding a glass of her homemade peach iced tea.

I groaned inwardly. The only time she made her peach iced tea was when she was having company over. And since it was a Saturday afternoon I knew it was likely women from her bridge club who were with her. Sure enough, a few paces behind my grandmother stood two women looking to be in their early fifties like my grandmother, both of whom I was familiar with.

"I'm sorry," I mumbled, staring at my grandmother's golden hue that was about two shades lighter than my own copper coloring.

"Oh, Dottie, you know how these teenagers are," Betsy stated from behind my grandmother's five-foot nine inch frame, before smiling over at me.

I gave her a small smile in return before lowering my gaze.

"Sandra will be nineteen in a few months. She is almost out of her teenage years. It's time she began acting like it."

I bit my tongue to keep from reminding my grandmother that I had spent nearly my entire teenage life *not* acting like a teenager. I was president of numerous clubs in school including the debate team, chess team, and the honor society. I had just graduated two months earlier as number one in my class and I was on my way to a very prestigious university on a full academic scholarship. Yet, somehow all of that was negated by the fact that I'd raised my voice a few octaves too high for my grandmother's liking.

I sighed and I had to ball my hands into fists and shove them into my pockets to keep from clutching my belly. I never wanted my future child to feel like they weren't good enough.

"We were finishing up anyway," Amy, the second woman with my grandmother, stated. "Dottie, the tea was lovely as usual."

"As were the pastries. We'll see you next week."

I nodded and mumbled partings to the women as they passed by me, along with my grandmother. Taking a few steps into the living room, I listened as my grandmother said her good-byes to her friends. I swallowed and inhaled deeply, mentally preparing myself for what needed to be said. I couldn't keep this secret. I was terrible at lying, and knowing that my baby was growing inside of my womb every day would kill me not to say out loud.

"Did you and Randy have a good time at the movies? He'll be heading off to Notre Dame soon."

A wave of nausea overcame me. It wasn't from the pregnancy. It was due to hearing *his* name. I'd made up a story about going to the movies earlier, and my grandmother had just assumed it was with him, my supposed boyfriend.

"Um, he got sick so we didn't go."

She paused, her forehead wrinkling. Her perfectly arched eyebrow raised. Not for the first time I noticed how well my grandmother was put together. At five nine she couldn't weigh anymore than one-hundred and twenty-five pounds, due not only to the healthy diet she fed the both of us but also the strict exercise regime she kept up five to six days a week. Her golden skin glowed healthily and her dark hair was pulled back into a neat bun at the nape of her neck. She wore a light grey, crew neck, cashmere sweater as well as black pants. This was her "around the house" attire. She never let anyone see her with a hair out of place.

"That's odd. I hope he's well enough to start practice soon. They begin well into the summer months for football season, don't they?" she inquired.

I shrugged.

She tutted. "Sandra what have I told you about shrugging? It looks sloppy."

"Sorry. I honestly don't know when R—" I broke off, unable to even speak his name. "He and I broke up weeks ago," I lied.

My grandmother tilted her head. "You told me you were going to the movies with him just this morning."

I shook my head. "I said I was going with a friend." I never said who. She'd assumed since *he* was the only friend I had. But, well, he wasn't that either.

"Well, who did you go—"

"I'm pregnant!" I blurted out much louder than I'd intended. I needed to say it before I lost my nerve. And it took a full ten seconds for my grandmother to fully process those two little words. But once she did, she repaid my surprise with one of her own. She hauled back with her right hand and smacked me clear across the face.

I gasped as my hand flew to my left cheek. At first, I was too stunned to feel anything. My grandmother had never hit me. But within seconds my cheek went from stinging to throbbing.

"All of these years," she began through clenched teeth as she took another threatening step toward me, "I sacrificed and took care of your ungrateful ass. I endured the shame of your birth and raising you after your mama ran off."

I flinched at her words. They stung more than the slap had.

"I sheltered you. Had you live in one of the best communities and sent you to a great school, and this is the way you repay me?"

I blinked, trying to hold back the tears, but it was useless. I knew she'd be upset, angered, but the vitriol I heard in her voice, I hadn't expected. I knew the story of my wild child mother who'd gotten pregnant at sixteen and stopped only so long as it took to give birth to me before she was out the door. I'd only met my birth mother twice in my life.

But I wasn't her.

"Does Randy know?" my grandmother demanded.

I swallowed, shaking my head. "I-it's not h-his," I stuttered.

"That's why you broke up, isn't it? Bad enough you went back on your purity promise, but you broke that poor boy's heart cheating on him! Just like your tramp mother!"

I gasped again. I'd never heard my grandmother use such harsh language. Especially, about her own daughter.

"I-I didn't—"

"Didn't what? Open your legs and act like a complete whore?"

No. I hadn't done that. But for some reason I couldn't let the words come out. I could see it in her eyes. She wouldn't believe me even if I did tell the truth.

"You're not keeping this baby!" she insisted.

My hands went to my stomach. "I can't give her up for adoption," I blurted.

"Her? You already know it's a girl?!" Her russet-colored eyes bulged as they dropped to my belly.

"I have a feeling." My voice had fallen to a whisper.

"Well, you're not keeping *her*. Nor are you giving it up for adoption."

My eyes swung upwards to meet my grandmother's. She couldn't be saying what I suspected she was saying.

"You're aborting it," she stated as if her word was final.

"What?" Ever since I could remember, my grandmother had been an advocate against abortion. She called it murder. Always said girls and women who got knocked up deserved to be forced to reckon with the consequences of their actions. She was one of the loudest proponents of a state bill that decreased the time period a woman could get an abortion to just twenty weeks. In short, my grandmother was the last person I'd ever expected to be standing here demanding I get an abortion.

"You heard me! You're aborting that baby!"

I was more scared than I'd ever been in my life. Add to that I was hurt by her words. But even those emotions didn't stop me from shaking my head in rebellion.

"I'm not killing my child." My voice shook but I held firm.

"Oh yes the hell you are!" she seethed. "I'm getting on the phone right now with Doctor Ludwig." The sentence was just barely out of her mouth before she whirled around and started toward the phone that sat on the shiny wooden end table next to the couch.

"No," I stated firmly.

My grandmother stilled, her spine straightening. Slowly, she turned to me. "No?"

"I'm not aborting my baby." Gone was the shakiness of a few moments ago. I'd made my decision. I was sure my once my grandmother got over her initial shock and disappointment she would come to see things my way. She would accept this baby.

"Then you will get out of my house."

Or maybe she wouldn't.

"Grandmo—"

"Don't grandmother me! You've made your decision. You wanted to spread your legs like a common hooker and dare to tell me no when I tell you how this needs to be handled?" She waved her hand in the air, shaking her head. "You will *not* embarrass me the same way your mother did. I will not raise that!" she spat out, pointing toward my stomach as if some alien life form was growing inside instead of a human baby.

"I'm not asking you to raise her. But I will be in school and—"

"I don't give a damn what you do. That child will never step foot in this house. Get out!" she ordered.

"Grandmother!"

"Now! I want you to pack your things and be out of my house within the next twenty minutes!"

"B-but where am I to go? I don't have anyone else."

"You should've thought of that before you got knocked up. Why don't you go live with whatever boy it was who did this to you."

A lump formed in my throat and my stomach lurched at the thought. That certainly wasn't an option. I'd rather die than do what she'd suggested.

"Of course, you can't go to him, can you? Well, you were grown enough to let this happen to you. Be grown enough to figure out how to raise this baby on your own. You have twenty minutes or I'm calling the police!"

I blinked as she stormed out of the living room. I knew she was serious. My grandmother would never get the police involved unless she meant it. And as a county court judge, my grandmother held a lot of sway in our community and with the police.

Resigning myself to the fact that I would have to find somewhere to stay for the night, I trekked my way through the living room and up the wooden staircase to my bedroom. Getting my duffle bag out of the closet, I stuffed as many of my clothes and belongings as I could into the bag. I grabbed a few of my books, my Vivaldi's Cello CD along with a few other classical CDs I loved, and some toiletries before heading out and back downstairs.

My ears perked up when I heard my grandmother's footsteps round the corner. Maybe she'd had time to think this over and realize how irrational she was being. I raised my gaze to meet her, hope filling my chest, but it was quickly extinguished. She brushed right past me, not even glancing my way. Instead, she moved to the front door, holding it open for me to pass through.

I opened my mouth to speak but nothing would come out. I couldn't tell her the truth—it was much better kept a secret I'd take to my grave. Besides, no matter what the truth was, I knew I was keeping my child. Come hell or high water.

My grandmother refused to look my way as I passed over the threshold to the outside. And as soon as I did, she swung the door closed to my back.

The loneliness I'd always felt growing up was even more pronounced in that moment. My grandmother had never been the most affectionate or loving person but she was there. She'd kept a roof over my head and kept me well fed, made sure my basic needs were tended to. Now that was gone.

I had no idea what I was going to do as I slowly ambled down the stone steps of the brownstone.

CHAPTER 1

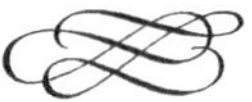

S*andra*

"Monique! Let's go. You're going to make Mommy late!" I yelled down the hall to my nine-year-old daughter, who I was sure had her face glued to her tablet playing one of her video games. She loved those things. And though I tried to limit the amount of time she spent in front of a screen, she got plenty of time in when I wasn't looking.

"Coming, Mommy!" she called back in that saccharine sweet voice of hers that let me know she was *definitely* playing her game when I'd specifically told her to go to her room to finish getting dressed.

"Monique, if you're not up this hall in tw—" My rant was cut short by her stampeding foot stomps as she ran up the hall from her bedroom toward the kitchen, fully dressed, her Dora Milaje Black Panther book bag hanging off her right shoulder.

"I'm here!" she sang with a grin spreading wide over her cinnamon-toned face.

My own heart smiled back though I tried to keep my face neutral. To think I used to spend my nights while pregnant wondering if I could truly love this little being the way a parent was intended to love a child. All of those thoughts were eradicated the moment her squirming body was placed in my arms while my legs were still in the stirrups. They'd never returned. It truly was love at first sight.

"Did you pack your insulin?"

She nodded. "Yup."

"Let me see."

"Mom—"

A lifted eyebrow and cocking my head to the side cut off her whining.

Pushing out a frustrated breath, she shook her head—reminding me of a woman with decades more life behind her who was trying to summon her patience with an unruly youngster. I smirked but hid it behind my hand. My daughter truly cracked me up sometimes.

"See. Plenty of insulin to last me all day. Just as I said."

I narrowed my gaze. "Watch your tone, little girl." I swatted her with the dish towel I'd been holding after cleaning up our breakfast dishes before turning back into our small, albeit comfortable kitchen with the wooden cabinets and drawers.

"Sorry, Mommy," she mumbled before heading to the living room.

Out of the corner of my eyes, I saw her reaching for the remote control.

"Don't you dare turn that television on."

"I just wanted to check the weather."

How could I forget? This month my daughter's obsession had been watching the weather forecasts. She claimed she wanted to be a meteorologist when she grew up. Like I said, that was *this* month. The previous month she wanted to be a rocket scientist, and the month before that it was a veterinarian. Those changes came after I had to tell her that no, we couldn't actually *go* to Wakanda so she could train to be one of the Dora Milaje. That was after I'd informed her that she couldn't shave her head to look like them either.

"All right, but just five minutes," I insisted from the kitchen as I rooted around in the refrigerator, packing up her snacks for the day.

"That's all I need. Last night I read there was a cold front moving over the Rockies. I wanted to see how that turned out."

"Un huh," I muttered while packing apple slices, a juice box, and the baked chicken and brown rice mixture we'd had the previous night into her lunch bag. I then moved on to packing my own lunch to take to work with me. It was a Saturday morning, but due to the high-profile case the attorney I worked for had taken on, a weekend day in the office a couple of times within the month had become the new norm. And I'd only been with this particular firm for about six months.

"I hope you remembered to compost that apple core," I heard behind me.

I turned to look down over my shoulder to see Monique's pensive brown eyes glancing between myself and the white bucket we kept in the corner of the kitchen for our food scraps.

"Would I forget such an important task?"

She smirked and shook her head.

Monique was serious about saving the environment also. Hence, her interest in the weather. Two years prior she'd come home from school having learned about just some of the destruction faced by our planet and asked me to help her do some research. Since then, we made recycling a natural part of our routine and found a company that collects our food waste to sell to local farmers instead of sending them to the landfill.

"Ready to go?" I questioned while zipping my lunch bag closed before handing Monique hers.

She nodded. "I get to spend the day with Aunt Kayla and Uncle Joshua," she sang excitedly. "You think Diego will be there, too?"

I made a face, uncertain. "I'm not sure. He might be spending the day with his parents at his house, sweetie." I turned to shut off the kitchen light.

"Okay." Her voice held a certain resignation.

Diego was the nephew of my physician turned friend, Kayla Reyes, now Kayla Townsend. I'd met Kayla about nine months earlier when I went to the doctor's office she worked at as an alternative doctor, seeking help on how to handle Monique's type one diabetes. We quickly went from patient and doctor to friends. Now, Kayla was married and expecting her first child with her husband, and she'd graciously offered to babysit Monique while I spent the morning and most of the afternoon working. Monique had developed a friendship with Kayla's nine-year-old nephew, Diego, as soon as they first met at the wedding rehearsal. Monique had been the flower girl and Diego had been the ring bearer.

"It's cold outside. Zip your coat up all the way," I insisted, just before opening the door of our apartment and stepping aside to let Monique pass through.

"Thank you, Mommy." She smiled. She was so polite sometimes.

"All right, let's go," I stated, reaching for her hand. Although she was nine, going on ten, I couldn't help the protectiveness I still felt to hold her hand even as we walked the halls of our apartment building.

We made it out to my building's parking lot and into the car in record time. Despite my rushing Monique, the truth was we were early enough that I had plenty of time to drive across town to the Cedarwoods community where Kayla lived with her husband, and back downtown to get to my job by nine-thirty. I rushed simply because I was a worrier and hated being late for anything.

Monique climbed in the back door of my old, white Cavalier before I shut it and opened my own door.

"Play Yo-Yo Ma's 'Unaccompanied Cello Suite,' Mommy," Monique requested from the backseat as she buckled herself in.

I smiled. "Coming up." What nine-year-old requested classical music? Mine did. Not that that wasn't my fault. I'd played it the entire time I was pregnant and around the house since Monique was born. I loved it and was grateful that she'd grown a love for it as well.

When I turned the key to start the car up, I could hear the engine making a coughing sound. It didn't alarm me at first, seeing as how it'd done the same thing for months now, but that day it lasted longer than previous days.

"Please turnover," I mumbled while releasing the key and turning it again.

"That doesn't sound good."

I frowned but ignored smarty pants in the back. She was right, however. It didn't sound good.

"Ha!" I yelped as soon as the engine turned over and my car started. But in the back of my mind, I knew my car had seen better days. I was finally at the point in my career where I was making decent enough money that I didn't need to drive around in a nearly twenty-year-old vehicle. Especially considering all of the maintenance I had to do just to keep it on the road. I really needed to start car shopping. *Maybe after work.*

"What time do you get off today?"

I peered up into the rearview mirror just after turning onto the main street leading to the highway that would get us to Cedarwoods. "No later than two, I think."

Lowering my gaze back to the road, I prayed inwardly that I wouldn't be stuck at work all day.

"I really wanted to go to the zoo."

I frowned. "I know, sweetie. We can go in a couple of weeks. The law firm Mommy works for is working a big case and they need me to help on weekends to get all of the work done." I tried to keep the bitterness out of my own voice. I enjoyed my job, but I would've much rather preferred going to the zoo with my daughter or doing pretty much anything else with her than going into work on a Saturday.

I pushed out a hefty breath.

Oh well.

These were the sacrifices parents made. I did my best not to complain. I had a good job that didn't require extreme hours most of the time, and it allowed me to take care of myself and my daughter reasonably well. Add to that the health benefits were great, which took much of Monique's extra medical costs off of me. Nope. I didn't have the right to complain. We'd come a long way in the last ten years.

"Tomorrow we'll sleep in and make veggie omelets with the home-made granola bars," Monique concluded.

I nodded. "Sounds like a great idea to me." Since Monique's diagnosis, I'd worked hard to clean up our diets and follow the healthy meal plan Kayla had devised for her. I ate the same things she did, and have grown to enjoy most of it. Add to that, I'd lost the ten pounds I'd managed to hold onto since Monique's birth, and in her early years when a meal was anything leftover from the diner I worked at. To top it off, I used my company's in-house gym—often during my lunch break along with a twice a week Pilates class that was discounted through my work—and I was in better shape than I'd been in in years. But the most important thing was that Monique's diabetes was managed and getting better.

"We're here," I stated in a sing-song voice to rouse Monique who somehow had fallen asleep during the ride.

Her eyes the color of maple syrup opened up, reminding me of my own.

"I wasn't asleep, Mommy," she insisted.

Lifting an eyebrow, I laughed. "Are you sure? You appeared to be sleeping to me," I teased as I held the door open for her to get out.

"I was just resting my eyes."

I tossed my head back and laughed because she'd gotten that lie from me. All of the nights she'd come to me to read her a story after I got off work, I'd be asleep on the couch but would tell her 'Mommy was just resting her eyes.'

"Hey!" Kayla greeted as she opened the huge glass door of her and Josh's massive home.

"Hey, Kayla. Thank you so much for this." I rushed everything out in one breath.

"I already told you about giving me thanks where none is needed. Hey, Monique." Kayla's cinnamon eyes sparkled as she looked down at Monique. She let out a giggle when Monique responded by wrapping her arms around Kayla's mid-section and laying her head on Kayla's protruding belly.

"Hey, Aunt Kayla," she greeted.

When we first met Kayla she said it was all right to call her by her first name instead of Dr. Reyes. I wasn't comfortable with Monique using just her first name, so I had her call her Dr. Kayla. Eventually, as Kayla and I became friends and Monique participated in Kayla's wedding as the flower girl, she eventually took to calling her Aunt Kayla. That worked for me.

"Come in." Kayla stepped back, allowing us entry.

"I packed Monique's lunch. I know" I began, hand raised to stop whatever retort was on the tip of Kayla's tongue, "I didn't have to bring anything, but I didn't feel right dropping her off without any food and snacks."

Kayla frowned. "I should fight you for thinking I wouldn't feed my niece."

I giggled as she turned her back, starting toward the hall following behind Monique.

"You and that six months pregnant belly?"

She glanced over her shoulder at me, her auburn curls swaying with the movement. "I can still fight. My husband taught me everything he knows."

I smirked and looked around. "Was that one of his cars parked out front?" There was a dark blue BMW—at least I thought it was a BMW —parked out front. Joshua had an array of cars, according to Kayla.

"No, that's Damon's. Those two are downstairs talking about God knows what. Hey, Monique, you want to help me …"

Kayla's words trailed off as my mind went racing. My heartbeat quickened at just the thought that I was in the same house as Damon Richmond.

"Sandra? Did you hear me?"

"Wh-what?" I questioned, turning back to Kayla, blinking.

Her eyes narrowed on me.

Uh oh.

"I asked if it was okay to take Monique to the park later? It's supposed to get a little warmer."

I swallowed. "Uh, yeah, of course." I shrugged, trying to play off my initial absent-mindedness. It was mid-February but the forecast did call for temperatures getting as high as the fifties later on in the day.

"You know you can go downstairs and say hello."

My eyes bulged. "No." I shook my head adamantly. "I don't want to disturb Josh. He's busy. But please give him my thanks for helping to babysit Monique. I thought I might have to bring her to work with me when my sitter told me she was sick with the flu."

"I wasn't talking about Joshua."

"I have to get going." I looked around the kitchen for Monique.

"She's in the great room."

I nodded and passed by Kayla who I was sure was smirking.

"Give me a hug, baby. I'm getting ready to go."

Smiling, Monique ran over from the coffee table where she'd already set up her tablet. "Bye, Mommy. Have a good day at work."

I kissed the top of her head before smoothing down the little flyaways that'd already escaped the fluffy ponytail I'd brushed her hair into that morning.

"You enjoy Aunt Kayla and Uncle Joshua. Be good for them."

"She's always good. Right, Mo?"

I turned, startled by the deep male voice. I pushed out a breath, relieved to see Kayla's husband instead of his friend.

"Uncle Josh!" Monique squealed, excited. "Is Diego coming over today?"

Joshua tossed his head back, laughing, his green eyes shimmering with delight at the apparent friendship developing between my daughter and his eldest nephew.

"How'd I know you were going to ask? We might be able to arrange that. We'll have to call his mother."

"Monique, I told you, Diego might have plans with his family today. I'm sorry, she's been asking all morning." I lifted my gaze to meet Joshua's.

"Diego's been asking the same thing. They were over last night for dinner."

I dropped my gaze to Monique who was obviously excited about the news.

"Well, I have to get going. Thanks again … I know, I know. Kayla already told me to quit with the thank yous, but I can't help it."

Josh chuckled.

I started past Josh and smiled at Kayla who was coming up the hall from the kitchen. Out of the corner of my eye I saw a shadow behind her and opted to pick up my pace toward the front door.

"I got it."

"Thanks, Kayla." I gave her a quick hug before practically sprinting out the door to the parking lot and back inside my car where I felt a little safer. I sighed in relief at not having come face-to-face with Damon. That man was … everything. Way too much for me. One dance was all I needed to tell me that.

Pushing thoughts of six-foot-three, mahogany skin toned, solid framed men out of my head, I turned the key to start my car and … nothing. I tried again and that time a little noise sounded before it died.

"No, no, no," I whined, trying again.

Nothing.

She was dead.

I started to lower my head to the steering wheel when a knock on the driver's side window scared the living daylights out of me.

I turned and my throat instantly went dry.

With his large hand he pointed in a downward motion, indicating he wanted me to lower my window. My hand was shaky as I used the lever to lower the window.

"Need some help?"

Oh god. How could a man's voice be smooth as silk but laced with steel at the same time?

My gaze trailed from his full lips that were a shade darker than his mahogany skin, to the dark hairs of his beard, up to his, noticing—not for the first time—that while both were brown, they were different colors. The left eye was the color of coffee, and the right eye was the color of warm honey. Raw, unfiltered honey, not the fake stuff sold at most grocery chains.

"Huh?" I asked dumbly.

"Your car." He motioned with his head to my vehicle. "Won't start?"

I turned my head as if taking notice of my vehicle, the one I was sitting in and had owned for the last ten years, for the first time.

"N-no."

"You need a jump?"

"Y-ye— No … Huh?" Where was all of my good sense?

"For your car. Do you need a jump? Do you have jumper cables?"

I blinked and came back to myself. "No. It's not the battery." I'd just gotten a new one a few months earlier.

"Then it's something else. I don't know much about cars, but I know a couple of mechanics who could tow you out of here to their shop. Unless you have one of your own?"

"Uh, no, I don't. But I really need to get to work. I'll just catch an Uber and find a tow truck once I get back." That, of course, relied on whether or not Kayla and Joshua minded my car taking up space in their driveway.

I sighed.

This was a mess.

Suddenly, I felt a whoosh of air. I turned and realized my car door had been opened.

"Kayla and Joshua won't mind your car hanging out here for a few hours. No need for an Uber. I'll take you wherever you have to go." And without another word, he was holding out his hand, nearly identical to the way he'd held it out to me when he'd asked me to dance at Kayla and Joshua's wedding reception.

Placing my much smaller hand in his for the second time felt just like it had the first time. Perfect.

I stepped out. "You don't have to. I'm sure you have other things to do. I can just get an Uber and then be on my way." I started digging around my bag for my phone. Anything to avoid looking in his eyes. "I'll just phone work and let them know I'll be a few minutes later than I'd intended. I'm sure it will be okay. I might have to stay a little later than I expected. Monique might be a little miffed about that but—"

"Put your phone away."

And just like that my little rant was cut short. My belly fluttered at the subtleness of his command. And despite the lightness of his voice it *was* a command.

"I'll take you. Your car is fine where it is."

I swallowed. I hadn't even realized I'd voiced my concerns out loud. Unless this man was a mind reader? Then I was in *serious* trouble.

Get real, Sandra, I admonished. People weren't mind readers. I just wore my emotions on my sleeve. Always had.

"Thank you," I stated since it was the only thing that seemed to fit at that moment.

"No problem," he responded while moving to pull out a key fob from his dark jeans.

A second later I heard the distinctive sound of car doors unlocking. Damon strolled—the man didn't walk, he strolled—over to the BMW I'd originally thought belonged to Joshua and opened the passenger side door for me to get in.

I swallowed and told my pacing heart to chill out.

He's safe, I reminded myself as I got in the car. According to Kayla, Damon and Joshua had been friends for years. She trusted him. I tried to let that knowledge guide my decision-making as I lowered myself into the vehicle. But trust was difficult to come by. I flinched a little when the car door closed and Damon's long legs carried him around the front of the car to the driver's side.

"Where to?" he asked as he started the car.

I turned, feeling captivated by this thick beard. I briefly wondered if he moisturized it like I'd seen some men do on Youtube videos. Coconut oil. He definitely used coconut oil, at least. The shimmer of the hairs in the beard told me so.

"Sandra?"

"Huh?"

"Where are we going?"

Anywhere you want.

"Oh, uh, Mansfield, Duval, & Mason Attorneys at Law. The address is …" I paused as I dug through my tote bag for my wallet. I always forgot the actual address of my company.

"Don't bother. I know exactly where that is."

"Thank you," I said, my gaze straight ahead as we pulled out of Joshua and Kayla's driveway. My bag was clutched tightly to my lap.

"You say that a lot, huh?"

My eyes shifted to the left to peer over at him. I tried to stop it, but my head followed, obviously needing a better look at the specimen that sat next to me.

"Say what?"

"Thank you. That's the second time you've thanked me in like five minutes. I also heard you thank Kayla and Joshua at least twice. And that was only what I heard before you sprinted out the door."

I could've sworn that last sentence held a tiny amount of accusation behind it. As if he was suggesting I was running from him.

Well, he was right.

But I would never admit it out loud.

"I like to show my gratitude when people are kind to me or go out of their way on my behalf." Lord knows there hadn't been many throughout my life.

"Mm," was his response.

I wrinkled my forehead, wanting to ask what that meant, but I kept my mouth shut. The less talking the better. The more we talked the bigger the possibility I might do something stupid like develop a crush on this man or something. I was certain he was just being kind to a friend of his friend. Same as for the wedding. For a brief moment, I suspected his asking me to dance, and what I thought was him watching me throughout the night, spoke to a deeper interest. But those suspicions were put to rest when I watched him leave with another woman who was the total opposite of myself.

"So, you're a lawyer?"

His question pulled me from my thoughts which was good since they were starting to veer off into resentment territory. Which was silly since he wasn't anything to me.

"No. Paralegal."

"That's cool. You like it?"

"I do."

"What do you like about it?"

"Researching. That's one of my favorite aspects of the job."

"Working Saturdays doesn't bother you?"

I shook my head. "I don't usually work weekends. We've got a big case and are possibly taking on another."

Damon nodded. "Which lawyer do you work for?"

"I work for more than one, but Emma Leslie is who I'm working a couple of cases with."

"I've heard of her."

I wondered how but again, opted to mind my business. However, in the interest of not being rude I decided to say, "Kayla tells me you're involved in real estate?"

"That and more," he responded.

I wanted to ask what he meant by *more* but his cell phone beeped and soon was ringing through the speakers in the car. I glanced at the display and read the name "Scarlet." I thought back, trying to remember the name of the woman he'd left with the night of Kayla and Josh's wedding. Was it Scarlet? From what I recalled that woman had been as sultry as her name indicated.

Like I said, nothing like me.

I ran my hands down my thighs, smoothing out imaginary wrinkles of my dark denim. Weekends were the *only* time I wore jeans. But to keep it as professional as I could, I'd paired the jeans with my white, ribbed turtleneck and my Badgley Mischka crystal pointy toe flats, which I'd managed to score for less than half the retail price, at my favorite online thrift store that sold high end names. This morning I hadn't had any problems with my outfit, but as I sat next to Damon, I started to regret not wearing my usual high heels to the office, giving my five-foot-one frame more height. At least when I stood.

I was so caught up in my own head, I hadn't even realized Damon had sent the caller to voicemail. Probably not wanting me to overhear a private conversation with his lover.

"We're almost there. Do you need a ride back?"

"No. I'll just catch an Uber or something. Hopefully by then I'll have the name of a mechanic I can send it to get checked over."

"I can do that for you."

My eyelids raised. "Why?" I blurted out.

Deep creases formed in Damon's forehead as he looked at me questioningly. I realized how accusatory my question had been.

"I mean, you don't have to. Really. I can find someone—"

"Who'll probably try to rip you off."

My mouth snapped shut. He was right. I had enough experiences with mechanics to have been scammed a time or two … or five.

"My friend owns an auto shop and a dealership. Worse comes to worst, he can help you out with a great deal on a new car."

Taking a deep breath in, I looked down at my hands in my lap. I should've been grateful for Damon's help. I was. But I was also just a touch … embarrassed. I was sure the car we were driving in was a 2018 model, if not newer, and was much more advanced and in better shape than my run down eighteen-year-old vehicle. It made me suspect that maybe Damon thought I needed help, especially since I had a kid. In other words, he felt sorry for me. That stung.

"We're here. You sure you don't need a ride back home?"

"N-no," I blurted out, fear rising up my throat. I blinked and shook my head.

Calm down, Sandra.

The man was just offering a ride.

"I meant thank you but no. I'll give my mother a call and she can come get me," I lied.

"Your mother?"

"Yes," I answered, nodding my head but avoiding eye contact as I reached for the door handle. I rushed to get out of the car that was pulled up in front of my office's main entrance, so fast that I didn't even realize Damon had gotten out as well. Just as I fixed myself to stand upright, he was there, holding the door open for me.

I swallowed as my eyes made contact with his broad chest. Even through the dark sweater he wore, I could tell what lie beneath that cashmere material was solid enough to bounce a quarter off of.

"Thank y—"

"That's the second time in the last sixty seconds. Don't thank me again."

I clenched my lips, feeling admonished.

His body brushed past mine as he leaned down, shutting the car door. The whiff of cologne I got filled my nostrils with a smell of strength, cardamom, and spice. A smell I knew was only written into this man's DNA, not whatever bottle he'd used. I remembered it from our one and only dance.

"Well, you enjoy your day," I stated, taking a couple of steps backwards. I bit my tongue to keep from thanking him yet again.

"You also." He nodded in my direction but thankfully didn't move any closer.

I stood there for a few seconds too long, making it awkward. At least, with another person it would've been awkward, but Damon simply stared at me, patiently waiting for me to turn and head inside. Those different colored eyes were hooded, unreadable, which made him especially intriguing. A second later he ran a strong hand down the right side of his face and through his beard.

That was when I finally got my brain to communicate with the rest of my body. It was time to go into work.

I gave a small smile through shaky lips and turned, nearly stumbling over my own two feet. I ambled toward the door, inhaling and feeling deeply grateful that my nose wasn't filled with the smell of his any longer. Grateful yet yearning at the same time. He wasn't good for me. There probably wasn't a man alive who was, but Damon Richmond sure as hell wasn't it.

CHAPTER 2

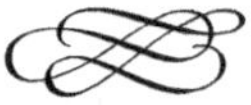

*S*andra

"Well, well, well, look who finally decided to show up," Kayla chimed as she opened the door.

"Mommy!" Monique screeched as she ducked underneath Kayla's arm to embrace me around the waist.

Smiling, I lowered my face to kiss the top of her head. I'd been at work much longer than I had originally planned. An appointment with a relative of a former client had landed a new case in our laps. And the complaint of the new client was with a company I was very familiar with. But I didn't want to think about any of that as I hugged Monique.

"Hey, baby. I'm so sorry," I began, looking up at Kayla. "The case we were working on—"

She held up her hand. "Don't even think of apologizing. You gave me more time to spend with my niece."

She tickled Monique under her chin, causing her to giggle.

"Come in. I was thinking of ordering Thai so we could have an early dinner. I don't much feel like cooking."

"You don't have to. I'm sure Josh wants some alone time with you."

"Josh is out working. An issue came up at one of his developments.

He went to check things out. He's so hands-on. Anyway, I'm starving and don't really want to eat alone so you'd be doing me a favor."

"Okay, but I'll pay since—"

"I'll slap any money you try to give me out of your hand," she stated firmly, hands moving to her hips.

I laughed, knowing she'd definitely try to slap my hand.

"Thanks, Kayla. I'm hungry, too. Monique wasn't a problem, was she?"

"Not at all. Diego came over and we took them both to the park. He had to go back home since he was going over his grandmother's to celebrate her birthday. Then Nique-Nique and I did some decorating of the nursery, didn't we?"

"Yup. Mom, they're doing an 'Under the Sea' theme for the baby's room," Monique informed me.

I nodded even though I already knew that.

"Oh, and your car was towed to the mechanic on 35th."

"Thank you so much for doing that, Kayla."

Kayla looked up from the Thai menu she'd just pulled from one of the cabinet drawers. "Me? I didn't call."

"Oh. Well, Josh then."

Before the sentence was fully out of my mouth, Kayla was shaking her head. "That was all Damon. He insisted on covering the bill as well."

I frowned, having forgotten about our conversation just that morning. I'd gotten so wrapped up in work I'd actually started for the garage where I normally parked before remembering I hadn't driven in. I lifted an eyebrow realizing that he'd been serious about helping me with my car. I knew the mechanic he'd sent my car to was one of the best in the city of Williamsport. Which also meant he was one of the most expensive.

"You could call him and thank him."

I lifted my gaze to Kayla's before shifting a glance over at Monique who was now looking down at the menu.

"Monique, do you know what you want?" I questioned, ignoring Kayla's last statement.

"Yeah, I want a spring roll with the curry chicken and rice."

"Too many carbs," Kayla and I stated at the same time.

We looked at each other and laughed. As her doctor and mother, Kayla and I both knew keeping Monique's carbohydrate intake at a certain level was important.

"Then I'll skip the rice," Monique negotiated.

"How about half of a spring roll and a small portion of the rice … brown rice, to go with the curry chicken?" Kayla quickly amended.

"Deal!"

After Kayla and I decided what we would have, she placed the order and we followed Monique up the hall to the great room, to talk for bit while we waited.

Monique turned on the television and immediately found the weather channel.

"She's still on the meteorologist kick, huh?" Kayla asked as we sat down on the unbelievably comfortable black couch.

I rolled my eyes. "Every morning before we leave the house she has to check the weather. If rain is in the forecast and I even thinking of not picking up my umbrella to take with me, she's all over me like a dog with a bone."

Kayla laughed. "She's so grown."

"Girl, I have a hard time remembering who's the parent and who's the child sometimes."

We talked some more about Monique and then I told Kayla a little bit about my cases at work.

"Speaking of work, how was your ride in, this morning?"

Pushing out a breath, I allowed my gaze to bounce around the room, avoiding Kayla's eyes.

"Sandra."

"It was fine. Damon was very friendly."

"Friendly?"

"Yes. How else would he be?"

"I don't know, flirtatious, like he wants to jump your bones."

I looked heavenward. "He doesn't see me that way."

I jumped when Kayla's hand tightened around my arm.

"Please tell me you're joking."

I looked down and over at my friend. "I'm serious."

She shook her head. "After the way he was looking at you at the wedding?"

"And then left with someone else." I slapped my hand over my mouth. I hadn't meant to say that out loud. I didn't want anyone to know I'd been watching Damon intently that night, least of all Kayla.

"You did notice him. And I don't know what happened after the wedding, but according to Joshua, Damon doesn't have a girlfriend."

I thought about the woman he'd presumably taken home that night. She was tall and thin almost to the point of being modelesque. She walked with her shoulders back and head held high. Though her skin tone was shades darker than my own, she wore red lipstick like it'd been made with her in mind. If he was interested in her, then I surely was not his type.

"Stop it. I can tell you're in your head comparing yourself to her."

Squinting at Kayla, I sighed, hating that she was able to read me so well. Close friends had been far and few between in my lifetime. Kayla was the closest thing I had to a best friend, and I'd only known her for less than a year.

"I wasn't," I lied.

"You were. You're a terrible liar."

I laughed at that. She was right.

"Anyway, I don't know what went on between him and that woman, but a man like Damon Richmond doesn't look at you the way he looks at you, then offer you a ride to work and pay to have your car towed to one of the best mechanics in the city because he's *not* interested."

"But interested in what? I can't be anything more than friends with someone," I stated, feeling inadequate. I'm sure Scarlet could be more than friends with a man like Damon.

"Sandra …" Kayla's voice dropped to an empathetic note as her hand rested on my arm.

I swallowed.

"I know what you've been through—"

I shook my head. Kayla knew a lot of my story, but I hadn't shared everything with her. And I certainly wasn't brave like she was.

"Can we talk about something else?"

At that moment, the doorbell rang.

Kayla peered down into her phone at the app that let her see the front door through the camera that'd been installed there. Joshua didn't play about the safety of his family. "Food's here."

"I'll get it," I insisted so she wouldn't have to get up. I knew how much of a pain in the butt it was to have to get up once comfortable while you were six months pregnant.

I met the delivery man at the door, Monique on my heels. Apparently, she was hungry, too.

"Smells good," I chimed excitedly to my daughter as I shut the door.

"Let's eat in the great room!" Kayla called from her position still on the couch.

I frowned, looking around at all of the expensive decor that accompanied the dark sofas and glass coffee table. "Are you sure?"

"Why wouldn't I be?"

I shrugged. "I wouldn't think you'd want to make a mess in here."

She waved me off. "No worries. If anything gets messed up we can have it cleaned. Besides, I don't feel like getting up from this couch and slugging this belly all of the way down the hall to the dining table."

I giggled. "I understand that."

Although we ate in the great room, I had Monique bring us a few placemats and napkins just to keep things as neat as possible.

"You should really switch to cloth napkins, Auntie Kayla."

"Monique, we don't talk with our mouth full, right?" I lightly scolded, hating the mouthful of rice she'd neglected to swallow before speaking.

"Sorry, Mom," she apologized, still without finishing the food she was eating.

She made a show of bobbing her head as she swallowed—for effect

—before opening her mouth again. "They're better for the environment. Right, Mom?"

"Monique, it's not nice to tell people how they should live."

"I wasn't. I—"

"It's okay, Nique. I was just telling Josh the other day that we waste a ton of paper towels and napkins."

"Right. And they all go straight to the landfill, taking years to decompose, and since—"

"She gets it, Monique," I cut her off before she started spouting environmental statistics.

"Mommy can make you some. She made ours."

I raised my eyebrows across the coffee table at Monique who was sitting on the floor. "Thanks for volunteering my services."

She shrugged. "I was just saying."

"You made your napkins?"

I glanced over at Kayla. "They're easy to make. Just purchased some patterned cloth from the fabric store that was on sale and used my sewing machine."

"I thought you bought those from some store. I saw one in Monique's lunch bag."

I shook my head. "I didn't like the ones sold at the store, and since they're napkins and will get all stained I wanted patterned cloth that would help hide the stains over time."

"Unfortunately, I don't know the first thing about sewing, but I'll buy some cloth napkins the next time I go to the store. You've convinced me, young lady!" She smiled over at Monique.

"Yes!" Monique cheered as if she'd scored a winning goal. And for her, it was a win. She loved nature, and saving the environment had turned into a real passion project for her.

Over the course of dinner Monique offered more tips on how to reduce waste. By the time our meal was finished I was pretty sure she'd have Kayla and Josh signed up for trash pickups, volunteering, and building a compost in their own backyard despite the fact that neither one of them was a gardener of any sort.

"Thanks for spending the day with me, Nique-Nique," Kayla stated as we walked to the doorway, preparing to leave. I smiled at the nickname she'd given Monique.

I'd requested an Uber to pick us up, even though Kayla had offered to give us a ride home.

"Thanks, Auntie Kayla. Thank Uncle Josh for me, too, please. And tell Diego I said bye."

Kayla grinned in my direction. Smiling, I shook my head, remembering how young and innocent she was. If I could, I'd wrap her up in bubble wrap to preserve that innocence.

"Those jeans look great on you, by the way. I meant to tell you earlier."

Kayla's compliment pulled me from my wandering thoughts.

I glanced down at the dark denim pants I wore. They were skinny leg and stopped just at the ankle.

"I would've thought it'd be difficult to find petite jeans that fit you just right."

"It is," I confirmed. "I had to dart these at the back, and I cut and altered the length myself. But it was worth the time. I got these for less than twenty dollars."

"They look amazing on you. Maybe you should teach a class." She grabbed my arm, turning me this way and that, looking over the fit of my jeans. With anyone else I would've been super self-conscious. My body shape had always been an issue for me. Not only was I short but my top half was small while my bottom was, shall we say, curvaceous. I'd always gravitated toward a more conservative style of dress, and I loved the classic look of turtlenecks, tweed skirts and dresses, button-up blouses with bows, and the like. But I'd learned from my grandmother that fit and material took an okay outfit to amazing. I'd learned to sew as a teenager and it served me well in my early years as a single mother. And while I now took most things to a tailor near my apartment to be hemmed or altered, I occasionally took the time to do it myself … when I had time, of course.

"Maybe when Monique's in college and I have more time," I retorted to Kayla's comment.

"I'd be the first to sign up. Oh, your Uber's here."

I glanced over my shoulder and saw the compact SUV, which the app had told me was coming, pulling up.

"Thanks again. I owe you dinner."

"You owe me squat," Kayla returned as she pulled me into a hug.

"Fine. I'll see you at Pilates on Tuesday?"

She nodded. "I'll be there."

She gave Monique a hug and kiss good-bye, and we climbed into the Uber to head home. On the way there I lost myself to thoughts of tall specimens with thick beards and different colored eyes.

CHAPTER 3

*D*amon

"We're working on a huge project. The Williamsport Bridge is in need of a great deal of work. The last thing this city, or country for that matter, invests in is its infrastructure. Which is crazy and makes absolutely no sense."

I kept my face placid as to not alert my date to the fact that I gave absolutely no damns about what she was saying. Scarlet was a civil engineer and never failed to drop that tidbit of information into any conversation she was a part of. Sure, she had every right to be proud of her accomplishments. Lord only knew how difficult it was being one of a few women, let alone black women, in her field. However, what I didn't feel like doing was smiling and nodding as she talked about the Williamsport Bridge and all of its structural integrity issues when all I really wanted from her was a few great orgasms. On that account, Scarlet delivered.

"Tell me about the next project you're working on. It's an apartment complex, right?"

I lifted the glass of bourbon, which I'd been nursing throughout dinner, to my lips. By choice, I wasn't a heavy drinker. I never liked the out of control feeling being intoxicated filled me with. I could count on one hand the amount of times I'd been drunk or high off of weed. And I'd still have fingers left to form a handmade pistol and aim it at someone's head. I'd seen too many people taken out by their own addictions to let any drug become mine.

"Yeah, we're working to purchase the abandoned Lakefront building to fit about sixty condos on the top ten floors and businesses on the bottom floor."

"That's a lot. Are you sure you have the right engineers working on the job?"

I squinted at the woman across the table from me as I lowered my glass.

"You don't think I know what I'm doing?"

A coquettish smile broke free on her wine-colored lips, showing off her brightly whitened teeth. The color was a sharp contrast to her dark brown skin tone. A move that had me licking my own lips.

She leaned forward, allowing the low cut, sparkling red dress she wore to show off her considerable amount of cleavage.

"Of course you know what you're doing. I just thought you might want some recommendations. I know some great engineers in the area." Her voice had taken on a sultry note. One that my body wasn't immune to. Granted, it wasn't quite the same response I'd had a few days earlier in my car while driving Sandra to work.

Wait.

Where the hell had my head just gone?

I was in front of a beautiful woman who was making it obvious that she was down for whatever once the check was paid for, and here I was thinking about a woman who was Scarlet's total opposite. Where Scarlet was long and lean, Sandra and petite and thicker, particularly her bottom half. While Scarlet's skin could be described almost as midnight in tone thanks to her Sudanese heritage, Sandra's skin mirrored that of a shiny penny with huge, maple syrup colored eyes that held so much emotion they practically spoke for themselves. And where Scarlet knew who she was and what she wanted, Sandra could best be described as … skittish.

"I don't need any recs. My team is solid," I replied to Scarlet, pushing thoughts of Sandra out of my head.

"There is something else you could help me with, though." I lifted and motioned with my hand for the waiter to bring our check. I wasn't the usual type to eat at the French restaurant we were at but Scarlet had requested we come.

"And what's that?" Her voice dropped noticeably and her dark brown eyes were transfixed at my center as I rose from my seat.

"You already know what it is," I responded, holding my hand out to help her stand.

No more words were needed. Once the waiter brought my card back, I returned it to my wallet, placed my wallet in my pocket, and wrapped my arm around Scarlet's waist, leading us out of the restaurant.

* * *

THAT WASN'T IT.

My mind screamed those three words at me as I laid next to a lightly snoring Scarlet, covered by her silk bed sheets. Spending the last few hours with Scarlet's long legs wrapped around my waist and more than one orgasm hadn't quelled the agitation that seemed to have lived with me over the past few days.

I briefly thought of waking Scarlet for another go-round but quickly killed that idea. Fucking wasn't going to extinguish whatever this was, so it was on to the next best thing. I sat up, grabbed my boxer briefs from the floor, and stood to step into them.

"Where're you going?"

I looked over my shoulder at a groggy Scarlet before turning and pulling my pants from the rocking chair in the corner of her room.

"I've got some business to handle."

"Business at …" she leaned her head over looking at the clock on her nightstand, "one twenty-three in the morning?"

I paused, staring at her before going back to buttoning the shirt I'd worn on our date. "I said what I said." Scarlet wasn't my girlfriend. She knew this. I knew this.

To prove she knew this, her lips twisted into a dissatisfied frown but she didn't press me any longer.

"I'll give you a call," I stated as I leaned over and pressed a kiss to her forehead. I wasn't a whole asshole. But without a backwards glance, I moved over the threshold of her bedroom, checking my pockets and making sure I had my keys and wallet before heading down the spiral staircase. I briefly admired the high ceilings of Scarlet's loft style apartment. I made a mental note to have my team research this neighborhood.

In less than two minutes I was out the door and reached my car in five minutes. Within sixty seconds I turned and aimed my vehicle for the highway that would carry me to my destination.

* * *

"You hit like a pussy!" I taunted the guy circling me, the same as I was doing to him.

"Fuck you!"

"Tough talk gets you knocked on your ass," I warned just before I ducked and moved in, quickly sending a hook and then an elbow to his ribcage.

"Unf!" he pushed out, breathing heavily.

I pondered whether or not to taunt him some more or to just do a takedown and end this bout quickly. Around me I could hear the rumblings and cheers of the spectators egging either one of us on. This was what I needed. A good energy pumping, blood flowing, and possibly bone crushing fight in the ring, with the Underground—a secretive fighting club I'd been a part of for a number of years.

"What the hell is taking you so long? Getting slow in your old age?"

I grunted at the sound of Joshua's voice. I briefly thought about hanging around for the next fight just to enter it with him to shut his ass up. Best friend or not, he could get this work, too.

Suddenly, the dude in the ring with me, James, I think was his name, lunged at me. I hastily sidestepped his assault and aimed another hook, this time with my right hand, at his other ribcage. He stumbled, falling to his knees. Though, ordinarily I would've waited for him to get back up in order to defend himself, I was over this fight. I'd clearly won. So, instead, I grabbed his right arm, wrapping it behind him, and gripped the back of his neck with my free hand, forcing him face down into the mat, pinning him there with my knee at the center of his back.

"Enough! Enough!"

I felt the tap on my shoulder from the guy refereeing and released James, letting him up.

"Nice fight," he stated, holding out his fist.

I nodded and we bumped fists, a sign of our mutual respect. Down here things got gritty and raw but it was all respect. At least, most of the time.

"You looked a little tense out there."

I ducked underneath the ropes of the boxing square and hopped down before shifting my gaze to the right, glancing at a smirking Joshua.

"No more tense than your wife's gonna be when she curses you out for being down here," I quipped.

Joshua's green eyes narrowed, his face darkening.

I chuckled. The man didn't play about his wife.

"Don't mention my fucking wife."

I chuckled some more.

"Wanna try to beat my ass?" I challenged.

"I just might. Besides, she's staying at her parents' tonight. Her mom had surgery. Outpatient, but Kay wanted to stay with her tonight to make sure everything's okay."

My head shot back, surprised. "You let her out of your sight for a whole night? Good for you."

"Fuck no. I'll be picking her up once I leave here. She's not staying out of my bed for a whole night."

Shaking my head, I wiped my face and neck with the small white towel he tossed me. I followed him as he made his way toward the changing room behind the wooden door at the far end of the room. The building we were in looked like an abandoned building from the outside. We held our fights on the basement level, to not garner much attention with the lights. But the building had fully equipped electrical and plumping, which allowed everyone who was invited to partake in our fights to shower and change back into their normal, regular selves once they left. Each and every one of us were professionals and businessmen in our own right. The building was jointly owned by Joshua and Connor O'Brien, a former pro-fighter.

"You're crazy," I chuckled, shaking my head at Joshua's antics regarding his wife. Few people knew the lengths he'd gone to protect that woman. Though, I have to say, had my wife or someone I loved endured what Kayla had, at the hands of someone meant to protect and serve, I can't say I wouldn't have done the exact same thing.

Hell, I was no stranger when it came to getting revenge for harms perpetrated against someone you love.

"It runs in the family." Josh shrugged. "Speaking of …"

Here we fucking go.

I knew what he was going to say before he said it.

"Don't fucking ask."

"Shit, man, I can't even ask you about your—"

"My what?" I questioned sharply, tossing the used towel in the laundry bin at the corner of the room. Only Joshua Townsend would have a laundry bin in such a dingy ass place. The laundry was actually cleaned professionally.

"Your woman," he answered boldly, knowing it would piss me off.

"I don't have a woman." I had ladies who I entertained. Some I kept around more than others. But a woman? Hell no.

"Don't give me that shit, Damon. You and I both know you're into Sandra."

"*Into* Sandra? What the fuck does that even mean?" I shook my head.

"You know what the hell it means. You like her, want to do some very unsavory things to—"

"Watch your mouth," I warned, my voice dropping to an almost menacing tone.

And fucking Joshua ate that shit up. His eyes glinted and he gave me a dumb ass smirk as if he'd called it right.

"Defensive, huh? Weren't you *just* getting on me for being protective over my *wife?*"

Shit.

He had a point. Sandra was far from my wife. She wasn't even my *type.* I liked women who were bosses. Who could walk into a room—any room—and own it. The type of woman with not just the education and credentials under their belt but the savvy, skill, and know-how to back those credentials up, in and out of the boardroom. Sandra wasn't that. She was wholesome.

Why that thought had my heartbeat picking up speed, I had no fucking clue, but I didn't like it. I'd long since surmised the underlying agitation I'd been feeling for days—the very angst that'd sent me into the ring just now—had nothing to do with work and everything to do with her.

"She's not my fucking wife," I stated like a damn chump.

"Not yet. You buy her a new car yet?"

"What?" I yelled.

Josh lifted his eyebrows almost innocently. "I was just asking. You had it towed, insisted on taking it to the best shop in the city, *and* insisted on paying for it yourself. We both know her car has kicked the bucket. That thing's better off in a junkyard than on the road. I'm wondering when you're taking her car shopping is all?"

"Mind your goddamn business," I grunted before grabbing another larger towel and strolling back toward the showers. Joshua's laughter echoed off the ceramic walls and concrete floors as I moved through the doors that led to the shower.

Jackass.

What pissed me off the most was that Joshua was right. He knew it and I knew it. Sandra had been on my mind. And if I'm being really honest, she had been on my mind since his wedding, six months earlier. My driving her to work a week ago and paying for her car to get towed was more than me just being friendly. However, I'd done my best to stay away from her. Something in her eyes called to me, as if she was in need. I had more than enough needy women in my life. I wasn't going there with her.

CHAPTER 4

*D*amon

I brought the cup of coffee I was drinking to my lips as I let my eyes narrow on the building diagonal from my office's window. I'd chosen the particular office space for a specific reason. From the window I had a perfect view of the tall, brick building a few blocks away. More importantly, I had a view of the twentieth floor, including most of the comings and goings. The man who rented that particular space was so damn cocky he didn't bother using privacy window glass.

I snorted as my right hand twisted into a fist in the pocket of my pants.

"If you wanted an office in that building, you should've put in an offer when you first looked at it."

Rolling my eyes, I turned to the woman leaning against the door jamb of my office. She smiled and her heels sounded loudly as she made her way across the hardwood floor to sit in the black leather chair across from my own seat, which sat behind my glass desk.

"I didn't want that office," I stated, moving away from the window and taking my last sip of coffee before tossing the cup in the wastebasket.

"This office is nicer and has better views. But you keep looking at that other building like you wish you could have that office."

"I don't, Charlotte."

She sighed, shoulders slumping slightly. She quickly recovered, twisting her head and neck to move the long, bouncy curls of the weave she wore that particular week out of her face.

"What time is my meeting with Sean?" I questioned, looking down at the files on my desk, shuffling through them.

"Nine o'clock. It's only quarter of."

I nodded, my eyes going to the silver Cartier timepiece on my wrist that matched my suit. I didn't wear watches, they were timepieces.

"Mama wants to know why you haven't been over to visit her."

I lifted my gaze to meet Charlotte's. My baby sister stared me right in the eye as if she truly expected an answer.

"I was over not too long ago."

"Yeah, in like November. You called her for Christmas. It's February, Damon. She's our mother."

I snorted. "You think I need you to remind me who the woman who birthed me is?"

She rolled her brown eyes, pursing her lips. "She wants to see you."

"For what? She has no mortgage. She gets the money I put in her accounts every month. She gets the food I have delivered to her place every week. What does she need?"

"You," Charlotte screeched, sounding exasperated.

"Watch all that yelling in the office."

She huffed, uncrossing her legs and standing. In the heels she wore Charlotte was almost as tall as my six-foot-three height. At five ten, she was no shorty, but she loved to accentuate her height with heels.

"If you weren't my brother …"

"You'd what? Have to actually work for a living?"

"I work," she insisted. "This place couldn't run without me."

I chuckled at the preposterous notion. I decided against informing my sister that I'd successfully ran my business for the last decade, eight and a half of which had been without her. Charlotte had graduated from college after five years and then spent the next twenty months backpacking around Europe, Asia, and South America, on my dime, mind you. After coming back and deciding she had no clue what to do with her life, I took her on as my administrative assistant, seeing as how my previous one had just retired. Taking care of the women in my life had become a way of life ever since I was thirteen years old and my father was killed.

"If you say so, little sis."

"Anyway, Sean will be here soon. You know he's as much of a stickler for time as you are."

"What up, cousins?!"

Charlotte rolled her eyes. "See what I mean?"

She turned and gave Sean, my righthand man in my business a smile.

"Hey, Sean."

"Charlotte."

"You want some coffee?"

"Yeah, one creamer, two sugars."

"Coming up."

Charlotte moved past him and gave me a half smile.

"You finally got her acting like a real assistant?"

I pushed out a breath. "Trying to. What up?" I questioned as I held out my hand for Sean to slap it and pulled him into a half hug, our typical greeting. Aside from Joshua, Sean was my closest friend and ally. He was also family, though we'd only come to know each other in our later teen years.

"How was your flight back?"

Sean shook his dark head before sitting in the chair Charlotte had just vacated. "It was smooth, thank god."

I chuckled. Sean hated flying even though he probably took something like fifty flights a year with all of the travel we did for work.

"Hey, did you see the new mock-up our designer did of the watch?"

"Not yet. Been waiting on you to arrive to take a look."

"Man, it's a thing of beauty." He pulled out his tablet and tapped a few keys before setting it up and turning the screen to face me.

I leaned across the desk, from my still standing position, and brought the tablet closer. I whistled long and hard.

"Right? I told you."

This really was a thing of beauty. "He added all of the specifications I asked for."

"Asked? You mean demanded."

I shrugged. He was right. I was going for a specific look, and if this guy couldn't design it, then we'd get someone else. Like I said, I was interested in timepieces, not just a fucking watch.

"I know you've been planning a woman's watch. I was thinking it would have diamonds in the face floating. Not too many to make it gaudy but four or five just to make it appealing enough to the eye."

I nodded. "I like that." Sean and I both had a passion for watches. Apparently, it'd been something our grandfather had passed down to my father and Sean's mother. He wanted our first female timepiece to serve as a tribute to his mother.

"Imagine showing this off at SIHH one day," he stated, holding up the design of our athletic watch.

"That's the dream."

SIHH, also referred to as the Salon International De La Haute Horlogerie. In other words, the international gathering for those interested in high-end watchmaking. Each year it was hosted in Geneva. We were going in just a few weeks. While the watch we were staring at would not be ready by then, it would one day.

"That's a beauty. We'll discuss it some more later, but I have a meeting with the lawyers today to go over our exposure to liability. Since we've been adding more apartments, it only makes sense to review our insurances and whatnot."

Sean nodded. "I hear you. Sounds like a good look to me. I've been researching the loft apartments you asked me to."

I lifted an eyebrow, peering across my desk at Sean. After thinking over Scarlet's place, I had Sean do some research on the community and the owner of the apartment building. Always searching for more leads. Sean's official title in my company was that of vice president. He'd been with me since the beginning and enjoyed real estate—and now, watchmaking—almost as much as I did, but he was more than comfortable taking a backseat position. Though, he didn't need fancy ass titles or the recognition that came with them. For that, I respected him. And his hustle was truly unmatched, save for my own.

Sean and I talked and caught up for another thirty minutes before we both needed to head out to our respective meetings throughout the day.

"Tonight would be a good time to go see Mama," Charlotte pestered as I moved past her desk toward the glass door to exit.

I paused and looked at my sister like she was crazy.

"I'm just saying. Your last meeting is not too far from her condo."

"Whatever," I responded before heading out the door, keys in hand. She was right, but stopping by to see my mother hadn't been on my list of things to do that day.

Imagine my surprise when a couple hours later, I was standing at the desk of another woman's who also hadn't been on my list to see that day. Or any day, to be honest.

* * *

Sandra

The romance novels I love to devour often talk of the heroine feeling the presence of her hero before seeing him. I'd never had that experience in my life. Not once. Until that moment as I stared at my computer screen and a feeling crept through me, that I'd only felt in the presence of one man. The goosebumps rising along my arms told me I wasn't making it up.

"Hello."

Did his voice have to be so deep? And so silky? And so rich and full of … everything?

"Sandra?"

Oh shoot. I still hadn't said anything.

I turned, pulling the earbuds from my ear. They hadn't been on. I'd heard his "hello" loud and clear.

"Damon." My voice was breathless. I stood from my chair. "H-how are you?" I smoothed down the edges of the pastel pink pants I wore before unconsciously straightening out the belted bow of the pants.

His thick lips spread into a smile, displaying his perfectly straight and blindingly white teeth. He was obviously a man who believed in managing his appearance. I briefly wondered if he ever wore braces as a child.

"I'm doing well. Was in the office for a meeting so I thought I'd come visit."

"Office?" I glanced around as if I'd forgotten I was even at work.

"Yeah, but the real estate division. Connors is my head attorney."

"Oh, right." I nodded, my brain suddenly coming back to life. We did indeed have a real estate division in this law firm.

"How's your car?"

I frowned, my stomach dropping a little. There hadn't been any good news regarding my car. For the past week and three days I'd been using Uber to get around.

"That doesn't look good."

I lowered my head slightly then remembered that was probably rude. "It's not. The mechanic says it'll cost more to fix than it's worth. He's giving me a few days to decide what I want to do."

Damon nodded in understanding. "Then you need a new car?"

I pushed out a breath, my shoulders slumping. I really wanted to put off buying a new car. I'd been saving up for a new one but hadn't quite reached my goal just get.

"Looks like it."

"That's not a terrible thing."

I shrugged. "In the grand scheme of things—" I stopped short when my office phone began ringing. "Can you excuse me for one second?"

"Sure thing."

Turning, I frowned, looking at the time. It was almost a quarter after one which meant I was supposed to be on my lunch break. The receptionist usually held my calls during the hour, so to have my phone ringing surprised me.

"Sandra Robinson, how may I help you?"

"Ms. Robinson, this is Mrs. Green, at P.S. 150—"

"The school nurse!" I blurted out, my heartbeat starting to race. I immediately began opening my drawer for my bag and cell phone. "Is she okay? What happened?"

"There was an incident. Monique collapsed on the playground. It appears she didn't have her insulin with her."

"Oh my god! Where is she now?"

"She's being taken to Williamsport General. The school's social worker, Debbie, is with her."

"I'm on my way." I frantically hung up the phone, grabbed my handbag and cell phone, and spun around to let Emma know I was leaving for the day. On second thought, I'd tell Emma from the car. My baby needed me.

"Unf!" I let out as I walked into a damn brick wall.

"What happened?"

His big hand cupped my upper arm and I felt myself wanting to lean into that strength.

"Monique got sick at school. She's being taken to the hospital. I have to get to her." I said it all in one breath.

"I'll take you."

I peered up at him. "What?"

"You don't have a car, right? You'd have to wait for an Uber or a taxi."

I swallowed and nodded.

"Let me take you to your daughter."

I pushed out a breath and let him lead me by the arm down the hall of my office and out the door. It was only when we stepped over the threshold of the main entrance did I realize his hand was still firmly gripping my arm. I wondered if the shaking from my legs was from his touch or the fear running through me over the well-being of my child.

It took approximately twenty-minutes to get from my job to

Williamsport General. While on the way, I sent a text to Emma letting her know what happened. I was grateful when her response was to please keep her informed on how Monique was doing and she insisted I take the remainder of the day off. Past attorneys I'd worked for couldn't care less I had a sick child at home or in the hospital. All they cared about was billable hours and productivity.

As soon as Damon pulled up to the entranceway of the emergency department, I hopped out of the passenger seat, slammed his door shut, and ran inside.

"I'm looking for Monique Robinson, please," I stated urgently to the woman behind the nearest desk I could find. I didn't waste time waiting for her to respond as I glanced up and around at the people filling the room.

"And you are?" the woman asked.

"Mrs. Robinson?"

My head swiveled and I saw a woman I knew was a counselor at Monique's elementary school. I ran over to her.

"Where is she? How is she?" I demanded.

"She's better now. They had to give her some insulin. She's resting behind one of the curtains. Follow me."

I followed the woman to a far end of the emergency department that was separated into rooms by those hanging cloth shower curtain looking things that hospitals used.

"Hey, Mommy," Monique stated a little weakly. Her eyes were droopy as well but she was smiling.

"Hey, baby," I responded, rushing to her side, and smoothing the top of her hair back, pressing a kiss to her forehead. "How're you feeling?" I asked, my voice softening with concern.

"Tired but I'm okay."

I gave her a small smile. Monique could be feeling like she'd just gotten hit by a bus and she'd still tell me she was doing fine. She knew her mother was a worrier.

"What happened?" I asked her, pulling up the chair that sat in the corner, taking her hand in mine.

She shrugged. "I don't know?"

That didn't make sense.

"Did you not take your insulin outside with you?" The nurse had said she'd collapsed on the playground, so I'd concluded that she must've left her insulin in the classroom, forgetting it, and when her insulin dropped, she didn't have it to medicate with.

"She says she forgot it at home."

I looked from my daughter to the school counselor, eyes going wide.

"What?" I turned back to Monique.

"Mrs. Robinson, can I speak with you for a moment?"

"Yes, of course." I gave Monique another kiss before following the counselor out of the makeshift room. I pulled the curtain back.

"Mrs. Robinson, this was a very scary incident."

I was thrown by the accusatory tone in the woman's voice.

"I'm the last person you need to tell that to."

"I was advised that when Monique's teacher went to go search for the insulin in her bag, it wasn't there. *That* is what caused the issue."

I began shaking my head. "That can't be."

"It was, and I must say it is highly inadvisable to send your daughter who has such a delicate medical issue to school without the proper medications."

Is this bitch out of her mind? I rarely cursed, but when it came to my daughter …

"First of all, I'd *advise* you to check your tone when you're speaking to me about my child. Secondly, not a day goes by that I don't check Monique's bag to make sure her insulin, lunch, and extra snacks and juice are packed with her so that this very thing does not happen. So if insulin couldn't be found, it's because your incompetent staff couldn't be so bothered to help my daughter."

I pushed out a breath as my nostrils flared. I was furious. I'd lost count of all of the sleepless nights I'd had going in Monique's room checking and rechecking her insulin level while she slept. Not a morning went by that I didn't stop to make sure she had her medicines with her. Hell, I'd even fought the school district when they tried to force me to let the school nurse hold onto Monique's insulin throughout the day. While I'm sure the nurse was decent enough, she was responsible for the health of hundreds of students throughout the day. I'd much rather have Monique keep her insulin on her because she knew better than anyone when it needed to be checked or she wasn't feeling well.

"Maybe it's time for you to head back to the school."

I looked up behind the counselor at the sound of Damon's deep voice behind her. Both of his eyes appeared to be slightly darker than their usual color, although I could've just been imagining things.

"You must be Monique's father," the counselor stated, breathless.

"Who I am isn't really your concern."

Okay, if I had suspected before, I knew right then that he, like me, was pissed.

"Mrs. Robinson—"

"*Ms.* Robinson," I emphasized. "You can leave now. I will speak to the doctors about my daughter."

I stared the woman down right into those hazel eyes of hers until she finally lowered her head and turned to leave. I watched as she proceeded through the double doors of the ED.

Rolling my eyes, I turned to head back to Monique. I needed to check on her and speak with the doctor to make sure she was okay, and then ask her about her missing insulin. I wondered if some knucklehead child in her class could've stolen it from her as some sort of joke.

"Mr. Damon." Monique perked up, not at my entrance back into the room. No. That was saved for the man behind me.

"Hey, short stuff," he responded, his voice sounding much lighter than it'd sounded out in the hallway.

Monique giggled at the silly nickname.

I frowned, my gaze bouncing between the two of them. When the hell had they formed any type of bond?

"Mommy, Mr. Damon was over Aunt Kayla and Uncle Josh's house when they babysat me. He played video games with me and Diego."

Well, I guess I had my answer.

"Diego and I," I corrected.

"Short stuff almost beat me, too," Damon spoke up. "How're you feeling?"

"I'm fine."

I lifted an eyebrow and Monique looked over at me, her little face giving me an uncertain look. She knew that I knew she was telling a fib.

"Sweetie, what happened to your insulin? The counselor said the teacher couldn't find it."

Monique shrugged and peered down at her fingernails. Something she did when she was lying.

"Mo," I leaned down, cupping her chin, "you won't get in trouble. But I need you to tell me the truth."

"I am, Mommy."

I released the breath I'd been holding. I knew my little girl was lying and I don't know what hurt more—the fact that something was causing her to feel ashamed or the fact that she felt she couldn't come to me about it.

"Hey, short stuff," Damon called.

I looked over at him as he playfully wiggled her right foot.

"Your mom was really worried about you. I was, too."

I swallowed. He sounded so sincere as he moved up the side of the bed, standing at Monique's side, opposite myself. His six-foot-three body towered over my daughter and I, but it felt protective more than menacing.

"You were?" Monique asked, looking at me with eyes that were identical to my own and filled with worry.

"Of course I was. I dropped everything to get here. Mr. Damon was kind enough to give me a ride."

Monique swallowed and returned her attention to Damon. "Thank you, Mr. Damon, for helping my mommy."

She looked down at her fingers again. Just when I was about to ask her again what happened at school, she opened up.

"Some kids were teasing me."

I held my breath.

"They were calling me names. Saying I was a junkie because I knew how to give myself a needle. What's a junkie?"

I was stunned into silence. How did nine year olds even know such language? I shook my head.

"It's nothing you ever need to worry about," Damon stated firmly, cutting my response off before I could even muster the words.

"How long has this been going on?"

"Since the beginning of the school year."

I sighed. "Why didn't you tell me?"

She shrugged.

"And what happened to your insulin?" I knew without a doubt I had seen her put it in her bag this morning, just like I did every morning.

"Right before we left, I told you I'd forgotten my notebook."

I nodded, remembering.

"I went back to my room and took out my insulin pack."

"Monique," I sighed out. I fought hard not to yell at her. It was beyond a stupid thing to do. Not having her insulin could literally mean the difference between life and death. But I had to remember she was only a child. A child who didn't ask to be sick, nor did she ask for the little assholes in her class to make fun of her for being sick.

"I'm sorry, Mommy. I didn't mean to scare you."

My heart shredded at the pleading in her voice.

"It's okay." I stood and kissed her forehead again.

"Monique Robinson?"

I glanced up at the woman who'd just entered the room.

"Hi, I'm Dr. Walker."

I reached out to shake her hand. "Hi, I'm Sandra, Monique's mother. How's she doing?"

"Her blood sugar was dangerously low when she first came in. But from the looks of it, she's doing a lot better now."

Just then the sound of Monique's giggle had me turning and looking over at her. Damon had pulled out his cell phone and was showing her something on the screen.

A small smile creased my face before I turned back to the doctor.

"Will I be able to take her home today or does she have to be admitted overnight?" This wouldn't be the first time we had to pull an overnight at the hospital.

"We'll run the tests in another hour, and if all checks out you should be able to take her home."

I nodded. "Thank you, Dr. Walker."

"Do you ever get scared, Mr. Damon?"

I stopped short at Monique's bedside as she posed the question to the only man in the room. The same man who was now sitting in the other chair, leaning over Monique's bed. He looked so natural with his concerned expression.

"Not so much anymore. My pops taught me to fear no man. When I was just about your age and I told him I was afraid of doing something because of what other kids would think of me, he told me to *never* lie to myself to make someone else feel better. He said that betraying myself was the worst kind of betrayal. And that's what I was doing when I only followed the crowd instead of doing what I wanted or needed to do. Betraying myself."

I swallowed the lump forming in my throat as I watched those two.

"I don't have a dad," Monique responded, sadness peppering her voice.

The usual guilt and shame that came up whenever she asked about having a daddy formed like a dark cloud over me.

"But my mom tells me it's okay to be different. Sometimes I forget."

Damon's eyes shifted from Monique to me, paralyzing me in the spot where I stood.

"Your mom's right. Being the same as everyone gets boring. And you, short stuff, are far from boring." His voice lightened as he looked back at Monique, reaching a finger under her chin and tickling her, causing even more giggles.

I blinked after a few more seconds and finally got my wits about me again.

"Damon, can I speak to you in the hall for a moment?"

He raised a dark eyebrow and unconsciously ran a hand down his thick beard, smoothing it out.

Did he have to do that? And did he have to look so damn good?

"Hey, thank you for bringing me down here. I, uh, well, the doctors will have to take another test in a little while and wait for the results to come back. That will be at least an hour. Hopefully, I'll be able to take her home after that. You can head out. We'll just catch an Uber home. I can pay you for the ri—"

"Pay me?"

I inhaled sharply at the offense I heard in his voice. Obviously, I'd said the wrong thing.

"Like I'm a goddamn Uber driver? I don't need your money."

"I'm sorry. I'm just used to paying my own way." *Especially with men.* I never wanted to be made to feel like I owed them something I wasn't willing to give.

A small tick in his jaw moved, barely noticeable through the beard but I caught it.

"You don't owe me. I'll stay until she's cleared and take you both home. I just need to rearrange a few things." And with that, he turned, pulling his cell phone out of his pocket and moving back into the room where Monique was.

I stood there feeling thoroughly chastised and somehow ashamed for offering to pay him for bringing me to the hospital. Maybe it was a little rude. But how the hell was I to know that? It's not like he was a friend of mine. He was a friend of a friend. Barely an acquaintance.

And yet he's gone out of his way for you twice.

"Sandra? Is that you?"

An eerily familiar voice pulled me out of my musings about the man behind the curtain. The same voice that had been absent from my life for over ten years now.

I turned my head and looked up to see a ghost. At least, that's what it felt like. My mouth parted but I had no response to give.

"I thought that was you. You look … great." My grandmother's dark brown eyes moved down my body, her full, glossed lips spreading into an appreciative smile.

I ran my hand down the side of my pants, smoothing out invisible wrinkles because even though it'd been a decade since she kicked me out, I still seemed to yearn for her approval.

"Gr-grandmother," I finally eked out.

"How are you?" she questioned, lifting a smiling gaze in my direction.

I started to return the smile but then a flash of memory befell me, throwing me back to that summer day years ago when she tossed me out on my butt. The words she spouted at me and the look in her eyes, as if I was no better than the trash she'd often tossed in jail throughout her time as a judge, and a prosecutor before that.

I stood up straighter, squaring my shoulders and lifting my chin. "Fine."

The brevity of my response obviously surprised her a little.

"Are you all right?"

My eyes narrowed and I folded my arms. "Why wouldn't I be?"

She glanced around. "We're in a hospital."

I ground my teeth. "Not for much longer. We'll be leaving soon."

"We?" Her perfectly arched eyebrow rose.

"My daughter and I."

Her eyes enlarged. "Daughter? Y-you had a little girl," she stated as if she cared. "Is she sick?"

"She's none of your concern."

Her mouth snapped shut. I was expecting her to let me have it. I'd never spoken to my grandmother with anything besides respect. Even the day she kicked me out, though I was defiant in my wishes to keep my child, I pleaded with her to understand. But more than to under-stand, to still love me.

She'd chosen not to. And in doing so, she'd lost my respect. It wasn't until that moment that I even realized that.

"C-could I meet her?"

She took a step forward, and I moved directly in front of her, blocking her access to the curtain, and most importantly, my daughter behind it.

"No," I answered flatly.

"Sandra, I—"

"I really need to get back to her."

"Oh. Okay."

I started to turn my back on my grandmother.

"Sandra, wait."

In spite of my anger I turned back to face her.

"Please, I know … you have every reason in the world not to speak to me again, but please, just take my card. It has my home and cell numbers. I've changed them since …"

You kicked me out.

I let those four words hanging in the air, unsaid. We both knew they were there. Between us just like the past ten years.

Out of interest of getting back to Monique without any further delay, I took the card from my grandmother's hand and shoved it in my pocket. After giving her a curt nod, I turned back to enter the room where Monique and Damon were laughing together as if they were old friend.

I had no intentions of calling my grandmother.

CHAPTER 5

*D*amon

"Don't thank me again," I stated a little more angrily than I'd originally intended. I immediately felt like an ass when Sandra's eyes drooped as she sat in my passenger seat. We were on the way to her apartment. Monique had just been released from the hospital and was she in the backseat. She's fallen asleep within the first five minutes of our ride.

When, out of the corner of my eye, I saw Sandra turn to me to say something, that'd been my automatic response. I got the sense she couldn't help herself, but shit, to be honest, I was still pissed she even formed the words to offer to pay me for bringing her to the hospital.

"What the hell type of men have you been with?" I blurted out due to my own frustration.

Sandra gasped and looked at me, eyes wide. She then turned to the backseat, presumably hoping Monique hadn't heard the question. Feeling a little ashamed, I peered into the rearview mirror and sighed in relief to see that she was still sleeping peacefully.

"What type of question is that?"

"A real one. I just want to know what type of men you're used to that would make you believe it's okay to offer me money for bringing you to the hospital so that you could tend to your sick child."

She pushed out a breath, and just when I thought she was going to have some sort of response, she peered out of the passenger side window.

She was silent for the rest of the drive.

That was a real fuckboy move you just pulled.

I cursed my own self out in my head the entire ride to her place. I hadn't meant to be so harsh, but for some reason her feeling like she owed me something pissed me off. Or was it the knowledge that men in her past had made her feel like she owed them something that got to me more?

"Monique, we're home," Sandra called, sweetly, rousing the nine-year-old girl out of her sleep.

A few seconds later, Monique, Sandra, and I were entering her building's elevator on our way up to the fifth floor. Still, it was silent.

I followed behind Sandra because I wanted to walk them to their door and I was still trying to figure out how to apologize for my words in the car.

"Go ahead inside and change out of your school uniform. I'll be in, in a second," Sandra said to Monique as she unlocked and held their apartment door ajar.

"'K. Thanks, Mr. Damon." Monique gave me a sleepy wave.

"You make sure to take your medication, short stuff," I called after her, causing her to laugh. Even at nine it was obvious Monique took after her mother's height.

Speaking of …

"Sandra, I'm sorry—"

"You want to know about the case currently I'm working on?" she questioned, abruptly turning to me and folding her arms.

Feeling the anger suddenly rolling off her, I took a step back. Damn she was fine when she was pissed. Her brown skin glowed, full lips pinched, button nose flared, and those huge maple syrup saucers she called eyes took on a certain glow that sent my damn body on full alert. And it wasn't out of fear.

Shit.

"I'll tell you. A little over a week ago—the same day my car died, as a matter of fact—a twenty-two-year-old woman came into the office. She told us a story of how for the past four years she's worked as a waitress at a popular diner. And at said diner, her bosses have fondled her, locked her in a deep freezer when she refused to have sex with one, kept her late hours, and stolen her tips, refused to give her her paycheck unless she sat on her boss' lap while he got off and so much more. She'd recently been fired for finally standing up to one of her managers and threatening to call the police on him."

"That's wild."

"No. What's wild is that the same owner and manager have gotten away with this type of behavior for *years*. Because when *I* worked at the same diner while heavily pregnant with my daughter, I endured or witnessed the same treatment. So, I learned most interactions with the opposite sex were transactions. And these days, the *only* form of currency I'm willing to give is in the form of money. That is why I offered to pay you. Because I know very few men who do things out of the goodness of their heart or simply because they're a nice guy. I would apologize for offending you but I'm not sorry."

How the hell did her statement piss me off and turn me on at the same time?

I took a step closer.

"You *didn't* know any man like that, until you met me."

Her eyes widened, and I watched as the rise and fall of her chest increased beneath the white silk blouse she wore.

"I'm not willing to take what you aren't willing to give."

"I don't have anything to give besides money." She tried to sound firm and strong in her decision. But the wobble in her voice ripped her lie to shreds.

Leaning down, I brushed my lips across hers. "You sure about that?" I asked just before brushing my lips against hers again. She shuddered and then parted her lips ever so slightly.

Everything in my body wanted to move in for the kill. To pull her little ass into me and take possession of those lips, wiping away any ideas she may have had that I was only being nice to get a piece of ass.

Instead of listening to my base self, however, I placed a kiss to the corner of her lips before rising to stand straight again and taking a half a step backwards.

Her eyes held a considerable amount of confusion. I wondered if mine were a mirror of hers. But instead of voicing that concern, I said, "Saturday. We're going car shopping."

Her forehead wrinkled. "Car shopping? How did we get on that topic?"

"You need a new one, and to be shown not every man you meet is just looking for some type of transaction."

Her eyes widened. "My car—"

"Is dead and you need a new one."

"I thought you didn't know much about cars."

"I don't but I know people who do and can point you in the right direction."

"I have some money saved … for a new car. I've known for some time I'd be needing a new one soon."

I nodded, not bothering to press that issue.

"Saturday at ten a.m. I'll see you then."

"Saturday." She nodded reluctantly but confirming.

I released a breath in relief, glad she wasn't going to try to give some excuse as to why I couldn't help her car shopping. I pulled out my phone to get her number. Then I sent a text to her phone so she'd have my number.

I watched as she turned and opened the door to her apartment. A stronger man would've left but I stood there, watching her entire body from head to toe, from behind. It wasn't the first time I'd done that. At Joshua and Kayla's wedding, I'd noticed the short chick with the thick thighs and ass to match. But unlike the Instagram models of our times, this particular woman didn't flaunt the figure she'd gotten naturally. I could tell there had been no surgical enhancements where Sandra's assets were concerned. If the natural sway of her backside and thickness of her thighs didn't give it away, the reticent demeanor, bordering on an innocence that couldn't be faked, would've.

It was that innocence that had forced me to keep my hands to my damn self where Sandra Robinson was concerned. But shit, I had to remind myself she wasn't *too* innocent. After all, she did have a daughter. One who looked just like her so she had to have some type of experience.

And as soon as that realization formed in my head I had to shake it loose. The thought of another man … Yeah, every woman has a past. Whatever. But I didn't need to think about it. Because the level of anger that rose in me was irrational at that thought.

I forced myself to think on work matters as I strutted down the hall to take the stairs back to the parking lot where I'd left my car.

* * *

"You finally decided to show up."

Here we fucking go.

I pushed out my frustration through my nostrils while I stood upright, across from my mother as she opened the door I'd just knocked on.

"I don't know why you didn't just use your key." She shrugged and turned, leaving me to enter and shut the door behind me.

"Good to see you, too, Mama," I retorted, sarcasm apparent in my voice.

"I'm sure Charlotte had something to do with you stopping by. I told that girl to leave it alone."

I frowned, knowing the truth likely was that my mother told my sister how long it'd been since I'd last visited, ad nauseum, hoping that she'd get me to stop by. I loved my mother but she was difficult as hell to deal with.

"Charlotte didn't say anything. I wanted to stop by and see how you were doing. For myself." I glanced around the spacious two-thousand square foot condo I'd purchased for my mother about five years prior. The hardwood floors and open floor plan would've been anyone's dream home. The place was decorated in earth tones, and there were a number of paintings that lined the walls depicting various images of black men and women, either holding one another, cradling the earth and such. My mother had loved such images when I was a child. Now, however, the only thing she seemed to love was telling the world how much I didn't visit her.

"I told you over the phone, I've been fine." My mother, at five foot nine, extended her heavy arms, displaying the oversized T-shirt she wore and baggy grey sweatpants before she plopped down on the brown leather loveseat. My mother had let herself go in more ways than one since my father died.

"You quit going to that gym class you had been telling me about?" I moved fully into the living room space and sat diagonal from my mother on the long couch but angled my body to see her.

Her dark eyes averted, turning to the fireplace that she never used.

"All them rich white women going to that fancy gym. All they do is talk about where their child is going to school or what play he or she is in or whatever." She waved her hand in the air.

"What does a bunch of mothers bragging on their kids have to do with you not working out? I thought you liked it there? The gym is only right around the corner from here." Lord knows, she didn't get out the house to do anything else. Over the years, I'd signed my mother up to do so many different things she used to like. But she either found an excuse to stop going or never go in the first place.

"It's too cold to go out and sweat, and then have to walk back over here all wet in the cold."

I held my tongue, avoiding telling her that winter was winding down and had been mild this year. That just wasn't my place. If she wanted to spend her days inside, who the hell was I to force her out? My job was to make sure she had a comfortable roof over her head, food in her refrigerator, and money for the bills and any other spending she needed. I'd done my job.

"I don't like working out with other people no way. I'll just pop in one of those DVDs Charlotte bought for me and do it here. You staying for dinner?"

I wanted to say no but felt obligated since I knew she'd be eating alone. Charlotte lived in the same building but had an active social life. And from what she'd told me earlier in the day, she was going out with some friends for dinner.

"What are you having?"

"Some rice and gravy, peas, and fried chicken."

I cringed. I'd just have to put in a few more hours at the gym that week to make up for dinner.

"Yeah, I'll stay."

I saw my mother's eyes light up for just a second, but then the frown that seemed to be etched into her face permanently returned.

"Let me go heat this food up."

I nodded and stood, removing my suit jacket and tie. I didn't see the point in keeping them on since I was only having dinner with my mother.

As we sat down to the wooden dining table that sat right in front of the sliding glass doors leading to the balcony, I glanced up and admired the view from her window.

"What you staring at? Someone peeking in here?" My mother turned to look out the window. "This is why I keep the damn blinds closed. Charlotte always coming in here opening these damn things."

"No, Mama," I insisted, "I was just checking out the view. At the sunset."

"Oh." She waved a dismissive hand, turning back to the table.

I shook my head. "Thanks for dinner, Ma. You cooked this?"

Nodding, she shrugged. "Nothing else to do around here."

"That cooking class you signed up for last year still on-going? Since you like cooking—"

"I ain't going to no cooking class. Them people didn't even know what lard was."

I frowned.

The last thing my mother needed was to be cooking with some damn lard. It was a healthy cooking class that Charlotte had told me about, asking me to sign our mother up for it, aka pay for it.

"Tell me about business," my mother insisted as we ate.

I swallowed a forkful of the rice with gravy before wiping my mouth. "Business is business."

"And them watches you love?"

"They're coming along. Sean just dropped off a mockup of one today. We'll have a prototype of it soon, hopefully."

My mother rolled her eyes and planted her elbow on the table, pointing her fork at me. "I don't know why you keep that boy around. If he's anything like his mother ..."

"Sean's cool, Mama."

"Anita took that boy all the way to California. She didn't even come back when your daddy died. What type of sister is that?"

My hand tightened around the fork I held. Sean was my cousin on my father's side. My Aunt Anita was my father's sister. Apparently, either before I was born or when I was real young, my mother and my aunt had had some type of falling out. My aunt moved to California with her then husband when Sean was only a few months old. She didn't speak to our side of the family for years, even well after my father died. It wasn't until her husband died and she moved back to Williamsport when Sean was sixteen and I was seventeen that I even met them. But like I said, Sean was my right hand. Whatever was between my aunt and my mother was their damn business.

"She's selfish. Lamar was dead in his damn grave, his two kids starving after he died, and she ain't have the damn decency—"

"Mama, let it go."

"I'll let it go, all right. As soon as she apologizes for what she di—"

"Drop it!" I snapped, slamming my hand on the table.

Her tirade stopped abruptly, mouth parted and eyes bulged as if she couldn't believe I raised my voice at her. Shit, neither could I. I might not enjoy spending too much time with my mother but I always managed to maintain a certain level of respect. After all, she was the woman who'd brought me into this world. But when she started talking about my father? Well, that always brought up memories I'd rather forget.

Truth be told, Aunt Anita had apologized to both Charlotte and I for not being around when my father died. She'd tried to apologize to my mother, too, but got rejected. My mother much rather preferred sitting in her bitterness.

"I'm sorry, Mama—"

"No, no." She shook her head. "I see she done got to you too. I bet you think she's a better mother than I am. Wish she had raised you instead of me."

I bit my tongue and neglected to tell her that she'd barely raised me. Once my father was killed, for months she was barely able to get out of bed. And when she finally did, she might as well have stayed there.

"Bullshit," I mumbled as I watched my mother walk off down the hall, clearly pissed off. I wasn't about to run after her like my father had always done. I'd been taking care of her like I was the parent and she was the damn child.

I went over to the sink and scrapped the uneaten portion of my food into the disposal before sticking all of our dishes into the dishwasher. It was only then I discovered the damn thing was full with dishes that still had yet to be cleaned. I put our dirty dishes in the sink before turning the dishwasher on to clean what was already there.

I didn't bother saying bye to my mother. When she got like this, time and distance were the best remedies. I set the alarm before heading out to the garage where I'd parked. It'd likely be another few months before I was back over here.

CHAPTER 6

*D*amon
"Dad!" I yelled down the dark alleyway.

He turned to me, but in the dark I couldn't see the expression on his face.

"Son? What the hell are you doing here?" He sounded panicked even to my thirteen-year-old ears.

"I—"

"Shh!" He looked up as if hearing something. "Shit. Get behind that dumpster and don't come out until I come and get you."

"Dad, wait—"

"Damon, do as your father tells you!" he ordered. "And don't let nobody see you."

Moving quickly, assisted by his pushing at my shoulders, I ducked behind the dumpster, low so that I couldn't be seen by anyone who passed.

"Remember, stay there."

I'd never heard that tone of voice from my father. I'd heard him calm, in charge, even pissed off but never scared. And recognizing that in that moment, my father was scared, terrified me.

I worked hard to keep my breathing under control. I tried to move my head around to be able to see past the side of the dumpster, to spot my father, but I stopped moving when I heard another voice.

"You got the stuff?"

I wasn't familiar with the person who the voice belonged to.

"Yeah, I got it, but things have changed."

Somehow, I knew that wasn't a good thing.

"I'm not doing this anymore. I got a family—"

Laughter sounded.

"A fucking family? We all got families. You think you're the only one with skin in this fucking game?"

"My concern isn't for anyone else."

I swallowed as my heart raced.

"Fuck your family!" another voice sounded. A millisecond later I heard the distinct sound of spit hitting the ground.

"And fuck you," my father retorted.

"Is that necessary, Lamar? We been in business together, what? Fifteen years? Since you was a teen ya self. How old's your boy now?"

"Don't ever mention my fucking son."

"Temper. I'm just saying you weren't much older than him when you joined this game, were you? I bet he likes that fancy school and nice house he lives in. It'd be a—"

Whoever the man was that'd been talking about me stopped when a clicking sound went off.

"Lamar, put away your fucking gun."

"Nah, you wanted to mention my son so now this is what it's gotta be." *My father's voice hardened into what I recognized as his protective mode. He used it often when we were out in public and some dude tried to talk to my mother or some person would come up asking for something.*

A few more clicking sounds sounded.

"You're out gunned, Lamar. What'd you think you could take me on all by your damn self?"

"If need be," my father responded, defiantly.

"You thought wrong, motherfucker!"

I gasped and then quickly covered my mouth with both my hands and squeezed my eyes shut when loud popping sounds that sounded like fire-crackers started going off.

* * *

"Shit!" I sat up in bed sweaty and chest heaving as I woke up from my dream. Blinking a couple of times, I glanced around my darkened bedroom, before turning to the clock on my nightstand. It read twelve-oh-eight.

Fuck! I thought, running my hands through my low cut Caesar. I hated waking up in the middle of the night like this, though I was no stranger to it either. Pushing the blankets and sheets off of me, I grabbed my phone to check the date. It was a Thursday which meant I could easily find a fight down at our spot. And since sleep wasn't going to happen that night, I stood from my bed, stretching before grabbing a pair of grey sweats, a T-shirt, socks, and sneakers, and was out the door in minutes. I always kept a duffle bag of fighting clothes in the trunk of my car.

Twenty minutes later I was pulling into the underground garage that was connected to the basement of the building we fought in. I parked, hopped out of my car, grabbed the bag from my trunk, and within a few minutes was pounding against the metal door. Two knocks, wait a second, then another three knocks—the secret code to alert whoever was watching the door that night the person on the other side belonged there.

"Damon, what's up?"

I nodded and slapped hands with the young guy who'd opened up for me.

"Come to watch or participate?"

"Fight," I answered.

"That's what I'm talking about." Grinning, he rubbed his hands together.

"Who's here tonight, Rich?"

"Doc, Brick, and you so far to fight. A few of the newer guys just came to watch."

I nodded.

"Buddy's in the back."

"Cool." I strolled off and gave a couple of head nods to some of the guys who were sitting around the ring we'd set up, waiting for the next bout.

"Nightmares still keeping you up?"

I narrowed my eyes and turned to the five-foot-eight pain in the ass. "Mind your damn business."

Buddy grinned and laughed as if he cracked his own self up. Buddy was older, in his fifties, and had been a boxing coach and trainer for years. Now, he was the guy who refereed, supervised, and even helped patch up the fighters down here. I'd known him for years yet had never told him about the dreams that kept me up some nights. But I suspected I wasn't the only one who had trouble sleeping at night. Shit, why the hell would any other sane adult be out in the middle of the damn night fighting for nothing but the bragging rights within our underground circle?

"Doc's up tonight. I was going to put him in the ring with Brick, but I can save Brick for Daniel. You want a shot at Doc?"

"Hell yeah."

Buddy narrowed his pale green eyes that wrinkled at the corners and nodded. "Get changed."

I passed Buddy to head to the changing room where I threw on a pair of shorts. Buddy came in a minute later and helped me wrap my hands. Five minutes later, I was entering the ring and came face-to-face with the guy we referred to as "Doc."

The jackass had the nerve to grin when he turned and saw me.

"Want a rematch, huh? Last time wasn't enough of an ass whooping?"

I frowned. "Talking shit usually leads to trouble, pretty boy. Close your damn mouth and lets get this started so I can wear that ass out."

Doc chuckled.

I pictured myself dislodging one of his perfect pearly white teeth from his damn jaw. I didn't dislike the man or anything, but the last time we were in the ring together, he'd caught me off guard and I walked around with bruised ribs for a week. I'll also mention that that had been the night of Joshua's wedding. After I'd taken Scarlet home and fucked her but still wasn't satisfied because I hadn't had the woman I really wanted. Images of Sandra in that long, black dress that had held those curves of hers just right had danced around in my head even while fighting. That was how Doc aka Jacob was able to knock me off my square.

"Shit!" I grunted as I ducked a fist aimed at my temple. I'd done it again. Gotten lost in thoughts of her while in the ring. Hell, at least my mind was off the fucking dreams.

"Fuck!" Doc grunted just after my left hook landed in his ribs.

"Payback's a mother lover, ain't she!" I taunted, as I circled Doc.

We had one rule in the ring. No head shots. We'd recently implemented it. Like I said, we all were businessmen and professionals. We weren't keen on the idea of walking around with black eyes or bruised cheekbones and shit.

Doc and I continued to circle one another, bouncing on the balls of our feet, keeping ourselves light on our toes. It helped when it came time to pivot out of the way. Doc attempted to land a leg sweep, one of his signature moves, but I wasn't falling for that shit. He was a sneaky motherfucker in the ring. His speed was second only to Joshua's. Considering I was bulkier than Doc, I was a touch slower but my blows made an impact. So, when I did make contact it slowed his ass down.

We went three rounds until Buddy finally called it.

"Give someone else a turn, why don't you?" he yelled out, getting in between us.

Doc and I touched fists to signal the end of the match and then ambled our way out of the ring. Two more guys entered but I didn't bother to turn back to see who was fighting.

"Nice spin move to avoid the leg sweep. You been practicing," Doc stated as he tossed me a towel in the changing room.

I caught it with one hand. "The only reason you caught me off guard last time is 'cause I had shit on my mind." I pulled a bottle of water from the refrigerator in the changing room. Again, that was Joshua's thing.

"We all got shit on our mind."

I nodded and swallowed. "How's the cosmetic surgery business? Ass implants still taking up most of your day?"

He gave a half smile and rolled his eyes. "Not as much."

"Then breast implants."

"Those will never grow old."

I chuckled. In our out-of-the-ring life, Jacob was actually an up and coming plastic surgeon. I'd once asked him why the hell a surgeon would get into a goddamned fight club. There was a high percentage of broken fingers, sprained wrists, and the like. The absolute worst things for a surgeon. He'd only shook his head, shrugged, and said he had his reasons. Shit, we all did.

"I'm heading out. See ya' next week?"

I nodded. "Probably."

We slapped hands and Jacob exited.

I thought about heading home but then the memory of the dream that woke me came to mind. Getting back to sleep with that shit on my mind wasn't an option. So I chose to stay and watch another fight.

As I watched the next two fighters, my mind drifted from the dream I'd had earlier to the woman I was supposed to be seeing this Saturday. That'd been happening a lot lately. Getting lost in thoughts about Sandra and the brief kiss we shared. Hell, I wasn't convinced it could even be called a kiss. A mere brushing together of the lips was more like it, but I'd be damned if it didn't make me physically ache for more.

* * *

Sandra

"Just a minute!" I called from my bedroom. I twisted and turned in the full-length mirror again, making sure the black jeans and burgundy top I'd paired together were fitting correctly. After slipping my feet into a pair of three-inch black leather booties, I headed out, shutting off my bedroom light.

"Coming!" I yelled again to the knocking at the door. I opened the door and … *Damn!*

He looked good, dressed in a sweater turtleneck, and navy jeans with a pair of brown, low top sneakers that matched his top. The brown of the material brought out the deep mahogany color of his skin even more.

This isn't a date, I reminded myself over and over. It was the only thing that had kept me from picking up the phone and telling him thanks but no thanks when it came to helping me look for a car. But this wasn't a date. It was the friend of my good friend's husband who obviously wanted to help … for whatever reason. I had to tell myself he didn't want anything from me other than that.

But as I glanced up into those two distinctive eyes, I knew I was lying to myself. What was worse, was that *I* wanted more, too.

"Sorry I took so long to answer. Please come in." I took a step back to give him space to enter.

"Thank you. Where's short stuff?"

I squinted but then remembered he'd given my daughter a nickname. "Oh! Monique. She's with her sitter. I figured the last thing she wanted to do today was to spend it at the car dealership. She and the sitter went to the library first, and then they're meeting Kayla's sister-in-law, Michelle, and Diego at the Children's Museum."

He nodded, looking around my modest apartment before turning eyes on me.

"I'm guessing she's been feeling better."

I nodded, smiling. "She's been feeling a lot better."

"No more leaving her insulin at home?"

I shook my head. "What you told her about not trying to be like everyone else really stuck with her. Thank you fo—" I stopped when his head lowered and he pinned me with his gaze. "I can't help it, okay?" I laughed.

His lips parted into a smile before a deep chuckle emanated from his throat. And my body temperature rose by five degrees from the sound.

"Besides, we've decided to get her an insulin pump soon. Would you like anything to drink before we leave?" I needed some water.

"Some water would be great."

I nodded and moved from the living room to the kitchen. Only when I was out from under his immediate gaze did I inhale and exhale fully. I poured two glasses of water from my glass pitcher before setting it back in the fridge.

"Thank you," he stated as he took the glass from my hands. Our fingertips brushed against one another's and the charge of energy from the brief touch nearly caused me to spill the water.

This man was more than fine.

He was potent.

Like walking sex.

I swallowed a mouthful of water before I did something embarrassing like say my actual thoughts out loud.

"How long have you lived in this place?" he questioned, looking around the kitchen. The very same one in which his very presence was sucking up all of the oxygen out of. I'd never realized how damn low the ceilings were in my place until seeing Damon's head only about two inches from it.

"Five years."

"You like it?"

I shrugged. "It's okay. Affordable. The commute to work is sort of a pain but you can't get everything you want." After I took the last sip of water, I placed my glass in the sink.

"Says who?"

"Excuse me?"

"Who says you can't get everything you want?"

I paused. "People. Life."

"You need to hang around better people if they're telling you that bullshit."

My eyebrows rose and I stood there stunned as he lowered the now empty glass into the sink.

"Ready?"

"Yes."

The sooner we left the sooner we could get this over with.

I held the door open as Damon passed through and then shut it behind me, locking it.

"I parked out front," he corrected when I started toward the elevator that lead to the parking garage.

We took the stairs down to the lobby of my building, and I passed through the door as Damon held it open for me.

"Is your coat in the car?" I questioned as I tightened the collar of my own blush-colored wool coat that fell a few inches below my waist. We were still very much in winter.

Damon pressed the button to unlock his car and held the passenger side door open for me before responding with, "Didn't bring one."

"Why not?" I questioned as soon as he shut the driver side door.

"Don't need it."

"Why don't you need it? It's only thirty degrees out here."

"Only going from the car to inside usually. I don't like coats. Too cumbersome."

I shook my head. "That doesn't make sense. Plus, we're looking at cars today, so we'll be outside much of the time."

Smirking, he turned to face me.

"You volunteering to keep me warm?"

My mouth fell open. For the second time, I finally started to understand what the romance novels were talking about when they said something was panty-wetting. Sensations I'd only ever felt while reading some of my favorite authors were taken up a couple of levels at the flirtatious grin Damon threw my way.

"Relax," he urged, placing a large hand on my left knee. "I'm a grown ass man, not having a coat won't stop the show." With that, he pulled off.

I sank comfortably into the leather seats of his car. This was the third time I'd ridden in this same vehicle, and it got more and more comfortable with each ride. Or maybe, I was just loosening up in his presence.

"How's the case you're working on going?"

I'd forgotten I told him about the diner case. "It's going." I shrugged. "These things take time. We have to research old similar cases and interview those who were willing to speak up. But that includes somehow convincing those who are reluctant to actually come forward. Our main accuser has come close to backing out, which is understandable. She just wants to live her life, find a new job, and move on with it, which I completely understand. But she also deeply believes that what happened to her was unjust and unfair and she wants to prevent it from happening to other women. She's moved in with her cousin, who convinced her to come to us in the first place, to help her out financially. Otherwise, I'm not sure she'd still be ready or able to pursue the case."

"And you used to work for that same company?"

I wrinkled my forehead at the ominous lilt his voice had taken on with that question.

"For a little while, yes. But I'm sure it'll work out. What kind of cars does your friend sell?" I asked, changing the subject. The last thing I wanted was to think back on the time period I was pregnant and when Monique was really young.

Damon turned his head, briefly looking from the road to me and back to the street again. Somehow, I got the impression that he realized I was uncomfortable with the aforementioned topic.

"He sold me this car."

My eyes widened. "I can't afford a BMW." I glanced around the interior of Damon's luxury vehicle. *No way.*

"Chill. BMWs aren't the only type of vehicles he sells. Besides, we're just looking, right?"

I nodded and pushed out a breath. "Right."

"Anyway, Carlos is good people. His family has been in the car business in one capacity or another for three generations. Even if you don't like anything we look at today, he can steer us in the right direction."

He used the word *us* like this was a joint venture. As if he was more than just a friend of a friend who was invested in seeing me get the right car. That felt good for some strange reason.

"I don't even know what I want." I'd been saving for a car but hadn't actively been looking. My Cavalier had been the first and only car I'd had. That car had taken me a lot of hours on my feet at the diner to save for and it was the cheapest thing I could find.

"How'd you get your last car?"

"One of the waitresses I worked with, her brother liked cars. He would buy and fix them up. She knew I needed a car so she convinced him to lower the price on the Cavalier. Reluctantly, he did."

"What did you like about it?"

I shrugged. "It got me and my daughter to and from work and school."

Damon chuckled. "That's it?"

"Yeah. I never had an interest in anything else." I frowned at the idea that there even was anything beyond that to like about a car.

"A'ight, let's start with the color. What's your favorite color?"

"Magenta."

He looked to me as we came to a red light.

"What?"

He shook his head. "Nothing. I doubt you'll be able to find a magenta colored car."

"Well, you asked."

He nodded. "I should've asked what's your favorite color for a car?"

"Um …" I paused, thinking. "Black." It was simple, didn't draw too much attention.

"We can work with that. And I'm assuming you want a car for the same reasons as you did in the past. Reliability, correct?"

"Yes, of course."

"Price is obviously a factor. Now we've got three criteria to work around. Carlos will be able to help us."

As soon as he finished his statement, he turned on the left side blinker and turned into the parking lot of a car dealership. With those few questions he'd actually helped me to come up with some guidelines for what I wanted in my next car. It was also comforting to know that this time around, I wasn't at the mercy of just finding the cheapest thing I could get my hands on. That knowledge alone had me standing up straighter and walking taller as Damon held the door of the dealership open for me to enter.

CHAPTER 7

*D*amon

Damn she looks good.

I held my car door open as she folded her compact body into the passenger seat. While I was sure she hadn't intended the black skinny jeans and burgundy turtleneck she wore to be a turn on, they were. Especially paired with the pointy ankle booties she donned. Regardless, if she knew it or not, Sandra was sexy as hell. Without even trying. Hell, maybe that's what made her so appealing. She didn't carry herself as if she wanted extra attention from men, or anyone else, for that matter. In fact, at times it was as if she was doing her damndest to hide from additional attention.

But she stuck out.

The thick yet well-toned thighs.

The blemish free copper skin tone that she coated with just enough makeup to enhance what was already there while not completely transforming her facial features.

And the way she dipped her head when put on the spot, which made me want to assure her nothing bad would ever come her way again.

And just when my perception of her being skittish and possibly too needy spiked, she bowled me over when she'd let the counselor from Monique's school have it. Then she'd let *me* have it in the hallway of her apartment complex. Which was why my lips had landed on hers. Hell, it couldn't even be called a kiss. But it did have me hungering for me.

"I can't believe I'm getting a new car. Well, not *new* but a 2017," she gushed as I got in the driver's seat of my car.

"Believe it. I still think you should've gone for the 2018."

She giggled and lightly slapped my shoulder. "Too much. The 2017 Accord was perfect. And I can't believe your friend's prices were so reasonable. I thought I'd be paying nearly double for the make and model that I bought. And it only has five thousand miles."

I wouldn't tell her that Carlos' usual price was indeed much higher than what she was paying for it. And I damn sure wasn't going to tell her that I'd promised Carlos I'd make up the price difference to him. We'd spent hours at the dealership looking at so many different cars I'd lost track. Sandra test drove three different cars. All different makes and models.

"I thought we were going to be stuck there for another eighteen hours," I teased.

Sandra threw me a sideways look. "We were not there that long."

I dramatically shot out my arm and lifted my wrist to my face, staring at the time. "It's damn near five-thirty. We got there around ten-thirty this morning." Carlos had even ordered lunch for us in between test drives.

"I really wanted to get it over with. I asked if you needed to leave and you said no."

"You did and I didn't. I was more than happy to spend the day with you." *Shit. That was a little too honest.* The time had literally flown by.

"Well, thank you for spending the day with me."

"What did I tell you about that thanking me shit?"

"My apologies."

I chuckled. Her ass sounded so formal sometimes. "Are you hungry?"

"Yes. Starving."

"Restaurant Row isn't too far from here. You up for an early dinner or do you need to get back to Monique?"

She shook her head. "Her sitter doesn't mind staying."

"What are you in the mood for?"

"My favorite Greek restaurant is on the Row."

I nodded. Restaurant Row was a nickname all of the locals called a particular area of downtown Williamsport that had a variety of restaurants along this one street.

"I know the one you're talking about." It was a tiny spot toward the end of the street but the food was delicious.

Ten minutes later, after winding through traffic, I pulled into the parking lot at the back of the restaurant.

"It's early yet, so it's not too busy for dinner," Sandra commented as I held the car door open for her.

"Good. I hate waiting." Usually I made reservations but this particular outing had been last minute.

"Mm, it smells divine in here," Sandra declared as we entered the restaurant.

After telling the hostess we needed a table for two, I tucked my right arm around Sandra's lower back and guided her as we followed behind the waitress to a table right next to the window.

"Oh wow!"

"What?" I glanced up after pushing in Sandra's chair for her to sit. I rounded the table to find her staring behind her out of the window.

"See, that's why magenta is my favorite color."

I looked up and noticed the perfect sunset. The sky, off in the distance, was lit up in an array of blues and pinks. My eyes landed back to Sandra who stared with a little grin on her face, admiringly.

"You're a fan of sunsets?"

"You aren't?"

I chuckled. "I am, actually. Spent a lot of late nights and early mornings up working in the first years of building my business. Gave me an appreciation for sunrises and sunsets."

I finally sat down and within seconds our waitress arrived at the table to take our orders.

"That's a nice timepiece."

I raised an eyebrow at Sandra across the table who was eyeing my watch.

"I meant to mention it earlier. It doesn't look like anything I've seen on the market."

"Because it's not," I responded as I removed the watch from my wrist. I bent in closer, holding up the watch for her to see better. "It's a Richmond & Raines original. A prototype actually. We had our designer build it out to give it a try. I wanted to see how it felt."

"We?" Sandra's maple syrup saucers rose to mine.

I nodded. "My cousin, Sean, and I."

"You're in business together? Wait, I thought you were involved in real estate."

The confused wrinkle that popped up between her eyebrows caused me to chuckle. She looked so damn curious and cute at the same time. Lord, save me, I didn't *do* women who were *cute*. Especially women who held so much emotion behind their eyes that it radiated out of them. And definitely not women who pressed every single one of my internal buttons to protect. I hadn't even realized I had those types of buttons for women I wasn't related to. But as Sandra's fingers brushed against mine, as she took the watch I proffered, I started to realize that maybe I didn't know my own damn self as well as I thought I did.

"To answer your question, I am in real estate. Richmond Real Estate is the company I've built up over the last decade. We own and manage a couple of different properties as well as invest in commercial properties, and we've even begun building a few places in recent years. However, I've always had a thing for luxury timepieces. I get it from my pops." I shrugged casually.

"He has a passion for collecting luxury watches also?"

I glanced down at the white linen cloth covering the wooden, circular table, before taking a sip of the lemon water the waitress had brought to our table.

"He did," I responded as I sat the glass back down.

Sandra's eyelids lowered in embarrassment, and I'll be goddamned if my heart didn't stumble over itself a little just to tell her it was all good.

"I'm sorr—"

"Don't be. You didn't know. Anyway, he always had a thing for time. He always said to be on time is to be late and to be late is to be left. He gave me my first Calvin Klein watch for my thirteenth birthday. It wasn't too flashy or anything, but he said he wanted to see how I cared for the watch and if I did well, he'd get me my first Rolex in a few years."

"Whoa," Sandra stated with raised eyebrows. "So how'd you do?"

I shook my head. "I bought my own Rolex on my eighteenth birthday. He died five years earlier just a few months after giving me that Calvin Klein." I grinded my teeth after admitting that out loud to the first person in years.

Sandra cleared her throat. I knew I'd made the conversation awkward as hell but something in me felt okay confiding in her.

"I never knew my father." A soon as the words were out of her mouth, she slapped her hand against her forehead and lowered her face, shamefaced.

Cute as hell.

"I have no earthly idea why I just admitted that."

I chuckled. "It's cool. We're delving into our collective daddy issues."

Raising her head, she gave me a funny look before laughing.

"But in all seriousness, I bet he'd be proud to see all that you've accomplished. This watch is amazing," she stated as her eyes closely examined the stainless steel case with black silicone band. "The hands are stainless steel?" she inquired.

"Observant. Yes." I nodded. "The dial is made of quartz but I'm looking to change that. It reminds me of another brand I already own."

She nodded.

"It's shock resistant as well."

"So you can wear it while working out."

"Exactly. It's meant to be a weekend or off-hours piece. Not a wear to work piece."

She nodded. "I can see that. It looks like you spent a lot of time thinking about and designing it."

"Close to twelve months."

"Any idea when you'll begin selling it?" she questioned as she handed the watch back to me.

"That's up in the air. Like I said, some changes still need to be made. But we've already got one retailer interested. We'll see."

"I would wish you luck, but I don't think you'll need it." She smiled, and I believed that she had total faith in me, which somehow deepened my own faith in myself.

"Now that I've shared a passion of mine, tell me one of yours," I requested just after our waitress placed our plates in front of us and walked away, leaving us to enjoy.

"Me? Um, well, I'm not starting a fortune 500 company any time soon."

I chuckled. "Maybe one day."

She shrugged. "Not likely. But you've already met the main thing I'm passionate about."

I swallowed the forkful of the chicken kabob over rice I'd ordered. "Monique?"

She grinned widely.

Anyone with two eyes could see how much she loved that little girl. At one point, I thought I was going to have to step in front of that counselor at the hospital to keep Sandra from taking her head off. Which is such a departure from the woman I'd thought she was. I mean, yeah, I'd heard most women had that motherly, protective instinct thing going on—we've all heard shit about the mother who lifted an entire car off her toddler—I just hadn't experienced that type of motherly protection in my own life. At least, not when I really needed it.

"She's my world."

"But there has to be something else you're passionate about."

She thought for a minute. "People."

I frowned, curiously.

"Groups of people, why they behave the way they do. I've always wondered. I wanted to go to college and get my PhD to become a professor of sociology."

"And what happened?"

Biting her lower lip, she glanced off out the window. Every protective alarm in my body went off.

Slowly, she turned her head back to me. "I got pregnant and plans changed. Suddenly, spending the next decade as a full-time student didn't seem like the responsible thing to do."

"And Monique's father wasn't around to help out?" *Why did I ask that question? Why the fuck did I bring that shit up?* I had a rule if I happened to date a woman with a kid—*never* ask about the father. It wasn't my business, and I damn sure wasn't trying to make it my business.

Now here I was holding my breath, waiting for Sandra to spill all of the details about the motherfucker that'd gotten her pregnant. He was a motherfucker. I knew it because the terrified expression that covered her delicate face when I'd asked that question almost had me leaping out of my skin to go find him.

Breathe, Damon.

Fucking breathe.

Sandra wiped her mouth with the white linen napkin and I didn't miss the shakiness of her hands.

"N-no. He wasn't around."

A muscle in my jaw flexed as I grinded my teeth for the second time. There were few things I found more abhorrent than deadbeat fathers.

"But I've recently taken up Pilates. I like it, though I wouldn't consider it a passion of mine." She was trying to change the subject.

I'd let her ... for the time being.

"Exercise can be a passion."

She shook her head. "Not for me. I mean, I enjoy it. Kayla and I go to the same classes on Tuesdays and Thursdays after work, and I walk on the treadmill on my lunch break at the gym in my office's building.

Being active help keeps my brain sharp, according to some of the articles I've read on exercise."

"Articles?"

She nodded. "Yeah, I like to research things before I do them. There was an article in the *New England Journal of Medicine* on the importance of movement, especially for those of us who work in offices five days a week for eight or more hours."

In spite of the tension from earlier, I chuckled. "You seem like the type to research everything."

She covered her mouth as she giggled. "As a kid I loved spending my weekends at the library looking up all kinds of facts and history."

I chuckled.

"No wonder I didn't have many friends, huh?" She laughed.

I shook my head. "They just weren't good enough for you," I responded, my voice deeper and slightly thicker than I'd intended.

She looked up at me through lengthy lashes that, at first glance, could've been fake. But Sandra didn't do fake lashes. She wore makeup but it was subtle, not over the top.

We finished our meal, Sandra telling me some of the facts she remembered learning in her spare time as a kid. I got the sense hiding out in the library felt safe for her. She was used to hiding. That I definitely picked up on from the first moment I saw her. Someone should've told her long ago that she was meant to stand out.

"Monique's probably thinking I abandoned her," Sandra stated, laughing as we walked down the hall toward her apartment. She'd just checked her phone and had received a second text from her daughter asking what time she'd be home. "Sometimes I forget who's the daughter and who's the mother in this relationship."

"Short stuff's demanding, huh?"

"You're still insisting on calling my child short stuff?" she questioned, hands on her hips as we stopped in front of her door.

"Hell yeah," I chuckled. "She's short just like her mama."

Sandra lowered her head, laughing.

"You should watch out, you know the little ones have that

Napoleon Complex." As soon as I made the quip, the door opened behind Sandra.

"Mommy! You're home. Oh, hi, Mr. Damon," Monique's little head popped out of the crack in the door.

"Hey, short stuff."

"Monique, where's Ms. Oralia?" Sandra inquired.

"Right here, Sandra. The little one was anxious to see her mommy," an older, Latina woman answered, pulling the door open a little more from behind Monique.

"Mr. Damon, did you buy my mommy a new car?"

Sandra gasped. "Monique, why would you ask that?"

Monique blinked, looking back to her mother with a confused expression. "That's where you went today, right? To buy a new car?"

"Yes, but I—"

"No, short stuff. I helped your mommy look for cars. She bought it herself," I stated, crouching low.

"Is it here?"

I looked up at Sandra.

"It's being cleaned and ready for me to pick up tomorrow."

"Yay!" Monique declared, clapping.

"Come, Monique. Let's let your mommy and Mr. Damon talk."

"Aww," Monique sighed.

"She's a trip," I chuckled, standing upright.

"Lucky me." Sandra rolled her eyes playfully. "I would say thank you for helping me with the car and for dinner but I don't want my head bitten off."

I gave her an incredulous look. "I should be the one afraid of getting their ass handed to them like you did the last time we were standing in this exact same spot."

"I didn't—"

"You did. But it's all good." I took a step closer. "It actually turned me on a little." And just as I suspected she would, a tiny gasp escaped her lips, leaving them parted.

I licked my bottom lip as my eyes remained planted on her full, luscious lips. Forcing myself to look up, my gaze rose to her wide eyes. They were begging me to do exactly as I had done the last time we were standing here, as well. Her shyness just wouldn't let the words fall free. Bending low, I reached out, lowering my right hand to her waist, pulling her into me. I took it slow just in case she wanted me to stop but those words never came. Next thing I knew, my lips were covering hers.

This wasn't the same kiss as last time. No, this was a real fucking kiss. My hand tightened around her waist, and my tongue swiped over hers, tasting both the remnants of the Greek salad she'd eaten for dinner and a taste so damn syrupy sweet it could only come from her. She was hesitant. Out of practice. That I could tell. But when she pressed her little body against mine and let out a short moan into my mouth, I knew she wanted it just as badly as I did.

I pulled back before I got too lost. Before I failed to remember that just on the other side of that two inches of solid wood was her nine-year-old child.

She was breathing heavy, her small hand clutching the front of my sweater, as if hanging on for dear life. I covered her hand with mine. It was trembling slightly.

"Have dinner with me this Tuesday."

Her head raised to meet my gaze.

"Tuesday?" she repeated, as if trying to remember what a Tuesday even was.

I would have laughed if I hadn't felt the same way.

Suddenly, the door I thought was closed widened, and a high-pitched voice announced, "We're having dinner with my new grandma on Tuesday. Right, Mommy?" Monique's big brown eyes shot to her mother.

"Monique, go inside!" Sandra insisted, hurriedly, turning to her daughter, pushing her inside and pulling the door closed behind her.

"I'm sorry about that."

I shook my head. "Don't be." I paused, knowing I shouldn't ask, but like with most things where she was concerned, my common sense flew out the window. "Her new grandmother?"

Monique's eyes widened. "Long story."

"You can tell me about it on our next date. I'm heading out of town on Wednesday, but I'll be back on Sunday. How's next Monday sound?" And when it looked like she was trying to come up with some excuse to say no, I planted my lips on hers again.

She responded immediately, opening up again, letting me taste her. I wanted to bite her lower lip, to suck it into my mouth and run my tongue along that plump lip, but that would lead to more. And I knew, like I knew my own name, she wasn't ready for more. Hell, maybe I wasn't either.

"Monday?" I questioned against her lips.

She swallowed but nodded. "M-monday."

I was a grown ass man. No way I should've felt as excited as I did at a woman agreeing to a mere date. I had at least ten women in my contacts list right now that would've agreed to a date with half the effort. But the only woman I wanted to take out, was the woman I had sworn was off limits to me.

Like I said, maybe I didn't understand myself as well as I thought I did. Least of all, when it came to her.

CHAPTER 8

$\mathcal{S}$andra

"This was probably a mistake," I mumbled to myself in the mirror as I wrung my hands around one another. Yes, this was a total error in judgment on my part. I needed to cancel it before it got—

My thoughts were cut off by a knock at the door.

Too late.

"I'll get it!" Monique yelled from her bedroom.

That's when I sprang into action, out of my fearful stupor.

"No!" I yelled, halting Monique in her tracks as she sprinted up the hall. "I told you, Mommy or an adult opens the door. Not you. Besides, you forgot to put your shoes on, little girl," I admonished. I stared at her as her shoulders slumped and she turned, marching back into her room to put on the black pair of flats I'd matched with the red and black striped dress she insisted on wearing. She wanted to look nice for tonight's dinner.

"Coming!" I called as the knock sounded again. It wasn't a loud or insistent knock. Which didn't surprise me. It wasn't her style.

"Hi." My grandmother smiled as I opened the door.

I'd done it.

I'd saved the card she'd given me, after my intentions were to throw it in the garbage as soon as I got home from the hospital that day. But then I'd shared my first kiss with Damon and my brain went to mush. The next day I found the card stuffed awkwardly in my pants' pocket and I got curious. I wondered why she had given it to me, why she wanted me to call her. And then I started thinking about Monique. As her only family, I ached for her. I wanted my daughter to have a larger family support system but had no idea how to make that happen. Seeing Kayla with her husband and his large family sometimes made me envious—not only for Monique, surprisingly. I found myself wanting a larger family for me, as well. A husband to share my days and life with, and who knew, possibly more children. I'd always wanted at least two kids so they would always have a sibling to depend on, unlike I had.

And since I couldn't give Monique a sibling right then, I made a decision. I picked up the phone and dialed the number for the only family I had ever known, at least to some extent. Though the conversation was brief, I invited my grandmother over to dinner to finally meet Monique. She'd wanted to. I felt defensive at first, but I remembered I wasn't the eighteen-year-old child she'd thrown out. If she had anything negative to say, she'd be out on her backside and that would be that.

"Hello," I responded, rather formally.

"Hi!"

My gaze lowered to Monique who'd come up beside me.

"Well, hello," my grandmother replied in a voice I'd never heard before. At least, I couldn't ever remember her using the sweet, high-pitched tone most adults used with children. She'd never spoken to me that way as a child.

"I'm Monique. Mommy says you're her grandmother which makes you my great-grandmother. Right, Mommy?"

I nodded. "Right, baby. Come in," I stated, stepping back.

"Thank you." My grandmother smiled over her shoulder at me as I helped her remove the long coat she wore.

I frowned. She seemed … different. She was the same height; her golden skin complexion was the same though slightly duller than I remember. But she appeared even skinnier than the last time I'd seen her all those years ago. Her hair was cut short, something I never thought I'd see on my grandmother. And the few strands of greying hair at the temple were a huge departure from what I remember. Throughout my childhood my grandmother had had a standing bi-weekly hair appointment.

"This is for you." She handed Monique a gift wrapped box with a purple bow on it.

"Can I open it, Mommy?" Monique asked excitedly.

I nodded.

"Thank you!" The two words weren't even out of her mouth before she was tearing at the paper. Underneath was a grey gift box. When Monique opened it, I saw a light blue globe that looked something like a paperweight.

"It's a birthstone wishing ball. Your mommy told me your birthday is at the end of next month. And this aquamarine is the birthstone for the month of March."

"I know. My mommy gave me an aquamarine ring last year for my birthday." Monique held up the globe, a pondering expression in her face. "What do I do with it?"

"You can do whatever you want with it. Leave it to sit out on your desk, or hold it in your hands and make a wish. Or meditate with it."

"I make wishes on sunsets like my mom taught me. If I use this will my wish come true?"

My grandmother's gaze moved up to mine. I gave her a short smile, not bothering to explain about sunsets and wishes.

"You'll have to try it and see."

Monique's smile was as big as the globe. "Thanks, Great-Grand-ma!" she exclaimed, throwing her arms around my grandmother's waist.

I moved to pull Monique off of my grandmother, knowing she wasn't a hugger. But then she shocked me when she put her arms around Monique and smiled widely as she looked down on her.

"I'm going to put this in my room. Mommy, can you please escort my great-grandma to the dining area?"

I rolled my eyes as she dashed out of the room, down the hall to her room.

"She a lively little thing."

"She is."

"And she looks just like you."

I narrowed my gaze on my grandmother, wondering if she was trying to imply something, or build up to asking something she had no business inquiring about. Instead, she simply stared at me for a heartbeat.

"It's been a long time, Sandra. Could I give you a hug?"

My eyes bulged before I caught myself. "Uh, sure." I awkwardly stepped closer with my arms outstretched.

My grandmother moved closer, her arms wrapping around my back, pulling me in. It didn't feel natural at first. Felt nothing like the embraces I'd shared with Damon. I blinked and silently scolded myself for even comparing. Of course, a hug with my grandmother wouldn't feel the same as an embrace with a man like Damon.

"Thank you," my grandmother stated as we pulled back.

I nodded and gave her a half smile. "Are you hungry?" I questioned.

"Yes. I also brought something for you as well."

I stopped. "Oh." I took the book she handed me, nearly dropping it. It was my senior yearbook.

"You left it when, um …"

You kicked me out.

"I thought you might want to have it."

I hadn't even thought about this thing. I hadn't forgotten it. I'd left the book on purpose. It seemed less important than ensuring I'd have enough clothing and linens with me wherever I went, rather than a yearbook full of pictures of students who barely knew I was alive even as we sat in the same classes together. The book was even less relevant now, more than ten years later. But she was trying, I guessed.

"Thank you." I placed the book on my shelf next to the mounted television, amongst the magazines and other books I kept there.

"I'm back and I made my first wish. But I'm not telling you what it is because then it won't come true. Right, Great-Grandma?" Monique looked up at her grandmother, slightly breathless from running up the hallway.

My grandmother nodded. "Yes, I believe that's how it works. Once your wish comes true you can tell us what it was."

"Let's eat. We made a creamy wild rice and sweet potato soup," I stated over my shoulder, to my grandmother.

"Sounds delicious. Can I help set up?"

"No!" Monique interrupted. "You're our guest. Come with me."

I giggled at my bossy daughter, before disappearing into the kitchen. I overheard Monique directing my grandmother around the wall divider that split the kitchen off from the dining area.

"This is your seat. This is Mommy's, and this one is mine."

I imagined her holding onto the backs of the wooden dining chairs as she meticulously pointed out where everyone would sit.

I went about the business of ladling the soup into three separate bowls and placing them on plates. As soon as I had finished, Monique came into the kitchen from the second entrance closest to the dining space.

"I'll help." She didn't wait for me, instead picking up one of the plates with a filled bowl on top and moved to the dining area. Right before she exited, she paused. "Alexa, play 'Six Evolutions' by Yo-Yo Ma," she called.

A half a second later the stringed sounds from Yo-Yo Ma's masterfully played cello began to fill the room. I smiled at the soothing sounds of the music while picking up the two remaining plates and carrying them to the dining table. We'd already set up placemats and silverware earlier. I went back in for a pitcher of my homemade lemon iced tea while Monique grabbed three glasses, placing them in front of us.

I glanced up as I sat down, seeing my grandmother's eyes shift from me to Monique and back again. It seemed almost as if she was amazed. A light smile touched her lips.

"You are quite the little hostess, Monique. I am not sure if your mother told you but Yo-Yo Ma is one of my favorite musicians," my grandmother remarked as she unfolded the purple checkerboard patterned napkin we'd set out and placed it in her lap.

"Really? Ours too. We listen every night at dinner."

My grandmother looked to me, surprised. Yes, it was a habit I had picked up from her. One of many that had stuck. And apparently would stick for the next generation as well seeing as how Monique was often the one these days insisting that we listen while eating.

"I hope the soup isn't too hot. I tried to cook it early enough that it'd cool off a little before we sat down to eat," I explained.

"It's great. Delicious as well. You used coconut milk for the broth?" she questioned before taking another spoonful.

"Yes, just one can, and combined it with my homemade vegetable broth."

"Completely plant-based," Monique declared.

"Oh, are you vegan?" My grandmother looked toward me.

I shook my head. "No, although we do a lot of plant-based meals."

"Aunt Kayla said it was okay for my diabetes."

I looked to Monique before turning to see my grandmother's reaction. Her spoon had paused halfway to her mouth.

"Diabetes?"

"Yeah, see." And without prompting, Monique turned and lifted up the sleeve of her dress to reveal the insulin pump on the back of her arm. The pump was a new addition to our life. Ever since our last trip to the hospital, I finally conceded that the pump would be a better alternative for Monique.

"Monique, put your sleeve down."

She gave me a surprised look. "What? You told me not to be ashamed of my illness, right?"

I barely kept my eyes from rolling. Leave it to my child to use my own words against me.

"Right. You have nothing to be ashamed of because you have diabetes. You just don't have to show everyone, especially if they didn't ask."

"But she's not everyone. She's my great-grandmother which makes her family. Right, Great-Grandma?" Monique turned her big doe eyes on my grandmother.

"Right."

My eyes flew to my grandmother who had just agreed. She gave me an almost bashful look, as if she was trying to earn *my* approval in the matter. My, how the roles had reversed.

"Monique, I don't want you to be ashamed of diabetes, but just have a little more consideration before raising your sleeve in the middle of dinner. Okay?"

She nodded. "'Kay, Mommy."

We ate in silence for a few more minutes before my grandmother asked Monique about school and her interests. She seemed to keep her interest on my daughter. I'm hundred percent certain that was due to the somewhat icy reception I gave her, as evident by the one word answers I responded with when she did ask me a question. Monique, on the other hand, seemed to be thrilled at having met another relative. She was more than pleased to give long, drawn out answers to any and all questions. Her chatting, along with the background music that continued to play, were the dominant sounds of that dinner.

"Thank you for coming to dinner, Great-Grandma. I'm sorry I have to go, I promised my best friend, Diego, we could play Fortnite together for thirty minutes before Mommy makes me turn it off so she can read with me before I go to bed." Monique sounded truly apologetic.

"Fortnite?" My grandmother looked down at Monique with a questioning expression as we sat in the living room where we'd chosen to eat the lemon bars I'd made for dessert.

"It's a videogame," I interjected.

"Oh." My grandmother nodded. "Well, it's rude to keep your friends waiting. Thank you for being a great hostess."

"Thank you for coming over." Monique threw her arms around my grandmother again. "And for the wishing globe," she added before running off down the hall.

My grandmother stared at her retreating back until Monique turned the corner.

"She's amazing."

I pushed out the breath I'd been holding and gave my grandmother a sincere smile. I nodded in agreement because it was true. My daughter was nothing shy of amazing.

"We can sit and finish dessert," I stated, not wanting to be rude and push her out the door, now that dinner was over, and Monique had left us to go play her videogames. Though I'll admit it was nice having her there as a buffer between my grandmother and myself.

"I truly appreciate you inviting me. Dinner was delicious."

"I'm happy you enjoyed it."

"How've you been?"

"Been?" I questioned.

"Yes. How are you? I, uh, wanted to ask at the hospital, but—"

"I was really short with you."

"Which I can't blame you for."

Now that, was surprising.

"Your face still reveals exactly what you're thinking. You're stunned I can admit my wrongs."

"Yes, actually, I am."

She nodded, her head lowered as she looked down at her hands in her lap. "I've been thinking for a while now to try and get in contact with you. I kept your high school yearbook all of these years, hoping one day you'd return for it. Silly, I know. It's taken me a long time and some not so nice realizations to see my mistakes. I was a hard-headed woman. It took waking up in the hospital from surgery, alone, to see the errors I'd made."

"Hospital?" We'd ran into each other two weeks prior at the hospital, but she hadn't looked sick or like she'd just had surgery. Her words indicated a much longer stay than when we'd seen one another a couple weeks before.

"Last year, around this time, I was diagnosed with stage three breast cancer."

I inhaled sharply, sitting back in my chair.

"I had a double mastectomy and went through chemo and radiation. Just before this past Christmas I was declared cancer free. I was back at my doctor's office a few weeks ago for a check-up."

"Where we saw each other."

She nodded. "The oncology department is right next to the emergency department. I was cutting through to get the parking lot where my car was parked when I saw you."

"Oh my goodness." I covered my mouth with my hands. I had wanted to be so angry with this woman in the hospital that day. It had been on the tip of my tongue to give her the curse out I'd fantasized about for years. And now to know why she was even there to begin with, I felt nothing but guilt.

"Don't feel guilty. The last time you and I spoke, I said some horrible things to you about …" She looked off toward the hallway. "I'm sorry, Sandra. I was wrong for so many things. I was afraid you'd turn out like your mother that I kept a tight rein on you to the point you could barely breathe. Then, I kicked you out and abandoned you just like your mother did when you were a baby."

Lowering my gaze to my own hands in my lap, I listened to the words I'd wanted to hear for so long. I hadn't thought much about my biological mother in years. Growing up, I just got used to the fact that she hadn't wanted me. My grandmother's rejection upon finding out about my pregnancy had reopened that abandonment wound and I'd tried hard to block it out for years.

I inhaled, thinking about the loneliness I'd felt since my grandmother kicked me out. I'd been on my own for so many years. I swallowed back the tears. Now wasn't the time for them.

"I probably don't deserve your forgiveness, but—"

"You have it," I lifted my head and said. It probably was too quick to give but she had my forgiveness. It may have been the thought of losing the only relative who had ever shown me at least some sort of love throughout my life, or the idea that Monique came dangerously close to not ever meeting her great-grandmother that did it, but all I knew was that the space in my heart which had disliked my grandmother for so long was gone.

That night was the beginning of a new relationship for us.

* * *

Damon

I stared down at my phone, my thumb hovering over her name. It was about a quarter after eleven here in Geneva which meant it was only quarter after four in Williamsport.

"Shit! It's cold," Sean cursed as he got in the backseat of the chauffeured car we were taking back to our hotel.

"It's fucking Switzerland. What did you expect?" I shot back.

"Not this! Damn. You know I was raised in Southern California. Not this Ice Age shit!" He clapped and rubbed his hands together, blowing in them because he'd forgotten his gloves back at the hotel.

Chuckling, I shook my head as we pulled off. "Hey, you ever call someone just because you wanted to hear their voice?"

I kept my eyes trained on my phone, but out of the corner of my eye I saw Sean turn to look at me.

"What?"

"You heard what the fuck I said." I grunted, not caring for his tone.

"Hell no. Wait … there was one time. I was sixteen and Sherie Sharp was feeling me. She was eighteen and all of the dudes was digging her. I do remember looking forward to her call."

I rolled my eyes before turning to stare at the passing lights. That wasn't the same thing at all. He'd had a crush on Sherie based out of male competition against one another.

"You want to call her?"

No sense in lying. "Yeah, but it's not even five over there. She's still at work." It was a Friday and Sandra would still be at work at this time.

"So leave a message," Sean suggested.

I gave him a blank stare. That would defeat the purpose of the call. I wanted to hear her voice. Her voicemail was the automated message that most people used because who the hell checked voicemails in 2019 anyway?

"I'll call later," I mused out loud.

"Speaking of calls, I got one while you were out looking at the newest Cartiers." Sean's voice had lowered.

I took that as a hint. Reaching over to the door on my left, I hit the button to raise the partition for privacy.

"What's up?"

"That was our guy …"

Our guy was code word for the PI I'd hired who only worked special cases.

"He says Russo Jr. is on the outs with his pops. Has been for years, and in fact, has been looking for a way to take his own father down."

I raised an eyebrow and leaned closer to Sean.

"He's also looking to get an invite to that weird fight club shit you're part of."

I ran my hand through my beard. Sean didn't understand my underground fighting and I didn't feel the need to explain it to him. But Mike Russo Jr. wanting to be a part of the club was interesting. Very few people even knew about it because the ones who did know kept their mouths shut.

"I'll see he gets an invite," I stated, sitting up and scrolling through my phone's contacts. This time I knew who I was calling and it wasn't to hear his voice.

"I thought you were still in Geneva," Josh answered as soon as he picked up the phone.

"I am."

"Than this must be important. What's up?"

"Word on the street is Mike Russo Jr. is looking to join the Underground."

There was a pause on the other end.

"You want me to let him in."

I nodded even though he couldn't see me. "That's exactly what I want."

"Russo." I could just picture his eyes narrowing as he glanced upwards, mentally searching for a connection with the name. "*That Russo?*"

"Not quite. His son."

"The son of *that* Russo."

"The one and only." I hadn't given Josh too many details of my true connection with Mike Russo. Shit, I hadn't given *anyone* details on my real interest in Mike Russo, not even Sean. They just thought he was someone from the days I used to hustle on the street instead of in boardrooms.

"I better not regret this."

"I'll make it up to you, if you do."

A dry laugh sounded at the other end of the phone.

"How's Kay doing?"

"Who?" His tone sharpened, causing me to laugh.

Josh was adamant about being the only person calling his wife by her nickname. He was possessive as hell.

"Kayla. Your wife. How is she and the baby?"

"She's just about over being pregnant and stressing over this damn baby shower. She actually wants me to be there."

"Ah, hell, no."

"Right? I'd tell her there's no need for me to be there but with the mood swings she's been having while carrying this damn child, she'd either try to take my head off, or worse, not give me any pussy until after this kid is born." He grunted.

I shook my head, laughing at his apparent misery. "Better you than me."

"You'll be here one day. And sooner than you like to think. Anyway, I'll tell Connor to let Russo in. I gotta go."

Josh's bitch ass ran those last two sentences together and quickly hung up before I could curse him out. Marriage wasn't something that was on my mind.

Is it?

That two word question had me pausing as I got out of the car door that was held open by our chauffeur. I brushed it off as I stood upright. Josh was wrong, marriage was a long way off.

"Hey, I'm meeting a couple chicks in the lobby for drinks and whatever else they're into. You coming?" Sean asked as we entered the lobby of our hotel.

My answer was immediate. I began shaking my head. "Got a phone call to make."

Sean lifted a dark eyebrow, eyeing me suspiciously but didn't say anything. Again, I wasn't in the mood to explain myself either. We slapped fives and parted ways, him heading in the direction of the restaurant, and me toward the elevators up to my room. As soon as I stepped into my hotel's suite my phone buzzed in my pocket. My heart rate spiked at who it might be. When I saw the name "Scarlet" appear on my screen, my hopes were dashed. I hit the decline call button and tossed my phone on my bed before removing my clothes to take a shower.

We'd spent the last twelve hours meeting with various watchmakers, brands, executives, and timepiece experts and fans. I only collected a handful of business cards, knowing that most of the ones I passed off on to Sean I wouldn't need. He would give the to his assistant to have her organize them in his rolodex for future use. Aside from wanting to get a look at what was coming down the pipeline within the next year, in the world of luxury timekeeping, our main purpose was to get the word out about our new brand. We'd done so.

And as I showered, it occurred to me that I was more excited about getting to have a twenty minute conversation with Sandra as she left work and drove home, than about any of the watches I'd seen all day. Watches, business, branding, marketing—all of that shit fell away as I dried myself off, sauntered into my room to get a pair of boxer briefs from the dresser I'd unpacked my clothes into, stepped into them, and then laid across the bed, grabbing my phone.

"Hi," her breathless voice answered after three rings.

"Were you rushing?"

"Yeah, I had to step out in the hallway to take your call."

"You're still working?" I glanced at the clock. It was quarter after midnight, which meant she should've been leaving work about fifteen minutes ago.

"It's either stay late tonight or come in tomorrow. And I have to take Monique to the doctor's tomorrow morning so they can monitor how her new pump is working."

My lips formed downward, hating that she sounded as if she was being pulled in two different directions.

"You need to go?" I didn't want to let her go at all but it sounded like the gentlemanly thing to ask.

"No. I can talk for a few minutes. How was your day? Did Cartier offer to buy your prototype?"

She giggled and I laughed. She'd sworn up and down one of the brands here were going to either offer to buy us out or copy our watch before we even got a foot off the ground. I highly doubted either scenario would play out, but I hadn't worn our prototype to any of the events over the last few days just to avoid the possibility. I wasn't looking to be bought out, nor was I looking to have our watch copied before we could bring it to market, on our own.

"Not yet but we've still got another day ahead of us."

"That you do."

"Your case is picking up steam, huh?"

She sighed. "Thankfully, yes. Two more waitresses have come forward and admitted to being victims of the same type of sexual harassment our first client told us about. But these things take a lot of time and man hours. Luckily, our previous case ended in a settlement so we can dedicate most of our working hours to this one."

"There's no one better for the job," I stated with total assurance.

There was a short pause before Sandra spoke again. "I'm not the one trying the case."

"You might as well be. I know damn well the lawyers you work for at the firm couldn't function as well as they do without you."

I didn't hear anything at the other end of the phone but I pictured her dipping her head low and biting her lower lip, the way she did when she was at a loss for words. Or embarrassed. Or both.

"Don't say things like that if you don't really mean them."

I sat up in the bed. "What?"

"Please don't fill my head with nice compliments if you're just looking to—"

"Before you finish that sentence let's make a few things clear. One, if I say it then I mean it. Two, I don't know who it was in your past that filled your head with lies and betrayed you but he ain't me. And third, don't forget the first two."

There was silence on the other end but I knew she was still there. I could hear her breathing.

"I have to go back to work."

"All right, just don't forget what I said. And say hey to short stuff for me, when you get home."

"Bye, Damon." She hung up.

I pulled the phone from my ear, staring at it. I wondered what the hell had gotten me so riled up. The notion that she was either subconsciously or consciously comparing me to some dude in her past. Likely, the same one that'd gotten her pregnant and left her to fend for herself. That shit pissed me off, so much so, that I couldn't get to sleep. And since I wasn't home and unable to do what I normally did when I couldn't sleep, which was fight, I chose to workout instead. The hotel we were staying at had a twenty-four hour fitness center.

I hopped out of bed, threw on a pair of black sweatpants, a T-shirt, and sneakers, and exited my room, taking the stairs to the floor above my suite where the gym was housed. I started with a short warm up before working my way into a grueling ninety minute workout. By the time I was finished with my workout, I was too wired to get back to sleep, and my instincts had me wanting to call Sandra again, which was ridiculous. It was Friday, our date was the following Monday. I could go a few days without talking to the woman … right?

As I stared at my phone on the bed, I decided against picking it up and calling the woman who was beginning to drive most of my waking thoughts. I opted, instead, to sit my ass down at the desk in the main area of my suite, laptop in hand, and get some work done. I had a ton of emails to send out, notices on some properties that were for sale, including an abandoned building on Lakefront Drive in Williamsport, which I'd been finagling and trying to get ahold of for years. That plus a few documents Charlotte had sent me that needed my signature. Work kept me occupied enough over the next few hours, long enough that I found myself fighting to keep my eyes open. At nearly four in the morning, I made my way to bed to sleep for a few hours before I needed to get up for another long day. But even though I enjoyed my work and various business ventures, as I drifted off to sleep, I remembered thinking that I couldn't wait to get back home on Monday.

CHAPTER 9

*S*andra

"Are you sure about this?" I questioned as I cast yet another dubious glance from my phone screen to the full-length mirror in my bedroom. When I looked back to the phone Kayla was frowning at me. Obviously frustrated with my uncertainty.

"Sandra, look at yourself in that mirror."

Sighing, I rolled my eyes, feeling silly as if she was going to have me do one of those daily mirror mantras people seemed to like. I'd tried doing those years ago and just felt like a fool talking to myself in the mirror.

"Go ahead and *look*," Kayla insisted.

"Fine!" I blurted out but did as I was told and rose my gaze to the mirror in front of me.

"You cannot tell me you don't see how gorgeous you look. That burgundy peplum top fits you perfectly, and the black skinny jeans hug your hips nicely, thanks to your own tailoring. You look hot! If I swung that way and if I weren't already taken, I might try to get a piece of that."

"*What?*" I burst out laughing. Kayla said the craziest things sometimes.

Kayla giggled. "See, all you need is to hold that smile and Damon will fall all over himself for you … if he hasn't already. And that's a big *if*."

I frowned. "I'm sure he hasn't." I bit my lower lip.

"Stop that!" Kayla demanded. I was sure if she were standing in front of me she would've pulled my lip from between my teeth herself.

"I can't help it. I chew my lip when I'm nervous." I twisted around again in the mirror, this time admiring the curvature of my lower back and hips as they rounded out to a plump but toned backside. For the second time in as many weeks I started to admit I liked what I saw in the mirror. "You don't think it's too much?" I asked Kayla again, just for some reassurance.

"It's just enough. Damon will be eating out of the palm of your hand and begging to get between your thighs."

I gasped, my eyes shooting back to the phone in my hands. I started to shake a little bit. Just the idea of a man like Damon Richmond and sex was … I don't know.

"Sandra, please tell me you've thought about you and Damon and sex before?"

My eyes bulged. Why did I suddenly feel like a teenager whose mother was questioning her about the birds and the bees?

"I've thought about it," I hesitantly answered.

"You know it's a normal activity between two consenting adults, right?"

I swallowed.

Consenting.

There was a loaded word if any.

"Have you two talked about it?"

"Talked?" I asked, my voice rising to a near shriek.

"Yes. Two people who are attracted to one another and dating will often, or at least should talk about their expectations."

Running my hand over the high bun I'd decided to wear my hair in, I sighed. I even let a few loose curls fall down to frame my face. A departure from the typical tight, low bun I usually wore.

"I don't think that conversation will be happening tonight." I sure as hell hoped it wouldn't be. I didn't know if I was ready to go there.

"You'll be having it soon enough. I'd bet my medical license on it."

Pushing out a breath, I lifted my gaze to the mirror, staring at myself. I'd actually done a smokey eye rather than the usual plain makeup I wore to the office. A smile blossomed on my lips that were glossed with a nude color. I started to realize the idea of sex with Damon didn't put the fear of God into me like the idea had in the past. I'd dated a little here and there since Monique was born, but whenever it came time to take that next step I just couldn't do it. Most men weren't satisfied with just a few kisses here and there, so they eventually moved on. It was no real loss to me. And a few years earlier I'd decided to even give up dating entirely, or at least until Monique was eighteen.

And then in walked Damon Richmond.

The man had me reconsidering things I swore I had nailed down in my mind.

"That's him!" I blurted into the phone when a knock at the door sounded. "I gotta go."

"Bye. Have fun!" Kayla urged as she blew a kiss into the screen before disconnecting.

"Coming!" I called up the hallway to let him know I wasn't ignoring him. I slipped my feet into the burgundy stilettos I'd chosen, which matched my shirt perfectly, and quickly put the diamond studs into my ears to complete my outfit for the night. Glancing one more time in the mirror, I smiled wide at the woman staring back at me.

I hurried out of my bedroom, shutting off the light and making my way to the front door. I pulled it open just as Damon's large hand lifted to knock again.

"Sorry," I stated, breathless.

He didn't respond at first. Instead, those two different colored brown eyes trailed down my petite body, slowly, taking in every inch. His gaze was almost like a caress against my skin as it scanned the totality of my frame. I watched the Adam's apple in his neck bob up and down when his eyes reached my face again.

"Beautiful doesn't even begin to describe how damn good you look." There was such a guttural tone that emanated from deep in his throat, I had no choice but to believe the words he'd said. And again, I found myself realizing there was no fear on my part.

"These are for you."

My eyelids rose, and for the first time, I saw the beautiful multi-colored roses he held in his hands. How I'd missed the bouquet of a dozen rainbow roses was beyond me. The only explanation I could muster was that Damon himself had me transfixed.

"Thank you." I cleared my throat of the hoarseness. "Please, come in while I put these in water."

I stood back as he entered and then shut the door behind him. I moved around him, noting again how small my place felt with him standing inside of it. He followed me through the living room and stopped at the kitchen entrance, watching me as I dug under the sink for the glass vase I kept there.

"I half expected short stuff to come running to the door."

I stood up and glanced over my shoulder while filling the vase with water. "You do know she has a name right?" I joked.

My thighs tightened when a smirk broke through his thick, full lips. "I do but I like the name short stuff. It doesn't bother her, right?" He suddenly seemed concerned.

That had my chest tightening.

I shook my head. "She actually likes that you call her short stuff. She loves it when people give her nicknames. Joshua and Kayla call her Nique-Nique."

I had to look away when Damon chuckled. The deep sound caused my insides to quake. I busied myself with cutting parts of the stems of the roses off before placing them in the water. I felt him move in closer.

"It doesn't bother you, does it?"

I shook my head. "Of course not."

"Cool. Anyway, where is she?" he asked, reaching over my shoulder and turning the water off.

Somehow, I'd forgotten to do that. And when the trembling of my fingers, due to his nearness, almost caused me to drop the vase, Damon wrapped his arms around my arm from behind, helping me to steady the vase with his hands covering mine.

"Th-thank you," I stated once I placed the vase on the counter and turned to Damon. He was less than a foot away. "She's out with her sitter and my grandmother."

He lifted a dark eyebrow. "Both of them."

I nodded. "Monique's just getting to know my grandmother, and my grandmother wanted to take her out to dinner while you and I went out. I agreed but only if Oralia attended. She's a former pediatric nurse so I feel comfortable leaving Monique with her, in case something happens, with her diabetes."

He nodded and reached up, his hand grasping one of the curls that hung freely. "That makes sense. Your hair has specs of gold in it. Did you dye it."

I shook my head. It was a familiar question. It usually wasn't obvious because of my always keeping my hair tied up in a tight bun, but if I wore it down, the naturally gold or blonde streaks throughout my medium brown mane were more apparent.

"So if I kissed you no one's going to walk in on us?"

I shook my head. "Not a soul." Even if they did, I wouldn't give an iota of a damn, either.

When Damon dropped his head, I instinctively lifted my chin to meet his incoming lips. A moan broke free from my mouth as soon as our lips met. I sighed into his mouth, feeling an ease in tension release from my body that I hadn't even realized was there. The hairs of his beard tickled my chin but that only served to increase the sensational feelings that began coursing through me.

Damon's hands were at my hips, pulling me into him. I reached up to clutch his shoulders, clinging him to me like a thirsty cat clinging to her milk. My hands moved to the back of his head, and I reached up, fully pressing my body against his, seeking the safety of his kiss. I moved from his head to his beard, feeling its softness.

Just when I thought I would burst into flames he pulled back.

"We need to go." His voice was eerily calm, although I noticed he was breathing heavily as well.

I nodded. "Let's."

And a minute later, we were exiting my apartment for our date.

* * *

DAMON

Damn, she smelled good. Yeah, most women smelled good when going out on a date, but Sandra smelled like cotton candy and innocence. I don't know how to describe it. All I knew was that every time she got in my car, or she brushed past me, or we fucking kissed that particular smell lingered, reminding me of her presence even after she was gone.

"The African-American Museum?" she questioned as we pulled up to the parking lot.

I nodded. "I thought it'd be something you'd like to see. You said you wanted to study sociology in college. What better location to learn about groups of people than a museum?"

The fucking smile that spread over those damn lips was enough to have me gripping my chest with my hand. She made me ache in ways no one ever had.

"I haven't been here in years. Thank you." She squeezed my right wrist as she glanced out the window.

We'd just come from having dinner at a little Italian spot I loved, and thankfully, she had enjoyed it, too. Once I parked, I got out of the car, and circled the front to hold the door open for her, taking her right hand in my left to help her up.

She batted her lashes coyly, but I could tell the move came naturally. It wasn't an act.

"When was the last time you were here?" I inquired as I wrapped my arm around the small of her back. It was an instinctive move, one that she melted into.

"Uh, I think Monique was about four or five. I tried to take her on trips to museums when she was younger but I often worked so much or would pick up extra shifts as a waitress just to be able to afford what we needed, those trips became less and less frequent. And then when she got sick, we were in and out of the hospital and doctors' offices a lot. I became scared, too often opting to keep us home instead of going out on weekends, as a means to keep her safe, or so I thought."

I looked down at her as I held the door open. My eyes dropped to the sway of her hips while she walked over the threshold. My hand tightened into a fist.

"I bet that was tough. Seeing your daughter so sick," I responded, getting back to the conversation at hand and off my musings of all of the ways I wanted to feel those hips.

She nodded. "It was. It still is. I had to be told I don't know how many times by the doctors that her diabetes wasn't my fault or due to anything I did or didn't do. As parents we often blame ourselves for anything that goes wrong with our kids."

I nodded. "The good ones do, at least."

She gave me a look.

I jutted my head to the directory at the center of the main lobby. "Third floor has the information on pre-colonial Africa and Transatlantic Slave Trade, second floor goes into the abolition movement here in Williamsport up to the Civil Rights Movement—"

"And the first floor features artwork from the Civil Rights Movement until present," Sandra finished.

"Want to start on the third floor?"

She nodded.

Again, I placed my hand at the small of her back as we made our way up the stairs to the third floor.

"Monique's out with your grandmother? You didn't want to go?"

Sandra glanced up at me as we came to a stop in front of the first exhibit. It was a relic from pre-colonial West Africa.

"Well, she invited Monique and I out to dinner, and when I told her I was going out, she asked if Monique could still go. I agreed. I'm where I want to be." Her lips curled into a small smile.

Dammit. I both loved and wanted to strip her of all that damn shyness. Didn't she know that was the exact type of shit that called to a man like me?

"But you didn't feel comfortable leaving Monique alone with her?" That was odd and something I probably should've minded my business about but I was starting to conclude that anything concerning Sandra *was* my business. *Weird.*

"Not yet. Monique just met her a week ago. Plus—"

"The diabetes."

She nodded. "I felt better having Oralia there just in case Monique's blood sugar dropped or something else happened." She shrugged.

"And how come she's just meeting your grandmother?"

Sandra looked up at me, her feet stopped. We had been moving toward another exhibit on the third floor.

"I told you it was a long story …" She paused.

"I've got nothing but time."

I watched as her chest rose in her intake of air. Slowly she let it out. She glanced around before her eyes returned to me and she began talking. "My grandmother raised me. My mother was sixteen when she had me but wanted absolutely nothing to do with me. She handed me to my grandmother, and once she was discharged from the hospital, she left. I've met her twice since then and those encounters were brief. I don't even know who my biological father is. My grandfather died well before I was born. So my grandmother was all of the family I had. When I, uh, got pregnant …" She cleared her throat and averted her gaze.

There was something strange about the expression that covered her face. Was it shame?

"My grandmother wasn't too happy about it, as you could imagine."

I nodded. "History repeating itself."

"Or so she thought. I decided to keep my child and she became angrier than I'd ever seen her. She kicked me out and that was the last time I saw her until a few weeks ago when Monique was in the emergency department."

My head shot back. "Wow. So it's been a decade since you two have seen each other?"

"Yeah. At first, I wasn't too keen on seeing her but she gave me her card and I started to think that maybe it was time Monique got to meet another family member of hers. She seems genuinely apologetic for how she treated me, and wants to get to know both Monique and I." Sandra gave a one shoulder shrug as if to say she was still on the fence about how she felt, but willing to give her grandmother a break.

"You're the only family Monique has? Her father's side of th—"

"No." She shook her head adamantly, and just before she closed her eyes I swore I caught a glimpse of fear. What the hell was that about?

I wondered if her daughter's father had threatened her in some way. Maybe to keep her quiet about their daughter. I've heard of worse shit.

I angled my head when Sandra moved to stand in front of me, arms folded over her breasts.

"I don't tell most people what I've just told you."

"I'm not most people."

She nodded and looked down and then up staring at me again. "You're not, and I don't go on many dates or get caught up in relationships easily."

"Elaborate."

She glanced over my shoulder before pinning me with her gaze once again. "Do you know what you want with me? Because I-I'm feeling a little, or *lot,* off kilter here and it'd be nice to know that I'm not the only one."

I lifted my hand, cupping her chin, and stepped closer. "You're not, little one."

Her eyes widened at the new pet name that had just fallen from my lips as if I'd been calling her that for years. The tremble in her bottom lip forced me to lean down and suck it between my teeth, going over it with my tongue before releasing it. It was a quick move, not quite a kiss, but it solidified something for me—I'd been unsure right until that moment that I had actually wanted what was happening between Sandra and I to happen.

And I wasn't one for doubting.

Now the doubts were laid to rest.

"So your grandmother raised you?"

She nodded.

"And you don't have a relationship with your mother at all?"

She gave me a funny look, lifting her eyebrow before nodding.

"Just checking, 'cause that first day I dropped you off at your job, you said your mother was going to pick you up."

Her eyes widened and she covered her mouth.

I began chuckling. "It's cool."

"I didn't know you and-"

I laughed some more before saying, "It's cool. I knew you were lying then anyway. Finish telling me about growing up with your grandmother," I ordered as I took her left hand in my right, continuing around the third floor.

"What do you want to know?"

"Everything."

"Everything? That's a lot."

"I told you, I've got time."

Smiling, she averted her gaze, shrugging. "She was a district court judge and I looked up to her. She was very strict. Always demanded I participate in tons of activities and keep my head in the books. It wasn't too much of a chore, honestly, though. I loved reading and learning new things, which I've already told you."

"Right, your weekend trips to the library for fun," I joked.

Sandra laughed, nodding, before continuing. "I enjoyed being on the chess team and in the chorus much more than hanging out with the athletes or the popular crowd. Not that they'd have me anyway. I bet you were one of the jocks."

I glanced down, realized that my arm was slung over her shoulder and she was leaned into my body. The move had felt so casual and normal that I didn't realize we were locked arm in arm, with hers around the back of my waist.

"I dropped out of school at fourteen. But yeah, before then I was a jock, on the basketball team."

Her head popped up and I pushed one of the curls that'd fallen over her face out of the way.

"You dropped out?"

I nodded. "My pops died when I was thirteen and my mom fell apart. I had a younger sister who was only seven at the time. After months of notices and phone calls from bill collectors and the bank threatening to foreclose on our house, I figured my mom wouldn't do anything so I needed to. I connected with some of the people my father had worked for to earn money and eventually stopped going to school in favor of working."

Her head shot back, a wrinkle appearing in between her eyebrows, as we walked down the stairs to the second floor. "Your father's colleagues let a fourteen year old work with them? What did he do for a living?"

I chuckled. She really was as innocent as she appeared sometimes.

"He damn sure wasn't a judge." Like her grandmother had been. "He was a drug dealer. Granted, he wasn't an errand boy or the type that stood out on street corners, but he was what he was." I wasn't ashamed of my father's or my history. "He hadn't gone past the tenth grade but he was smart. He wanted to raise his family out of the neighborhood he grew up in. So, when my mom got pregnant, he married her, and worked his ass off to move us to a better part of Williamsport. He sent me to some of the best private schools in the city and pushed me to play sports and study hard. He didn't want the same life for me. For a long time, I didn't even know what he did for a living. He would often just say he was taking care of 'business.' I was thirteen when I found out the truth."

I ground my back teeth, hating the memory of that date and all of the horrible shit I'd said to him afterwards. Words I could never take back because soon after he was dead.

"He did what he had to, to take care of you all. It wasn't the best situation, but the way you still talk about him tells me he loved you all deeply and he did his best."

I paused, stopping in front of her so we were face-to-face, lifting her fingers to my lips, kissing them.

"We're even."

She gave me a perplexed look.

"You told me something about you that you don't share with others and I just did the same." I was about to go a step further. "My father wasn't the only one who had to make hard decisions. Once he died my mother could barely get out of bed. He'd been the rock of the family. All our extended family had made money through him. After his death, the family we thought had our backs either went to work for people who my father despised or they just fell off the face of the earth. We were all on our own. *I* was on my own. But I had my sister to look after. My father always said if something happened to him, I was the man of the house. So, I went to an uncle who I hadn't seen in a while and asked for a job. He didn't hesitate to put me on. I'm a hustler and as smart as my ol' man. It didn't take long for me to make money. I hated every minute of it, but I did it because the thought of Charlotte or even my mother starving sickened me more than selling poison."

"Don't be ashamed for choices you made at fourteen."

I shook my head. "I'm not. I stacked money for years, and as soon as I turned eighteen, I started looking for my first investment property. My business today is built on that same hustle and intelligence I used back then. But it was also built on blood money. There isn't a day that goes by that I don't remember that."

"Do you still …"

I shook my head. "I've long been out of that world, but I still have associates who never left that life behind." Keeping associates in that world came in handy when I needed to find out information about properties or their owners, but I didn't need to explain that to Sandra at the moment.

My brows rose when Sandra's hand lifted, cupping my cheek. A smile crossed her face. "We would've never ran in the same circles in high school."

I laughed. "Damn sure wouldn't have. I'll be damned if I was joining someone's chess club."

She giggled, lowering her head. "You're not going to let me live that down, are you?"

"Hell no. That or that bougie ass classical music you're always listening to." I always heard the music in the background whenever I called her at home.

"I'll make you fan of it."

I frowned. "Doubtful."

We spent the next forty-five minutes exploring the museum exhibits on the second and first floors. I didn't want the night to end. I wasn't even surprised by that feeling any longer. I'd come to accept that wanting to prolong my time with Sandra in any capacity I could was just a facet of this developing relationship.

"Thank you for dinner and the museum."

We were right in front of her door, yet again. She was whispering, certain that Monique was still awake and would open up the door once she realized her mother was on the other side.

"Thank you for wearing those jeans," I responded, eyeing the curvature of her hips in the pants she wore.

"Oops!" She blurted out, covering her mouth when her laughter bubbled out, louder than she'd intended.

"Shhh, you're going to get us in trouble by the warden!" I whispered, close to her face.

Monique had already sent her one text asking when she'd get home.

Sandra giggled. "I know, isn't she terrible?"

"Just like her mama."

Her eyes widened and she swatted my chest. I used that as an opportunity to grab her by the hand, pulling her into me. Lowering my head, I covered her lips with my own. Someone moaned. At that point, I didn't know if it was her or me, but the sound turned me on, shooting straight to my dick. My hands moved down passed her hips to that ass that'd been taunting me for the past three hours of our date. Sandra gasped into my mouth when I squeezed it and pulled her into me. I was sure she could feel the length growing in my pants.

However, she didn't back away, so I kept kissing. Allowing myself to get comfortable with the feeling of her in my arms.

When it became too much I pulled back, my hands going to her waist again. "You need to go inside."

Sandra panted, her eyes holding a glassy look. "Yes. Inside. To my child."

I nodded and swallowed. "What are you doing this Saturday?"

She frowned, thinking. "Taking Monique to the zoo. The weather is supposed to be in the fifties and she's been asking for months if we could go. Kayla's sister-in-law, Michelle, and her husband, Carter, are brining Diego." She hesitated. "Would you like to come? Wait, no, never mind."

My eyes narrowed.

"You probably have other things to do besides spend the day at the zoo with a bunch of kids. Forget I—"

"I'll be there. What time do you want me to pick you both up?"

Her mouth flapped open a little.

I tapped her chin with my forefinger, closing it. "How about ten a.m.?" I suggested when she didn't say anything.

She nodded slowly.

"I'll be here." I placed another quick kiss to her lips before taking a step back. I watched as she turned and pushed her key into the doorknob, unlocking it and then entering. She gave me a smile and wave over her shoulder before disappearing behind the door.

Yup. I was in this shit now.

CHAPTER 10

*S*andra

"I need an STD test."

Kayla's head popped up from her desk, eyes wide, and her mouth fell open. Obviously, my impromptu declaration in the middle of her office had surprised her. It was a Wednesday afternoon and I knew she stayed late on most Wednesdays seeing patients. I left work a few minutes early just so I could drive over and ask her to give me the test.

"You want an STD test?"

I nodded.

"You and Damon have already—"

I started shaking my head. "No, but it's happening." And soon, though I didn't say that part out loud. "You said he and I need to have a conversation, so I figured getting a test would be the first place to start."

Kayla nodded slowly, as she pushed back from her glass desk and stood. "Do you want to talk about this?" she questioned after she'd come around the desk, standing over me as I sat in the loveseat in her office.

I shrugged. "Not much to say." I rubbed my hands together, feeling stupid. "Why do I feel like this?"

Kayla turned the leather chair reserved for patients around so she could sit down, facing me.

"Feel like what?"

"Like a damn teenager. I'm twenty-eight years old for God's sake. I have a ten-year-old daughter. And yet, the thought of being physically intimate with Damon … I was the girl who swore up and down she'd remain a virgin until she got married. I wanted to do it perfectly. Fall in love, get married, then have the two point five kids and the white picket fence and all that."

"Life doesn't always work out the way we planned as kids."

"Psh. You're telling me." I frowned. "You know I have dated since Monique was born. Not frequently because I found most guys just assumed that because I already had a child that I'd have no problem spreading my legs to them without any sort of commitment. But Damon's different." I looked up at Kayla. "I didn't expect him to be but he's patient and has been vulnerable with me and let me be that with him. He doesn't treat Monique like an inconvenience. We went to the zoo last week and I swore she had a better time with him than me. Hell, I think *he* had a better time with her than with me."

Kayla and I both giggled.

"I'm sure that's not true."

I shook my head. "No." My eyes roamed up to the ceiling as I remembered when Carter and Michelle had taken the kids into one of the gift shops at the zoo, leaving Damon and I to see the gorillas. When one charged the window directly in front of me, I jumped back, right into Damon's awaiting arms. He held me tight and leaned down, getting close to my ear, his beard tickling the side of my neck. He whispered that he wouldn't let anything get to me. And I believed him.

"I'm not making a mistake, am I?" I asked, looking Kayla in the eye. I was much too far gone to determine this on my own.

Leaning in, Kayla cupped my hands in hers. "Only you can decide that."

I sighed, rolling my eyes. "You're no help. The last man I trusted …" I trailed off, looking over Kayla's shoulder.

She squeezed my hand.

"That was a long time ago and you were only eighteen years old. You're a grown woman now, who's been a single parent for a decade and been doing a pretty damn good job, if you ask me. And I'll remind you, you *did* ask me."

I laughed and then moved toward her, wrapping my arms around Kayla's shoulders. "I love you. Thank you for being such a great doctor and an even better friend."

"I love you back. Oh, and if Damon hurts you I'll just have Josh kick his ass in the ring, okay?"

I pulled back, my brows pinched. "Ring?"

Kayla's lips tightened. "Yeah, well, I have a patient arriving in five minutes."

"Wait, what did you mean by—"

"We need to draw your blood for those tests you asked for."

I'd almost forgotten my entire reason for stopping by. I nodded and then followed Kayla into the section of her office where patients had their blood drawn.

"How's that pump working for Monique?" she asked as she began inserting the needle.

I flinched at the first bite into my skin but then relaxed. "It's going well so far. I don't have to wake up in the middle of the night, every few hours to check her insulin."

"But I'm sure you can't help getting up still."

I nodded. "It's only been a few weeks. But I am getting better sleep and so is Monique."

"That's fantastic. I wished they had those things around when I was Monique's age. Would've saved me and my parents a lot of heartache and lost sleep."

I nodded. Kayla had been a type 1 diabetic as a child also. Unfortunately, her illness had worn out the organs in her body to the point that she eventually needed a kidney transplant. She got both a kidney and pancreatic transplant which ultimately cured her diabetes, alleviating the need for constant insulin shots. However, she still needed to take immunosuppressant medications to keep her body from rejecting the foreign organs. I didn't even want to think of Monique having to endure anything like that. Thankfully, my daughter's diabetes was well managed.

"Thanks. How long until the results come back?" I questioned, watching as Kayla carefully handled the vial of blood she'd just drawn from me.

"Why? Got a hot date?"

I grinned and looked down.

"You do, don't you?"

"I'm going over his place this weekend. He's having a special chef give us a private cooking class."

"That Damon's so damn smooth. I knew he'd wear you down. I'll put a rush on it and I should be able to have the results to you by Friday."

"Thanks, Kayla."

"Anytime. Give my niece a hug and kiss for me. I won't be a Pilates tomorrow. I told Patience I'd help her with the boys after work. Aaron's out of town until Friday."

Patience was another one of Kayla's sisters-in-law.

"Okay. You'll be missed but family is family."

She smiled.

I swallowed down the envy I felt. Kayla hadn't come from a big family. She was an only child to her two parents. But when she'd married Josh, his family became hers, and she got along well with her sisters-in-law. They were always having dinner at one another's homes and their ever-extending family was growing. Both her sisters-in-law had had recent births and Josh's younger brother, Tyler, recently revealed he'd secretly wed on their family's yacht while in the Caribbean, and his new wife, Destiny, was pregnant.

"I'll give you a call on Sunday," Kayla stated as we hugged. "Or maybe Monday. You might be busy Sunday."

I lowered my lashes, knowing what she was getting at.

"I'll definitely call by Friday afternoon so you can pick up your results."

"Thanks."

I wasn't worried about the results. I knew what they'd say. It was more that I wanted to have something to give Damon to show him what I was ready for. I pushed out a breath as I entered the elevator to exit Kayla's office building. At least, I hoped I was ready.

* * *

DAMON

I opened the door before she was even able to knock. The driver that I had pick her up from her apartment and bring her to my place had specific instructions to walk her up to my door. He texted me on the way to let me know they'd arrived.

"Good evening."

I laughed. She was so damn formal sometimes.

"Hey, little one," I murmured as I leaned down, pressing a kiss to the corner of her mouth. I inhaled that cotton candy smell of hers and my arm instantly went out, wrapping around her waist, pulling her into me.

"Thanks, Mike," I said over her shoulder to the driver. I passed him the cash I held in my pocket for his tip and he nodded and sauntered off.

Stepping back, I let Sandra pass through the door, shutting it behind her. I bit my bottom lip watching the black, ruffle dress she wore swaying side to side, lightly slapping the backs of her thighs. The heels she wore looked to be damn near six inches high, which showcased the toned nature of her legs.

Fuck milk. Apparently, Pilates did a body good, if her body was any indication.

"Mr. Richmond, did you want to begin now?"

I swallowed. Shit. I'd forgotten to do the damn introductions.

"Hey, Jeffrey Samuels, this is my date, Sandra. Sandra this is—"

"Master Chef Jeffrey Samuels. I know exactly who you are. I've seen you on the Food Network."

Samuels' eyes narrowed as he smiled wide.

I frowned and moved in close, wrapping my arm around Sandra and pulling her into my side as she and Samuels shook hands.

"Did I say date? I meant woman, as in my woman, taken," I corrected as I pulled her hand from his, eyeing him.

Samuels stood upright, giving me a smirk as if he understood my meaning. He was one of the most popular home chefs in the city of Williamsport. I had to pay a lot of damn money to have him available for the night. But I'll be damned if he tried to undercut me and put the moves on my woman right in front of me.

I lowered my gaze to Sandra to see a surprised expression on her face. Instead of answering her unasked question I leaned down and placed a kiss to those plump lips.

"You can set up while I show Sandra around," I told Samuels.

"Here, I didn't want to come over empty-handed. You said red is your favorite, right?" Sandra handed me an Italian Chianti wine. I wasn't familiar with the particular brand. "It's supposed to pair well with Italian dishes."

I nodded. "Thank you. We'll have to try it the next time you come over. Samuels is preparing a roast duck with potatoes cooked in the duck fat and a Brussels sprout salad."

"I thought we were going to be cooking."

I nodded. "We'll help with the salad, but the duck and everything else is all him. Takes too long."

She smirked. "You don't cook, do you?"

I lifted my brows. "Hell no."

She laughed.

Grabbing the hand that had gone up to cover her mouth, I held it in my own. For one, I was about to take her on a tour of my place, but also, because I disliked the way she sometimes used her hands to hide behind. When she laughed I wanted to see her entire face.

"Let me show you around." I pulled her away from the kitchen area. "This is obviously the living room." I held out my free hand and her eyes swept over the tan velvet couch, the oddly shaped copper coffee table, and the wooden chairs that sat across from the couch. The paintings on the wall behind the couch didn't hold any significant meaning but they added some color and dimension to the room.

"No TV?"

"Not in the living room. I'm not a big fan of television. I keep one in the den area which is down the hall. This, over here, is where we'll be eating dinner once it's ready."

"Oh wow. Look at that view," she stated as she lifted her gaze from the black wooden table and chairs out the floor-to-ceiling glass windows.

"That's exactly why I chose this place." I could've chosen to build my own home but I didn't want that. My company managed and had part ownership in this building for five years, and I'd owned my condo for almost four years and this view was the deciding factor.

"Do you get to enjoy the view often?"

It was a question I hadn't thought about in a long time. And since I knew Sandra was nothing if not genuine, I gave an honest answer. "Not as much as I'd like to. Maybe that'll change." And because she was there and it felt so damned good having her in my home, I leaned down and kissed her. It was quick but it was enough to tide me over until later.

I showed her the rest of my condo, including the two guest bedrooms, my bedroom, and my den which I sometimes used for working, on days I didn't feel like going into my actual office.

"You must've had help decorating," she stated as we made our way back to the kitchen.

I pulled out one of the wooden stools for her to sit at the bar that overlooked the kitchen.

I lifted my hand to my chest, affronted. "You don't think I'm capable of decorating my own home by myself?"

"Not at all." Her answer was quick and I found myself frowning over my shoulder at Samuels as he laughed with his back turned to us, stirring something at the stove.

"I'm offended."

Sandra giggled. "No you're not."

I chuckled. "Nah, I'm not. And yes, I did have an interior decorator design this space for me. Then I hired him to work for my company."

"A win-win."

"I'd say so."

"Do you prefer a red or white wine?" I questioned as I pulled out two wine glasses from my cupboards.

"Um, white."

I nodded, silently noting the hesitance in Sandra's voice.

She visibly relaxed when I pulled out a bottle opener.

"That's a new bottle?" she questioned, staring at the wine bottle in my hands. I'd just retrieved it from the holder where I kept a couple of bottles, most of which were unopened.

"Yeah," I answered cautiously, trying to remember if she'd ever said she didn't drink. Then I distinctly remembered her having a glass of white wine the other night we went out to dinner. She'd also brought a new bottle of wine over so I figured she wasn't opposed to drinking with dinner.

"Okay." She nodded, eyes still on the bottle as I poured the glasses.

Samuels came over to the counter and asked, "You two ready to start cooking?"

"Yes," Sandra responded, standing from the stool.

"First you both need to wash your hands."

Frowning at Samuels, I shook my head. "Nobody was planning on touching food with dirty hands."

He shrugged, chuckling. "Hey, I've worked in a lot of kitchens. You'd be surprised how many people skip that first, important step."

"See, that's why you can't eat at everybody's house."

Sandra giggled at my comment.

"Nasty ass people."

She nudged my side with her elbow, laughing.

We washed our hands and dried them before Samuels handed us a bowl of rinsed Brussels sprouts, walnuts, and dried cranberries for chopping. Sandra began slicing the Brussels sprouts. Her hands were half the size of mine but she wielded the knife with damn near the same expertise as Samuels. I admired the shiny lavender polish on her nails.

"How's the chopping of the walnuts coming, Damon?"

Glancing over my shoulder, I gave Samuels a deep frown. "Fine."

I looked back at Sandra who was now staring at me. Her eyes

dropped to the bamboo cutting board in front of me where the nuts remained untouched.

"I'll cut those." She reached for the cutting board, moving it in front of her and sliding the one she'd been working on out of her way.

"Why? You don't trust me with a knife?"

"I trust you." Her response had more to do with than just dinner.

I inched closer, so that our bodies were touching. "Good," I stated just before dipping my head and brushing my lips over hers. Her lips tasted like the wine she'd only taken a few sips of.

Stepping back, I licked my lips when Samuels began removing the duck from the oven.

Sandra inhaled deeply, turning to face Samuels as well. "That smells divine."

I smirked. Who used the word divine so casually? Sandra did. The way she talked made sense once she explained her background. Her grandmother being a judge, held her to a certain standard.

Over the next thirty minutes Samuel had us prepare a gravy to go over the duck and potatoes, a homemade vinaigrette for the salad that was tossed together in a large wooden salad bowl, as well as preparing the two individual chocolate lava cakes that would be served with ice cream for dessert. By seven o'clock I was finished setting up the dining table and was practically pushing Samuels out of the door. I was ready to have his ass out of my space so I could be alone with the woman I couldn't stop thinking about.

"Everything looks great. I hardly want to eat it. He made our plates so beautifully." Sandra grinned as she looked over the two plates Samuels had made for us. He'd garnished them with some shit that made it look pretty. And though I didn't give too much of a damn for presentation when it came to food, I did enjoy how much Sandra seemed to enjoy the aesthetics of it all. She had an eye for pretty things.

Coming up behind her, I rubbed my hands up and down her arms, leaning down close to her ear. "I don't know about you but I'm about to eat. I did not have that man all up in my place just to stare at this food."

I chuckled when she turned, swatting my way. Grabbing her hands, I pulled her to me, taking her lips because I felt like it. And just like every other time, she easily acquiesced to my hold. Her lips molding to mine. Her hands went up, tugging at my beard, not hurting but in an exploring way. She liked doing that while we kissed, I'd noticed.

When I pulled back, I paused and waited for her eyelids to flutter open. Those maple syrup saucers shone with a need so deep, I was ready to go back on what I'd just said, swipe all that shit off the table, and lay her on it so that I could feast until I was content. Then the thought occurred to me that I might never be content when it came to Sandra. And we hadn't even had sex yet.

"You need to eat," I ordered, moving around her to pull her chair out for her to sit. My voice was husky.

She smiled up at me as I pushed her chair in once she was seated. I moved around the other side of the table, thankful for the candles I'd let Samuels set up. They definitely helped give the area a romantic feel. This was the first time I'd ever brought a woman to my place for dinner. I liked to keep my space to myself, but for Sandra, everything was different.

"Mmm," she moaned after her first bite of the duck.

I damn near choked on the piece of duck I was chewing. "You really need to warn a man before you start making sounds like that."

She covered her mouth with the navy cloth napkin. "I'm sorry. I know it's rude but my goodness this is so good," she gushed.

I eyed her across the table halfway caught between amused and turned the fuck on.

"You aren't eating." She paused, looking at me across the table with those big, round eyes. "You're not hungry?"

"Hungrier than I've ever been in my whole life." That may've been an understatement.

Her chewing slowed as my words sank in. She swallowed and took another sip of wine.

"Tell me about your day," I insisted as I cut into my food.

I listened as she described her day at work. The case she'd been working on was picking up steam which seemed to make her happy.

"I think we've got a good chance of winning this one. I can feel it." Her voice rose in excitement.

"Have you ever considered going to law school?"

She paused for a heartbeat. "I thought about it very briefly. Again, I couldn't justify spending three years as a full-time student while I have a daughter to raise. Plus, the idea of taking out all of those student loans … You know I work with some attorneys who have six figures of student loan debt? It's crazy."

I snorted. "I've heard stories. Would you want to go back to school? If you could? If you had help?"

"What, like a scholarship?"

"Something like that."

Her lips poked out a bit as she considered it. "I might. But I'm so far removed from school now. I'm more concerned about saving enough for Monique's college fund."

Placing my glass of wine back on the table, I nodded. We ate and continued to talk some more about our days, life, and everything in between.

"You want ice cream on yours?" I questioned from the kitchen. We had finished our dinner and moved on to dessert. I was removing the vanilla bean ice cream Samuels had left to place on top of the chocolate lava cakes with some caramel and fudge sauces.

"Absolutely," Sandra responded eagerly from where she sat on a stool at the kitchen's bar.

"Come here."

Her eyebrows rose, questioningly.

I tilted my head, motioning for her to move closer. She rose from the stool, rounding the bar and fully entering the kitchen. I took a spoonful of the cake with the ice cream and held it up to Sandra's mouth.

"Open."

Her lips immediately parted, and I slid the sinful dessert in between those lips, slowly pulling it out. Dipping my head, I licked a drop of the fudge sauce that'd smeared a bit at the corner of her mouth.

Shit. The fudge tasted better eaten off of her than off of the damn cake. Slowly I inched forward, pushing her until her back hit the stove's countertop. I dipped the spoon again and held it up for her to eat from. She complied once more, savoring each bite I fed her. When the bowl was empty I placed it in the sink and braced my hands on the countertop on either side of her body.

"You're not having any?"

"I'm going to have my taste right now," I responded just before lowering my head to hers and taking my fill of what it was I'd really wanted all damn night. She moaned into my mouth, the same sound she'd made as she enjoyed every bite of her food. My hands moved from the countertop to her waist, squeezing, before moving around to her ass.

Our tongues licked and tasted one another, savoring every touch. One of Sandra's arms rose to wrap around my neck while her other hand went to caressing the hairs of my beard. I started to grow dizzy from our kisses alone. My dick hardened and began to strain against the pants I wore. I pressed myself into her, lowering my face to lick her neck. Her skin was so damn soft.

"Hsss," she hissed when I ran my teeth along the sensitive flesh there. "W-wait," she panted, pushing against my shoulders.

I pulled back, looking down on her.

"I need to get something," she stated, scurrying out of my arms and out of the kitchen before I even had time to respond.

I ran my hand down the side of my face. As much as I wanted to be patient with her because she needed it, I wasn't sure I could. Maybe inviting her over wasn't such a good idea. Because the last damn thing I wanted to do was simply cuddle up on the damn sofa and watch a movie, or worse, take her home. I wanted to rip that damn dress off and—

"This," she stated, walking back into the kitchen and placing a piece of paper down on the counter next to where I stood. I watched as she looked anxiously between the paper and myself, biting her bottom lip.

"What's this?" I questioned, gesturing to the paper.

"Read it."

I eyed her for a second before lifting the paper and reading it over. I swallowed. "Test results." I pinned her with my gaze.

She nodded. "Um, negative for … well, you can see for yourself."

I wrinkled my forehead. She'd actually gone out and gotten tested for STDs and brought the paper to me as proof. Maybe she was ready. Except …

"And this is supposed to mean what?" Placing the paper back on the counter, I looked at her expectantly.

Her eyes moved from me to the paper and back to me as if the answer was obvious. It was but she needed to say it out loud.

"That, uh, well, I'm ready. I mean if you are. Are you?"

Hell yeah.

"Ready for what, Sandra?" I questioned, moving closer to her, crowding her space.

"For you know …"

"I don't know." I took another step forward, bracketing her body with my arms again. I knew exactly what she was saying and what these tests were meant to prove. "You're going to have to say it, little one."

* * *

Sandra

Seven little words.

Seven.

That was all I needed to say.

I want to have sex with you.

That was all I needed to say for Damon to take away this ache. He knew it and I knew it and yet my mouth failed me. My body hummed when he moved a half an inch closer; the only thing separating our bodies were the clothes we still wore.

Dipping his head, he placed a kiss to my neck before rising again, looking me straight in the eye.

"When's the last time you had sex?"

My eyes closed as I inhaled. *Never.*

My eyes flew open and I thanked God I hadn't actually said that answer out loud. Sex was a voluntary act between two people, and well, that'd never been the case with me.

"A long time," I breathed out, instead of the truth.

He nodded. "Since Monique's father?"

My stomach plummeted. Casting my gaze down at the ground, I nodded.

"Do you want me to go slow?"

I pushed out a breath feeling comforted by his questioned. "Can you?"

He kissed my lips. "I can do anything you want me to. But if you're not ready for this tell me now. Because I'm letting you know my every intention is to have you screaming my name by the end of the night. If you're not down for that, it's probably best I take you home."

I swallowed the lump of fear that'd gotten stuck in my throat. Because more than anything, my body filled with the need of the promise it heard in his words and that was held in his eyes. I knew even before we'd done anything that Damon wouldn't let me down. I knew it with my entire being.

I nodded. "I'm ready."

His Adam's apple bobbed in his neck. "Then say it." Leaning down, he ran his lips down the column of my neck.

Goosebumps formed along my arms. I began trembling with anticipation.

"All you have to do it say the words, little one, and I can put us both out of our misery."

Aw hell.

"Damon, I-I want to have sex with you … Make love to me, please?" My question was borderline begging.

He lifted his head, his eyes taking on a new gleam, a mischievous smile on his lips. He stepped back, pulling his phone out of his pocket.

"Just for the record." He turned his phone screen to me.

I blinked, wondering what the hell was going on. My eyes zeroed in on the screen and once I finally realized what he was showing me, I smiled.

"Negative for everything also. This test is two weeks old."

Glancing at the date, I saw that he had had the screening just two weeks prior.

"Thank you."

"Don't thank me yet." He placed his phone on the counter behind me, his large hands rising to cup my face as he lowered his lips until they were just hovering over mine. "Do you need to be home by a certain time?"

I shook my head. "Monique's spending the night over Kayla's."

He nodded and swallowed before covering my mouth with his. I was stunned when he bent low, his hands moving under my thighs, scooping them up to wrap around his waist.

"Time to take this to the bedroom."

I tightened my arms around his shoulders, loving the feel of my body against his strong, muscled chest. I had the sudden urge to explore his entire body. Leaning down, I lightly bit his earlobe, causing him to shudder.

"Keep that shit up and I'll drop you and strip you right in this damn hallway."

I hummed against his ear, the pool that'd started in between my legs growing. Damon's strong hands remained on my thighs as we entered his bedroom. He turned on the lights, igniting the entire room. I noted the dark blue and navy shades that mirrored his living room furniture. Before I knew it, my back was being laid against the softest mattress I'd ever felt.

"I'm going to strip you naked so I can see this sexy ass body in its entirety."

Was he warning me or just telling me? Why did it sound like both?

He stepped back from hovering over me and took my right leg in his arms, trailing them down the length of my thigh and then calf until he reached the leopard print heel. He removed my right shoe then the left.

"These …" he held up the shoes, "are exactly what has had me wanting to bend your ass over my kitchen counter since I opened the door to your fine ass this evening."

I closed my eyes, sighing. He was so damn sexy. To know that a man like Damon was attracted to me was beyond my comprehension.

I didn't have long to contemplate his attraction when I felt his fingers moving up my thighs, underneath my dress, reaching for the top of the tights I wore. I raised my hips to assist him as he began sliding my panties and tights down my legs. I grew embarrassed when he tossed my undergarments over his shoulder and forced my knees apart, his eyes moving to stare at the core at the center of my legs.

I closed my eyes and attempted to pull my knees shut. I was ready to have sex, but the deep exploration of my body that Damon was doing would be my *undoing*.

"Uh uh," he warned, holding my knees farther apart. "I like to see my meal before I eat it."

Did he just …

"Ohh!" I gasped at the first contact of the hairs of his beard on my inner thighs as he kissed each side. He hadn't even made contact with the most sensitive part of my body yet and I was already coming undone. Easing the sides of my dress up, he pushed it over my belly so that it wouldn't obstruct his view or his actions. He kissed the top of my sex, the same spot I'd gotten waxed for the first time a week earlier, before moving lower.

Those strong fingers of his parted my sex, and the first swipe of his tongue had my hips rising off the bed.

I began to moan but covered my mouth with my hand, feeling embarrassed.

"Move your hands. I want to hear every damn sound you make tonight. I need to hear it. To know I'm giving you the pleasure you deserve."

My breathing increased and I slowly lowered my hand from my mouth, gripping the sheets beneath me.

Once again, Damon lowered his face between my legs and continued giving me pleasure I had never felt before, even with my battery operated toys that had been my only companions over the years.

I panted, and twisted my hands in the sheets, my hips rising to meet his hungry mouth. Sounds I had no idea I could even make emanated from deep in my throat. And just when I felt like my body couldn't rise any higher, I tumbled over into the sea of pleasure, all thanks to Damon's insistent mouth and tongue. He didn't even bother stopping. Instead, he grew even more persistent in his licking, tasting, and suckling. My body responded in kind, granting him a second orgasm. By the time he rose from between my legs, my thighs were trembling and I could hardly believe we hadn't actually had sex yet.

Damon stood over me, his chest rising and falling as he unbuttoned his dark shirt, tossing it to the floor.

"You taste good as hell. I could spend the entire night with my face between your thighs. But I'll save that for another time."

He leaned over, covering my body with his and pressing a kiss to my lips. I opened for him, but when I tried to deepen the kiss he moved back. He pulled me by the hands to sit up.

"I need to see all of you."

My hands went to his chest, my own need to feel him consuming me.

"Can I?" he asked, his hands rising to my hair.

I nodded.

Slowly and carefully he began removing the top bun I'd worn. As he massaged my scalp, loosening the strands of my curly, natural hair, it fell to my shoulders. He removed the numerous bobbie pins that had kept the bun in place.

"I've wanted to see you with your hair down since the first time I saw you."

"Really?" I don't know why that surprised me. Yes I did. Because he'd left with another woman the night we'd first met.

"No lie." His hands went around to my back, reaching for the bow that securely held my wrap dress in place. The dress fell to either side of my body, exposing the navy blue silk bra I wore that matched the panties he'd tossed aside earlier. He pushed the dress down my shoulders, causing it to pool at my knees. Seconds later the dress lie on the floor at Damon's feet.

The embarrassment and nervousness I'd felt earlier tried to come back, but the way Damon's eyes diligently studied my body, as if I were the only thing that ever mattered, there was no way I could feel anything but utterly captivating.

That was how he made me feel. Captivating. As if I were the only woman in the world who needed to be treasured and adored. I didn't even flinch when his hands moved, unclasping my bra, letting it fall to the floor with the rest of my clothing. His head lowered, taking my right breast into his hot mouth.

My neck arched and I cupped the back of his head as he ran his tongue around my turgid nipple. His hand went to my free breast, giving it the attention it needed. I covered that hand as well, never wanting this feeling to end. But it did when Damon stepped backwards.

Eagerness poured out of his body as he anxiously stripped himself of his pants and dark boxer briefs. My mouth watered at the hardlines and rigid muscles of his abdomen. I noticed a couple of scars that ran across his abdomen. They were flat and appeared to be years old. They didn't detract in any way from the beauty of his physique, instead doing the opposite. They seemed to fit naturally with the rugged energy Damon sometimes gave off.

My eyes dipped lower, passing the V of his waist, moving over the thick pubic hairs, down to his long …

Holy shit.

My eyes widened at the length of his cock. Fisting it, he stroked it slowly before moving away from the bed, over to the nightstand. He opened it and took out a condom before coming back to me.

He didn't say a word as he pressed a hard kiss to my lips. This kiss was more frenzied than the earlier ones. His control was breaking, I could feel it, and instead of it scaring me, it spurred me on. I kissed him back with all of the fervor I had coiled within my body. I ran my hands over his shoulders and chest needing to feel him.

He pushed me backwards, my back hitting the bed again, and he moved over top of me, surrounding me with his body heat. He lifted his head from mine, placing the condom wrapper between his teeth to tear it open with one hand. I watched as he astutely opened the condom and placed it over his hardness.

"I told you I can go slow—"

"Don't." I shook my head. "I don't need you to go slow anymore." I didn't want slow or careful. I wanted Damon and everything he could give me. "Please," I begged, my legs going around his waist as he lowered himself to me.

He kissed my lips and then to my ear, kissing it and my neck. Suddenly, I felt the tip of him as he began to breach my entrance. I pushed out a deep breath and tightened my arms around his shoulders.

"Goddamn," he cursed in a whisper as he continued to sink into my body.

"Hurry!" I urged, twisting my hips to encourage him further.

Instead of answering with words, Damon covered my mouth with his and kissed me deeply, letting his hips push all of the way into me. I gasped into his mouth. He pulled back almost to the tip before pushing all of the way in again. My back arched off the bed.

"Damon!"

Again, he didn't say anything. Instead taking either of my hands in his and planting them against the pillows while his hips sank into a comfortable rhythm.

"That feel good?"

"Yes!" I answered because holy shit did it feel good.

Damon picked up the movement of his strokes, causing me to breathe heavily. His hands released mine, as they moved to cup and massage my breasts. The extra attention to my breasts and nipples served to intensify the sensations happening in my core. I wrapped my hands around Damon's side, my fingernails clawing at his back because they needed something to grip and the sheets weren't enough.

He rose up slightly, staring down at me, watching me through those dark eyes of his. He wasn't just looking at me, he was watching, memorizing every moan, every groan, every time my breath caught when he switched up his movements. He was in it to ensure I received as much pleasure as I could. The knowledge of that overwhelmed me and my eyes glossed over. I raised up, pulling his head down to meet mine. I needed to feel his lips on mine. I didn't have the words to express what I was feeling, how treasured I felt at that moment, but I could show it with actions.

I put every thought and emotion I could muster into that kiss. Thoughts of fear or apprehension of being this intimate with a man disappeared with each kiss, lick, and stroke he gave. My body took over as my hips rose to meet Damon's ministrations. Our breathing, grunts, and moans were the only sounds

I hummed as the tension built in my body, alerting me of my third orgasm. Damon felt it too because he picked up the pace, his hand going to my clitoris, using his thumb to circle it.

"Ohhhh!" I bellowed as the orgasm crashed through me. My thighs clamped tightly to Damon's waist. I squeezed until I felt completely wrung out. Not long after I opened my eyes, I felt Damon's body tense, the veins in his neck straining as his orgasm coursed through is body.

Within seconds he collapsed on top of me, his large body trapping me between it and the bed. I pulled him in even tighter and leaned up to lick the trickle of sweat that ran over his shoulder.

"Cut that shit out before you get round two started."

Tucking my head into the crook of his neck, I giggled.

He rolled us, so that we were both on our sides, facing each other.

"How're you feeling?"

I grinned and kissed his lips before answering. "Hmm. Good," I sighed. My body still hummed from the aftershocks of the orgasms I'd had. I lifted my hand to run through his beard. I loved how soft the hairs there felt.

"Do you use coconut oil in your beard?" It was a question I'd wondered for weeks now.

He chuckled and moved my hand to his lips, kissing it before letting it go. "That's what you want to ask me right now?"

I nodded. "Mhmm. Do you?"

"It's a beard oil. A mix of coconut oil, vitamin E oil, and some other shit."

"I knew it. It's so soft."

I stared into his eyes, suddenly not shy about all of the other questions that'd lingered in my mind since the first day I'd seen him at Kayla and Josh's rehearsal for the wedding.

"Why are your eyes two different colors? Is it a family thing?"

He smirked. "I guess so. My sister's eyes are two different colors also. My left eye is the same color as my father's and my right is the same as my mother's. They literally went half on this baby."

I giggled. I enjoyed his sense of humor.

"Were you ever teased for having two different colored eyes?"

"Psh. By who?" Spoken exactly the way a man like him would answer. I bet he was one of the most popular kids in his class.

"What was it like to be popular in school? I was the outcast who never fit in any group. Even the nerds didn't really get me."

"Overrated." He shrugged. "Come here." He turned onto his back pulling me over him.

"You called me your woman earlier."

Damon's hand stilled in my hair, which he'd been stroking. "And?"

I stared at him. "What do you mean *and*?"

"You are. I know you don't think after tonight I'm going to call you anything else but mine, do you?"

I swallowed. I hadn't thought about it.

"I haven't seen or been with anyone else in weeks. I don't plan on seeing anyone but you for … Hell, for as long as you'll have me. That makes you my woman."

"Okay," was all I could say.

"Then it's done."

It was done.

I laid my head on his chest but popped right back up when I remembered the last question I'd had in mind to ask.

"Do you fight at the same club Joshua fights in?"

He lifted an eyebrow, questioningly.

"The scars on your body, are they from …"

"Fighting?"

I nodded.

"Yes."

I knew about the secretive fight club Joshua was a part of. Kayla had revealed it to me months ago and I always wondered but never asked if Damon was a part of the club as well. When I saw the scars it was easy to put two and two together.

"Does that scare you?" he questioned in the silence.

My gaze rose to meet his once again and slowly my head shook. "Why do you fight?"

His eyes rolled up to the ceiling and he ran his free hand through his beard, contemplatively.

I felt a muscle in his abdomen jump when I moved my fingers along one of the scars. It was faint but I could feel it. I waited patiently, wanting to know what drove him into the ring to fight in a place where he could obviously be harmed.

"Nights when I can't sleep," he finally responded.

Running his answer over in my head, I lowered back to his chest. "I know that feeling," I murmured.

His hand went to my unruly hair, lightly massaging my scalp. "You do?"

"Yeah. Can't sleep, feeling out of control of your own life or what's happening to it. Needing to regain control in some way."

"What caused that for you?" His voice had slightly deepened.

I opened my mouth and I started to tell him the truth, but instead I said, "When Monique first got sick. Feeling helpless to do anything. I hated that feeling."

"You were there for her," he said after a minute of quiet. "Trust me when I say that counts."

I shrugged. "It counts for something, I guess."

"Nah, being there when your kid needs you whether you can do anything or not counts for *everything*."

I lifted my head to stare at him again because his voice sounded far off, as if he'd gone back in to some place in his memory. I moved in closer, cupping the side of his face and pressing a kiss to his lips. It didn't take long before he took over the kiss, laying me on my back, covering my body with his.

"Told you, you'd be the one to get round two started." He chuckled deep in the back of his throat before his lips covered mine again, and my legs were opening up to wrap around his waist. So much for getting any sleep that night.

CHAPTER 11

*S*andra

"Oh my God! You scared me," I whisper-yelled to Damon behind me. I glanced around Kayla and Josh's kitchen, gladly seeing no one before I turned to face him.

He took advantage of the only alone time we'd had since we'd arrived an hour ago, to kiss me, placing his hands at my waist. It was rude to be at my friend's baby shower yet sneaking kisses in her kitchen, but Damon's lips always had me acting in ways that were slightly out of character for me.

"I should beat Josh's ass for making me come to this damn thing *and* for keeping you running around instead of sitting in my damn lap where you belong. He's got an extra guest room." Damon wiggled his eyebrows.

I dipped my head, giggling. "We are not sneaking off. All of the guests haven't even arrived yet."

"The hell I care about guests?"

I laughed, and Damon took the time to nuzzle my neck, licking it. "We can't," I whispered. "Besides, Monique's outside, too."

Damon's head popped up, an eyebrow raised. "And what do you

know about that Diego anyway? She seems attached to him." His eyes narrowed in a protective way.

"He's Josh's nephew. They're friends."

"Hmmm. Matter of fact, I should go out and check on short stuff and make sure everything's on the up and up with that little boy."

"Leave my nephew alone."

I peeked over Damon's shoulder to see Joshua entering the kitchen, staring at the two of us. I pushed Damon's hands from my hips and side stepped him.

"You sure he's only ten?" Damon asked Josh, his voice serious.

"Pretty sure, but you can go ask his father. Carter's right outside." Josh tilted his head.

My eyes widened when Damon nodded and said, "I'll go do that. I'll be back." He bent and pressed a quick kiss to my lips before moving through the kitchen toward the sliding glass door to enter the backyard. It was mid-March, and while it was typically still chilly this time of year, Kayla had wanted her baby shower to be outside. So it was.

I watched Damon's retreating back, and then my gaze moved to Joshua who picked up a deviled egg from one of the silver serving platters before popping it into his mouth.

"Don't tell Kay. She's had me running around all day for this thing and I haven't eaten anything. I'm fucking starving."

I laughed. "I didn't see anything."

He winked at me before taking another deviled egg.

I took one of the few opportunities I had alone with Joshua Townsend to say something I'd wanted to say for months.

"Joshua, I wanted to thank you for helping me land my current job."

His forehead wrinkled in confusion for a half a second before realization dawned on him.

"No big deal." He shook his head.

"It really was." I knew Kayla hadn't shared with him the details of why it was so imperative that I leave my last job but he'd been a lifesaver. He'd used his connections throughout the city of Williamsport to find a paralegal opening at the firm I now worked for.

"It meant a lot to me, and I'm sorry if it caused any problems for you that Kayla kept my secret."

Josh raised his hand. "Kay said you were in trouble and needed help finding a job. She trusts you and I trust that woman more than anything in this world. If she believes in you, so do I. I hear you're doing great at the new firm."

I nodded. "I love it. We're doing important work."

"Good. That's all that matters." He took another deviled egg and nodded in my direction before heading out.

I pushed out a breath but looked up to see Damon staring at me. His gaze was narrowed. Had he overheard the conversation between Josh and I? Of course he had. That was evident as Josh passed by him, but those two differently colored eyes remained transfixed on me, questioning.

"Josh got you the job at the firm?"

I looked around the kitchen. "Sort of."

"It's a yes or no question."

"My credentials got me the job at the firm. Kayla just gave him my resume in case he knew someone who needed a paralegal."

"And what happened with your last job?"

I shrugged and busied myself, organizing the cookies onto the free platter, avoiding his gaze. "I just needed a job that paid more and with better benefits. This one fit the bill." That was a partial truth and I was glad to have something to do to avoid looking up at Damon. I was thankful he hadn't heard the entire conversation I had with Joshua.

"There you are!" Kayla's breathless voice broke up the tension in the room. "Damon, I need to take the MC of this event outside with me for a while." Why on earth Kayla had begged me to be the MC of this baby shower I had no idea. I didn't like speaking in front of people. Most of these people were practical strangers to me. These were her friends, family, and colleagues, yet there I was hosting like I knew these people. But in spite of my uncomfortableness with my hosting duties, I was grateful to be out from under Damon's suspicious gaze. I wasn't ready to explain to anyone, but especially not him, what or rather *who* it was that drove me from my last job.

"Hey, you all right?" Kayla asked, gripping my wrist as I stared off into space while a handful of the men at the shower played one of the silly baby shower games. Four men stood at a table blindfolded trying to change the diaper of a baby doll that laid in front of them.

"Yeah." I nodded. "Fine. Are you enjoying your shower?" I smiled.

Kayla's cinnamon skin glowed from pregnancy, her cheeks much fuller than when I'd first met her, but she looked gorgeous. Happier than I'd ever seen her.

"Yes. Thank you so much for agreeing to host. I know it's a little out of your comfort zone, but I really appreciate it."

"Like you gave me much choice." I gave her a deadpan expression.

She giggled. "Sorry about that, too."

I shook my head. "No you're not."

Another laugh, louder this time. "You're right, I'm not. You're the perfect hostess even if you don't think so."

I rolled my eyes. "Whatever. You're lucky my daughter loves you, or else I'd be tempted not to speak to you after this."

"Yeah right. You can't get rid of me. Who else is going to babysit this kid once he or she is born?"

I laughed. Kayla had strong armed Josh into not finding out the sex of their baby until it was born. I didn't think I had that type of patience. I wanted to know as soon as I could when I was pregnant with Monique, even though I had the sixth sense early on that I was going to have a little girl.

Speaking of, I glanced over into the yard where the children played. Damon was out playing a game of catch with Monique and Diego. He'd opted not to participate in any of the adult games, insisting that he keep watch over Monique and *that little boy* as he now referred to Diego.

"They've taken to each other," Kayla noticed, staring out into the yard as well.

I bit my bottom lip. "You don't think it's too soon for that, do you?

I mean, it's still really early on in our relationship, and who knows what will happen. You hear all those horror stories—"

"Sandra," Kayla started, wrapping her hand around my wrist, "don't go making trouble where there isn't any. My grandmother used to tell my mom that when she got scared for me when I was a kid. Damon's a great man and you are a great mother. Trust in that."

I nodded and smiled at seeing Monique laughing as Damon picked her up, tickling her ribs.

"You're right," I agreed. Maybe I could let my guard down for once.

* * *

DAMON

"I still don't think you should've let her stay over for the night. I mean, what do you really know about the boy?" I demanded, as we entered my condo. I hung up the leather jacket I took just because Sandra had insisted I needed it, on the coat rack before taking her peacoat and doing the same. Why the hell Joshua's wife insisted we have a baby shower outside in March was beyond my comprehension, but that man gave his wife whatever she wanted, regardless if it made sense or not.

"You had no problem with Diego a few months ago. Now you're all suspicious. He's ten," Sandra retorted, her hands on her hips as she faced me.

I licked my lips, admiring those hips in the leather leggings she'd worn with a beige sweater. She'd also worn her hair down, letting the curls she'd set it in kiss the tops of her shoulders.

"That was before I saw how close he is with short stuff. You know those two have their own little secret code? Like their own personal language. I ain't know what the hell they were saying to each other this afternoon. They could've been telling all of us to kiss their asses and we'd never know it. He's trouble."

My head shot back when Sandra bent over, laughing. She didn't cover her mouth like she had in the past. Instead, I got to view her wide open mouth as she guffawed like I'd told a damn joke. But my name wasn't Chris Rock. I was dead ass serious.

"Fine. You laugh now, but wait 'til I dig up some info on that little boy. You won't be laughing then."

That made her laugh even more, and my damn heart kicked against the inside of my chest. There really was no use in fighting the inevitable. This woman and her ten-year-old daughter had stolen my heart. Something I would've thought impossible just a few short months earlier.

But I still had to act like I was pissed at her for laughing. I held strong until she walked over to me, wrapping her arms around my waist. My hand instinctively went to those full hips.

"Thank you for looking out for my baby. But I assure you, Diego Townsend is no threat to her."

I dropped a kiss to her lips before spinning her around so her back was pressed against the door. My hands rose to either side of her head.

"He better not be or I'll kick his, his uncles', and his daddy's asses, too."

She smirked. "You'd take on the whole Townsend clan for her, huh?"

"Hell yeah," I responded right before dropping my head and nuzzling the crook of her neck. I ran my teeth along the column of her neck when she lifted her head, giving me better access. It'd been two weeks since we first made love in my bed and I thought that that would've somehow weakened the constant need I had to be inside of her, but not at all. The only thing it did was make me want to keep her under lock and key, tied to my bed all day so I could slip in between those tight thighs of hers whenever I wanted. I spent many hours trying to convince my crazy ass brain that doing that would be akin to kidnapping.

"I have something to ask you," she stated, panting as I continued to run kisses over her neck, chin, and lips.

"So ask." I covered her lips with a brief kiss before moving to the other side, sucking her earlobe into my mouth.

"Hmmm," she hummed.

My dick responded to the moan, pressing against the zipper of my jeans.

"A-are you free next Saturday?"

I didn't even need to think about it. "For you? Always." I pressed another kiss just underneath her ear.

"Will you come over f-for dinner?" Her question came out on a moan when my hands moved underneath her sweater, touching the warm skin of her stomach.

"Just tell me the time."

She sighed. "I-I want you to meet someone."

I pulled back to stare down at her, my hands still wrapped around her body underneath her shirt.

"Who?"

"My grandmother. She's coming over for dinner."

Clenching my teeth, I pushed down the wave of anger that rose in my body. I wouldn't let Sandra see how I really felt about the woman who'd kicked her out of her home when she was pregnant.

I nodded. "I'll be there."

Her smile was worth putting my anger to the side. She looked as if a weight had been lifted off of her.

"Now ..." I began, pressing a kiss to the side of her neck before pulling back, "can we discuss something ..." I kissed the tip of her nose, "more important?" I kissed her lips.

"I think so." She nodded, smirking up at me, lashes lowered but not in a shy way. She'd slowly been dropping her inhibitions, at least with me. That felt comforting.

Reaching up, I wrapped my finger in one of the curls she'd worn her hair down in for the day.

"You're going to mess up my curls."

I grinned. "Hell yeah, I am. I'm about to have your hair all over your damn head."

The giggle that escaped her lips was cut off by my capturing her lips in a deeper kiss than earlier. I'd wanted to get my lips on hers all day and keep them there. If I hadn't had to keep an eye on Diego with

Monique, I would've taken Sandra in one of Josh's spare guest rooms and handled my business, but duty called.

Now, there were no overly friendly ten-year-old boys to worry about. Just me and my woman.

"I want to undress you this time."

My brows raising in surprise, I took a step back, holding out my arms. "Your will be done."

Sandra giggled, taking a shy step forward, but she didn't pause. Her hands went first to my beard, her personal playground. Tonight was the night I'd show her exactly how soft my beard could be when she used it as a seat. I licked my lips just thinking about it, my dick growing hard in my pants.

Her little hands moved down to my chest, unbuttoning the three collar buttons of the Polo shirt I'd worn before moving lower to pull the entire thing over my head. I had to help her a little with that. And as much as I wanted to hurry up and rush through this part to have her naked, writhing beneath me, I steeled myself against my own impatience. The deepest part of me told me that she needed to feel this. To feel some type of control in our coupling.

I sucked in air when her fingers made contact with my bare chest and abdomen.

"You're so beautiful," she stated in awe before pressing a kiss to the center of my chest. She rose, standing upright, and her finger outlined one of the scars on my stomach.

"Did you win the fight that earned you this scar?"

I stepped forward, advancing on her until her back was pressed against the door. "I always win." I dropped a kiss to her lips but pulled back before I got too lost in it. Raising my hands to the door, I bracketed her body. "Undo my pants."

Her hands went to the belt buckle holding my jeans in place. She trembled slightly before undoing the buckle along with the button of the jeans.

"Push them down," I ordered, still leaning over her.

Slowly she did as told, but stopped just as the tops of my pubic hairs emerged. She glanced up at me, biting her bottom lip.

I gave her a look through narrowed eyes. "Keep going."

She returned to what she'd been doing, pushing my pants and boxer briefs down past my waist. I sucked in air when the tips of her fingers brushed against my straining dick. I kept my gaze planted on her as she pushed my clothing all of the way down. I lowered my face to the crook of her neck, licking my favorite spot and causing her to shiver.

"Take it in your hands," I told her just before biting her earlobe.

"Wh-what?" It came out on a moan.

I pulled back. "You think it was an accident I told you to get that red nail color the other day? That's the color I like to see wrapped around my dick."

She gasped, and I captured her lips but didn't keep the kiss going too long. After guiding her hand to my erection, I pulled back, my gaze going to where her hand was now on my body.

"Now what?" she questioned, a little timid but there was an eagerness, an anticipation in her voice that called to me.

"Stroke it. The way you want me to stroke your insides when I get in between your thighs."

I dipped my head, biting her chin, eliciting another moan.

Slowly her hand began moving down my muscle.

"Now tighten your grip as you get closer to the tip."

"What if I—"

"You won't. Keep going," I demanded, my hand going underneath her sweater, to cup her breasts.

"That's it. Shit!" I grunted at the feeling of her hand on me. I took her lips, kissing her deeply. The movement of her hand faltered, which was fine because I much preferred coming while inside of her than in her damn hand. Stepping back, I removed my hands from underneath her sweater and kicked my pants and boxers to the side.

"Undress."

She gave me a surprised look, to which I kept a neutral face to. I wanted to watch her undress for me.

I took another step back, giving her some space. Her eyes circled the room around me, a contemplative gleam in her eyes. I wanted to rush her, to push her out of that deep insecurity I often saw in her eyes, but I knew she needed my patience more than my prodding. I could wait for her to get comfortable with me.

I was rewarded for such patience when her hands slowly went to the edge of her sweater, lifting it over her head. I held my hand out for the sweater and she handed it over. I tossed it over my shoulder, imagining that it landed on the couch or floor behind me.

"Pants next."

Her eyelids fluttered but her hands went to the waistband of her leather leggings. She'd looked good as hell all day in those damn things. I don't know what made it worse, seeing her in those leggings as she ran around hosting the baby shower, or knowing exactly how those thighs beneath the pants felt. Slowly she lowered the pants past her hips.

I frowned, realizing she'd have to take off the heeled boots she wore to remove her pants all of the way. I would've much rather preferred the heels stayed on during what I had planned that night but there'd be a next time. I aided her in removing the boots and leggings, leaving her in just her bra and panties in front of me.

I took my fill, letting my eyes trail over the smooth, copper-toned skin of hers.

"No," I shook my head, as her hands went behind her to begin removing her bra, "let me." I stepped forward, reaching around her body and feeling for the clasp. With a few flicks of my finger, the bra straps were sliding down her shoulders. I pushed them the remainder of the way down, releasing her breasts for my viewing. My hands went to them, cupping and squeezing her hardened nipples.

Sandra's head flopped back against the door as she let out a soft moan, biting her bottom lip. But this time it wasn't due to fear or doubt. She was turned on. Her breasts were particularly sensitive—something I'd picked up on the first time I'd touched them. To pull even more of those sexy ass moans from her lips, I dropped my head, pushed her breasts together with my hands, and ran my tongue over both nipples. Not only did she continue moaning but a purring sound escaped her lips. That shit turned me on even more, causing me to wrap my entire mouth around her left breast. I tongued her nipple while pinching and plucking the right one.

I squeezed and massaged her breasts, which were just large enough to fit comfortably in my hands. Her little compact body was perfect for me. A moan of my own escaped from the back of my throat from the softness and sweet taste of her skin. She had a taste that belonged only to her. For the life of me, I couldn't figure out how she tasted and smelled like cotton candy. Maybe I was just making it up because I was that fucking far gone over her.

My free hand trailed down to her left hip and I felt her thighs beginning to tremble.

"Damon." It came out as a pleading whisper, her back arched toward me, head lulled against the door and eyes tightly sealed.

She was coming.

From breast play alone she'd had an orgasm.

And from the looks of it, when she opened her eyes, glancing around and then up at me, she was completely taken by surprise.

"I-I had no idea those were real. I read about it, but ..." She trailed off.

I pressed a quick kiss to her lips. "They're real and you just had one." I kissed her again because I could, and then bent low, picking her up by the backs of her thighs to walk us both down the hall.

I stared into her eyes the entire time I carried her. She looked back at me, arms draped around my shoulders, looking as if she had a question to ask but couldn't figure out how to say it, or even what *it* was she wanted to ask. Hell, maybe that was my projection because I was feeling a lot of shit that I couldn't explain myself.

I placed her on the bed before opening the drawer of my nightstand and reaching in for a condom. Pulling one out, I handed it to her. Her eyebrows raised as she took the condom from my hands.

She sat up staring at me curiously. "You want me to ..."

"Yes. Open it."

With trembling fingers, she tore the wrapper open.

"Pinch the top."

She did.

"Place it at the tip."

Slowly she moved her hands to the tip of my hardness.

"Now roll it down."

As soon as she reached the base of my dick, I took her hands by the wrists, pulling them over her head and forcing her back against the bed. I moved to press my body against hers. Her legs instantly went up, wrapping around my lower back. I lowered my face to hers, kissing the tip of her chin, then the sides of her mouth, before fusing our lips together.

"Mmm," she moaned into my mouth as I began grinding my waist into her still panty-clad sex. Her hips began wiggling against mine, desperately seeking more.

I wasn't one to keep my woman waiting. Adjusting myself so that both of her wrists were in my left hand, I used my right to slide the crotch of her panties out of the way and began easing into her. Her moans grew louder and breathing heavier. I broke free of the kiss and lowered my face to the crook of her neck, licking as my cock moved deeper and deeper inside of her.

"Damon!"

"My dick feel good?" I asked, pistoning my hips, moving in and out of her body.

"Yesss," she hissed, her back arching off the bed.

I released her wrists and moved both of my hands to under her thighs, lifting them, and pushing them farther apart, giving myself more room to go an inch deeper.

Sandra screamed, tossing her head against the pillow, eyes squeezed shut.

"Open your eyes. Look at me when I'm making you come!" I ordered, my voice tight with my own pent-up sexual energy.

Slowly Sandra's eyes opened, those brown eyes looking into mine.

"You gonna come for me?"

She didn't answer, instead a gasp escaped her mouth as I pushed into her again.

"I didn't hear you. You gonna come for me?"

"D-Damon!" she yelled as her hands twisted in the pillows surrounding us.

"That wasn't an answer." I pulled out almost completely.

"Yes! Please!"

Goddamn I loved it when she begged like that. Other women I'd been with loved the power play involved with sex—wanted to try and see if they could get me to make promises I wasn't ready for or never would be, before they opened up sexually. Not Sandra. She didn't play manipulative games like that. And that made me want to please her in every way.

I lifted her knees and pushed them together at her chest, causing her thighs and pelvic area to tighten around my straining dick. I felt the trembling in her core and sped up the pace of my movements.

"Daamoon!" she yelled, moaning as her body released.

The tightness caused by the position I had her in, along with the milking from her orgasm, was my undoing. And before her release was complete, a ripple down my spine had the muscles in my body tightening and straining as my orgasm pushed through. I grunted and flexed my hips, working to release every drop of my cum into the condom.

I collapsed to the bed, rolling over so Sandra could lay on top of me. Our sweaty bodies were skin to skin, chests heaving as we strained to normalize our breathing.

"I had no idea."

I lifted my head, as my fingers continued to trail over Sandra's damp, bare shoulder. Looking at her head laying on my chest, her hand running through the hairs of my beard.

"No idea what?"

"Sex could be *that* damn good."

I chuckled and lowered my head to the pillow, tightening my hold around her body.

"Shit, me either."

CHAPTER 12

D amon

"Hi, Mr. Damon!" Monique eagerly greeted as she answered the door to her and Sandra's home.

Grinning, I stooped to get eye level with her. "What's up, short stuff?" I then leveled my brows, frowning. "I thought your mother told you not to answer the door."

She lowered her head. "Aw, man, I forgot."

I chuckled and tweaked her nose, making her laugh. "I won't tell."

"Tell what? That Monique is *not* supposed to be opening doors unless I specifically ask her to?" Sandra questioned as she rounded the hallway into the living room, approaching the door.

I scanned the length of her body, as had become my natural reaction every time I saw her. She wore a long, floral print dress, which had cutouts at the shoulders, displaying their bare smoothness. Those shoulders that I had licked and kissed just a few nights earlier.

"No," I responded to Sandra's earlier comment. "Short stuff and I have secrets all our own, that have nothing to do with you." I tossed Monique a wink and she giggled.

Sandra looked between the two of us. "Whatever. Monique, go finish putting your shoes on."

"'Kay, Mommy." Monique ran out of the room, and as soon as she turned the corner, I used the free moment to quickly wrap my arm around Sandra's body, pull her into me, and kiss those lips that always seem to taunt me. Even in my damn sleep.

Sandra was the first to pull back, which was probably a good thing, seeing as how I would often lose my ability to say enough where kissing her was concerned. She smiled up at me, her hands going to my chest, before one moved up to cup my cheek, my beard more specifically.

"One day I'm going to cut this thing off and find out how you really feel about me."

Her eyes widened. "You wouldn't."

"Don't tempt me. I don't appreciate being whored out for my beard."

She gasped and then covered her mouth, laughing.

I grabbed her hand, lowering it, wanting to see her entire face as she laughed.

"It's not the beard. It's the man behind the beard."

I nodded. "Uh, huh. You say that now. Watch when I cut it off, you'll be singing a whole different tune. Probably stop answering my calls and everything."

She shook her head. "Never."

Pausing, I looked her in the eye. There was no false pretense, no coyness, or manipulation. Just pure truth.

I dipped my head lower, placing a quick kiss to her lips before moving over to whisper in here ear. "Wait 'til you use my beard as a seat." That was the one thing I hadn't gotten to the other night that I'd kicked myself over. The next time I had her all to myself, I wouldn't be so damn forgetful.

"Damon!" she gasped, whispered, shocked, glancing over her shoulder I guessed to make sure her daughter wasn't around. I would've told her I already checked to make sure we were alone, but we were then interrupted from someone behind me.

"Hello."

I pulled back, looking over my shoulder, realizing that I was still part way in the hall of Sandra's apartment building. I narrowed my gaze at the woman behind me. She looked older, her skin a few shades lighter than Sandra's and she was about a half a foot taller, but there was an undeniable family resemblance. I didn't have to be told who this was. I steeled my face to a neutral position.

"Grandmother," Sandra pushed out. "Hi. This is Damon," she introduced, holding her hand out to me.

I looked toward the older woman and nodded.

"Damon, this is my grandmother, Dorothy Robinson."

"Ms. Robinson." I held out my hand.

She grasped it, shaking. "Please, call me Dottie."

I nodded but didn't say anything.

"Come in." Sandra stepped back, allowing both of us to enter.

I moved to the side, allowing her grandmother to enter first.

"These are for you. For dessert." I handed Sandra the brownies I'd ordered from the bakery not too far from my condo.

"Are these the brownies you had Monique raving about?"

Smiling, I nodded. I'd given Monique one of the brownies the other night when I'd picked Sandra up for a date. They were made with unsweetened applesauce and stevia instead of sugar which was supposed to be better for someone with diabetes.

"She loved them. Hasn't stopped talking about them since the other day. You are quickly becoming my little girl's hero."

I smirked and leaned down, pressing a kiss to her lips. "Yeah? And what about her mama's hero?"

Her eyelids lowered and her lips parted, but before anything came out the sound of Monique running down the hall occurred. "Great-Grandma!" she shouted. "Mr. Damon, this is my great-grandma. My mommy grew up with her." She pulled her grandmother by the hand over to where Sandra and I stood.

I nodded. "I'm aware but thanks for the introduction, short stuff."

She giggled and then looked up to Dottie. "That's his nickname for me. He says I'm short like my mommy but I'm only ten." She shrugged and we all laughed.

"I hope you're all hungry. Monique and I have been cooking.

Monique, Mr. Damon brought more of those brownies you liked." Sandra held up the white bakery box that was held closed by the red and white string.

"Yes!" Monique cheered.

"What do you say?"

"Thank you, Mr. Damon!" Monique moved over to me, throwing her arms around my waist.

My arms went around her. I swallowed the lump in my throat before looking at Sandra who smiled at the both of us. My eyes moved over to Dottie's who was watching me.

Monique and Sandra insisted that Dottie and I sit at the dining table, which had already been set up with plates, silverware, and napkins for four people. I watched as Dottie handed Sandra the bread she'd brought to accompany the chicken and vegetable soup they had prepared.

"Sandra tells me you're involved in real estate?" Dottie inquired, trying to make conversation.

"I am."

"That must be interesting."

I nodded. "It pays the bills."

She released a short laugh. "I'm sure it does more than that."

"You were a judge, correct?"

"Yes, I was a prosecutor for fifteen years before becoming one of the youngest judges in the city. I served for thirty years."

"Interesting," I said half-heartedly, taking a sip of the homemade iced tea from the glass Sandra had given me earlier.

"Here we are," Sandra announced as she entered the dining area, holding two bowls.

I stood, taking one of the bowls from her and placing it at the nearest place setting.

"Thanks," she stated before setting the second plated bowl in front of her grandmother. "I've still got it. Thought I might have lost a little bit of my strength since my waitressing days. I would've carried a third on my forearm, but I didn't want to show off," she joked.

I chuckled. "I bet you didn't."

"Let me go make sure my little helper isn't making a mess." She disappeared back into the kitchen.

I remained standing until she and Monique entered back into the dining area, plated bowls in hand. Only once they sat, did I take my seat.

I found myself annoyed when Dottie opened up the dinner conversation, asking how Sandra and I met. I let Sandra answer most of the questions her grandmother asked. Monique seemed to love her new great-grandmother. She talked at length about school projects she was working on, or wanted to work on, but had been told by her teachers she wasn't allowed.

"Ms. Jamison says there is no place for our school to do a compost even though I told them how harmful it was to keep wasting food and sending it to the landfill." She frowned as if truly puzzled on how to solve this particular issue. Sandra had already shared with me her daughter's passion for saving the planet. On a previous visit to their home, Monique showed me the composting buckets she and her mother used, which were picked up once a month to be sold to farmers around the state. She was very proud of it.

"And how are you getting along with the other kids at school?" Dottie asked.

I lifted an eyebrow, curious as well, considering Monique had ended up in the hospital as a result of the bullying she'd endured.

"Better," Monique answered. "Since Mommy visited the principal and my teacher the kids are nicer." She shrugged.

I remembered Sandra telling me she went down to the school the day after Monique's hospital visit to have a *talk* with the principal and teacher. I concluded that my little undercover spitfire had likely cursed those people at her daughter's school out for not being on top of the teasing she was dealing with. While that image had me smirking, I didn't say much during the conversation, even when Sandra and Monique stood to take our empty dishes into the kitchen. At that point, I rose.

"Let me, you stay and talk with your great-grandmother, short stuff." I took the plates from her hands and followed Sandra into the kitchen, placing the dishes into the sink, as she had done.

"You okay?" she questioned, a wrinkle in her forehead.

"Yeah, why?"

"I don't know, you just seemed quiet during dinner."

I shook my head. "Work stuff. No worries." Leaning down, I kissed her lips. "Thanks for dinner."

I followed her back into the dining room after she placed four brownies on four different plates. We sat down and ate dessert, Monique the most energetic out of everyone over the treat.

"These are great. Are they from the Smith Bakery, over on Lennox?" Dottie asked.

"They are."

"Oh, that's why they're so familiar. I used to stop over there on my lunch breaks sometimes during the day for something sweet."

I nodded and took a bite of my brownie, enjoying it more than I thought I would. When Sandra told me how much Monique loved the last one I'd brought for her, tonight's dessert choice had been a no-brainer.

We talked around the table some more before Sandra rose, needing to get Monique ready for bed.

"I can head out—"

"No," Sandra insisted. "Stay, it'll only take a few minutes. She's not going to bed. She just likes to have a few minutes on the tablet to talk with Diego before they both go to sleep. Hang on," she stated, following Monique down the hall.

I stood in the living room, looking around at the light grey and white furniture, and the pictures on the wall showcasing Monique at various ages.

"You don't like me very much."

My eyes lowered from the pictures on the wall to the woman standing to my left. I glanced over her shoulder to make sure Sandra and Monique were still down the hall.

"I don't know you well enough to like or not like you."

She gave me a small frown. "Any man of your stature has to be discerning, I would imagine. Which means you make split decisions on people every day in your line of work. I had to do it in my career. Which is why I'm able to tell when someone is just tolerating my presence."

I ran my hand through my beard before fully turning to Sandra's grandmother. "Like I said, I don't know you well enough to like or not like you. Now respect you?" I shrugged. "That's something different."

Her eyebrows raised. "Respect?"

I pushed out a breath. I'd been prepared to keep my mouth shut, to bite my damn tongue throughout this entire night, but since she'd asked …

"It's hard for me to respect anyone who kicks their teenage child out of their home when they need them the most."

Her mouth formed into an "O" realization or comprehension settling in on my problem with her.

"She was eighteen, fresh out of high school and you left her to fend for herself. With a baby."

Her eyelids fluttered.

My gaze narrowed. Was that shame?

"I thought she'd come back. Come to her senses. Or at the very least, marry the boy that'd gotten her pregnant."

It was my turn to gape at her in surprise. "Marry a dude who couldn't even claim responsibility for his child?"

Dottie shook her head, briefly averting her eyes, before turning back to me. "I was wrong."

"Yeah, you were."

"All right, Monique's settled in, talking with Diego. Those two could talk about nothing for hours."

I frowned, looking over at Sandra as she entered the room. "She has to talk to him so late at night?"

Sandra giggled. "It's barely eight o'clock."

"Exactly. Shouldn't his little ass be sleeping? Don't these kids have school in the morning?"

Sandra laughed as she moved fully into the room. "They're friends.

Calm down. Damon gets a little overprotective of his short stuff," Sandra explained to her grandmother.

Dottie turned to me. "It's not just Monique he's protective over."

My expression remained placid.

"Well, thank you for dinner, once again. I should get going."

"I'll walk you to your car," I stated. I may not have respected the woman's decisions, but I did have some form of home training.

"Thank you."

"I'll be back to say goodnight," I told Sandra.

After Dottie said her good-byes, I followed her out to her car which was out front of Sandra's building.

"You didn't have to walk me down."

"I did. Despite my feelings of what you did or didn't do in the past, I was raised to walk a woman to her car, at the very least."

She nodded. "I appreciate that, Damon. And, differences aside, I am thankful Sandra and Monique have someone like you."

I raised an eyebrow.

"You look out for them. Sandra needed that back then and I wasn't there for her. It's taken a long time and a cancer scare for me to see where I went wrong."

"It shouldn't have taken all of that."

"You're right. It shouldn't have. Have a great night." Turning, she pressed the button to unlock her brick-colored Mercedes.

I stepped back and watched her enter her car and drive off. She seemed remorseful over her treatment of Sandra in the past, I guessed, but I still would keep an eye on her. Just knowing she was living in a brownstone and driving around in a luxury vehicle while her granddaughter was struggling to raise a child with no help from anyone still pissed me off.

Swallowing down the anger, I made my way back into Sandra's building and headed up to her apartment.

"Thanks for doing that." Sandra smiled as I entered back into the apartment.

"Come here." I pulled her to me once I double checked to make sure Monique was still in her room. "Thanks for dinner."

"I'm glad you enjoyed it."

"We're still on for Saturday night?"

"Of course. Monique's staying over my grandmother's for the first time."

I frowned. "You sure that's a good idea?"

"You don't think so?"

I shrugged. "I'm not saying that, just asking a question. They've only known each other a few weeks, right?"

"Almost two months. And I've known my grandmother my whole life. I was worried about how she'd be taking care of Monique in case she got sick or something, but her pump has made it so much easier to maintain her glucose levels throughout the night."

I nodded. "That's good."

"Yeah, I'd forgotten what a full night of sleep actually felt like. Turns out it's not too bad," she giggled against my chest.

I raised an eyebrow, lifting her face by the chin to look up at me. "I sure as hell hope you don't think you'll be getting a full night's sleep on Saturday. I plan to have you up all night, just like last Saturday and the Saturday before that and the Saturday be—"

I jumped back, laughing when she swatted my arm with her hand. "Quit it before I tell short stuff you're trying to beat me up."

"She'd probably try and defend you, too. Telling me it's not nice to pick on people."

"And she'd be right. You know we're not with that bullying shit." I pointed at her.

She swatted me again, aiming for my abdomen.

"Speaking of, I should go tell her goodnight before I head out."

"You better. Or else, she'll be in here mad at me for making you leave after she went to bed."

I chuckled and made my way down the hall, knocking on Monique's half-closed door.

"Diego, I gotta go, Mr. Damon's here … Okay, bye!" She waved into the screen of the tablet before pressing a button to disconnect the video chat.

"Hey, short stuff. I'm heading out. I wanted to tell you that dinner you helped your mother make was delicious."

Her smile was just like her mother's. "Thanks, Mr. Damon. And thank you for the brownies. They were *really* good. I tried to get mommy to make them but she said she could just buy some. She doesn't like to bake."

I chuckled.

"Way to tell all my business."

I smirked at Sandra over my shoulder, as she stood leaning against the doorjamb of Monique's room.

I moved farther in the bedroom. "Don't blame your mom. I don't like baking too much either."

"But you're a boy. You're not supposed to like baking," Monique quickly countered.

"What?" Sandra shrieked. "Where did you get that?"

Monique shrugged. "It's just true. Everyone knows women are supposed to like to cook."

"She's right," I told Sandra who gave me a narrowed eye stare down. I laughed, shaking my head before moving to the side of Monique's bed, kneeling down. "Nah, that's not the truth, short stuff. Women and girls can like whatever they want," I stated in a serious tone, glancing up at Sandra and tossing her a wink. Her shoulders relaxed a little as she breathed a sigh of relief.

"Then how come it's always the mommies in the kitchen cooking? Even Diego said that's how it's supposed to be."

I glanced up at Sandra. "I told you I didn't like that little boy. See what he's filling her head with? How's she going to be the first black female president when he got her thinking stuff like this?" I shook my head.

Sandra rolled her eyes. "Leave Diego alone. I know for a fact that both of his parents do the cooking at their home."

"Yeah, but Diego said it's only because his daddy likes to cook. He has to because he works at the fire station. But he's not *supposed* to."

I sighed again. "That's that bullsh—" I paused, glancing up to see Monique's eyes, the same as her mother's, staring at me. "Uh, listen, short stuff. Diego's not wrong, just mistaken. Men and women cook and bake. It's not the responsibility of one or the other."

She gave me a funny look, as if she was trying to gauge whether I was the insane party in this conversation, or if she was.

Finally, she shrugged. "If you say. But can you bring me some more of those brownies when you come over again?"

"Monique! We don't beg for stuff. Mr. Damon was nice enough to—"

"You got it. They've got some lemon bars I hear are pretty good as well. I'll pick some of those up next time, too."

"Yess!" she screeched, clenched fist by her side as if she'd just scored a winning goal.

"You're going to spoil her rotten," Sandra remarked as we moved back into the living room. We'd just finished reading Monique a book she'd asked for. Something she and her mother, apparently, did every night. I was surprised when she requested I stay for the reading but one look and the word *no* just wasn't in my vocabulary. What the hell was going on?

"Nothing less than what she and her mama deserve," I responded, pulling Sandra by the waist to me. I gazed into her large eyes and the feeling was overwhelming. I wanted to know everything about her— past, present, and future. "Where's Monique's father?"

Her entire body language shifted with that one question. A haunted expression crossed her face as she pushed against my chest, silently requesting I release her. Reluctantly, I did so.

"Why are you asking about him?"

Was that a tremble in her bottom lip?

"You never mention him. Neither does Monique."

"He's not relevant. Never has been." She pivoted her head, staring down at the floor in the corner of the room.

I moved closer and lifted her face to mine by the chin. "He's completely out of the picture?"

She nodded before looking away again.

Something wasn't sitting right. The expression on her face was too full of fear. I knew what fear looked like, and to see it in the eyes of the woman who dominated my thoughts, over a simple question about the father of her child, it was hitting me square in the chest. A muscle in my jaw ticked as I ground my teeth together. I took a step back, running my hand through my beard, trying to calm myself down. She obviously wasn't ready for those questions.

But that didn't mean I was giving up.

"I'll drop the questions for now." I pulled her into me again, placing a quick kiss to her lips. She responded to the kiss but I still saw the whisper of unease in those maple syrup pools she called eyes.

As I headed out the door all types of thoughts crossed my mind. The main one being that once I caught the bastard who'd caused her to wear that haunted expression on her face, I'd wear his entire ass out.

✳ ✳ ✳

"HAVEN'T SEEN you in a couple of weeks."

I grunted as I passed over the threshold of the basement building where our fights were hosted. I held out my right hand for Connor to smack. Once he did, we tapped shoulders, as was our usual greeting. He closed the door behind me. Connor O'Brien was the actual owner of this building. He was also a former professional pro-fighter who'd retired some years earlier. And while he had numerous legit businesses throughout the city and state, few people knew that he ran one of the most notorious and far-reaching underground fighting rings in the continental U.S.

"Been busy," I finally responded to his earlier comment.

He looked down on me from his height of six-feet-five inches, with those hazel eyes, and nodded.

"Been there."

I lifted an eyebrow but didn't care to question what he meant by that. I wasn't in the mood for much talking. After leaving Sandra's that night, I found myself unable to sleep. If it wasn't the damn nightmares I'd had for nearly two decades, it was visions of that haunted expression on her face when I asked about her daughter's father.

Either I needed to get in the ring, or I'd be at her door at half past midnight demanding answers. The nightmares that'd haunted me for years I couldn't do anything about—I'd long since accepted them as part of my reality—but her ghosts I could fight … maybe. If she'd open up to me. But since I knew she was too sensitive to be pushed just yet, here I was, at the place where I could let out the part of me that felt like a caged animal, needing to break free.

"We've also got a newbie tonight. That should interest you."

I glared at Connor. "I don't fight newbies."

He nodded and stared at me over his shoulder. He'd begun walking closer to the ring where guys had already started to gather. "You'll want to fight this one, I'm guessing." He gestured with his head toward the ring.

Glancing up at the center of the ring, I saw someone who looked eerily familiar. I noted the dark, almost black, slicked back hair, the thick but solid frame, and six foot stature.

"Is that …"

"Mike Russo Jr. As requested."

My eyes shot over to Connor whose face was neutral as he stared at me.

"Joshua requested I let him in. For you."

I nodded.

"You ready to fight him now?"

"Hell yeah," I answered without needing to even think about it. My hand tightened around the strap of the athletic bag that I'd slung over my shoulder. My fingers literally itched to get into the ring.

"Thought so. Follow me."

I followed Connor into the changing room to ready myself for the fight. He helped me with my hand wraps since Buddy was already out in the ring.

"I trust you'll leave him alive."

I gave Connor a stern look. "I make no promises." I started for the door, but Connor's hand on my shoulder stopped me.

"You know who his fucking father is, right?"

I looked Connor dead in his eyes. "I know exactly who the fuck his daddy is." I tightened my fists.

Connor pushed out a breath. "Hell. I've never run a from a fight in my life, but if this shit goes wrong, I'm kicking your ass once the dust settles."

I snorted. "Like you could."

He grunted and tapped me on the back.

I made my way from the changing room to the ring, nodding at a few of the guys I knew. I passed underneath the ropes and came face-to-face with Mike Russo Jr. He squinted in my direction once he saw me. I didn't flinch. I took the opportunity to memorize his face. I wasn't surprised to notice that he looked like his old man. That caused my stomach to clench.

"You must be Damon."

Sounded like his fucking father, too.

This ain't him, Damon. I had to remind myself that this was Mike Russo's son and not the bastard I'd hated for eighteen years. The motherfucker who'd murdered my father as I hid behind a fucking dumpster.

"I must be," I retorted.

His dark eyes narrowed but he didn't say anything else. Good. I couldn't stand the sound of his voice just because it reminded me of his father.

"All right, gentlemen. You know the drill. No biting, no face shots, and make sure you're wearing your cups. Everything else goes," Buddy began his usual spiel.

I ignored everything around me, and focused entirely on Mike Russo Jr. Just before Buddy lowered his arm between both of our bodies, signaling the beginning of the fight, I wondered if this Russo knew what his father had done to mine. Did he know who I was?

And with those thoughts running wildly through my brain, I struck out the first opportunity I got. He'd left his entire right side wide open. Showing no mercy, I attacked his ribcage with a vengeance —with a right hook, followed by a left uppercut. The first punch stung and caught him off guard, but the second punch is what caused him to crouch low, the wind knocked out of his body. As he stood bent over at the waist I had every desire to throw an elbow at his face, effectively ending the fight before it even began.

But I backed off.

I reminded myself that junior wasn't my main target. He was a couple of years younger than I was, which meant that he likely had nothing to do with what his father had done to mine.

"Shit, I thought you were going to take it easy on me," he grunted as he rose, uprighting himself on his two feet.

"Why the fuck would you think that?" I countered, and immediately aimed a left cross at his face. He dodged that one.

"I thought we don't aim for the fa—" His question was cut off when I sent a knee to his right side ribs.

"Less talking. More fighting," I challenged, bending low and sending a swift side kick to the back of his knee, taking his legs from under him. He fell to his back, and before he could figure out what was happening, I pounced on top of him, locking his arms in a position that he couldn't last for very long in. He'd either have to tap out or risk suffocating. At that point, I didn't give a damn which option he chose.

Seconds later, Russo's hand, which was trapped between my legs, tapped my thigh. He'd made his choice.

Slowly I released him from my hold and stood. He moved even slower, needing to take his time to stand back up. Buddy moved between us, granting me as the winner of the fight.

"You're tough," Russo leaned in and said to me, holding out his hand for me to shake.

"I need to speak with you." I glared at him as I took his hands.

His brows raised.

"About your father," I stated, moving in closer so only he could hear me.

He glanced around before nodding.

I motioned with my head for him to follow behind me as I turned and headed straight for the changing room. Holding the door for him to pass through, I looked around to ensure we were alone. I nodded to Connor who moved in front of the door to make sure no one entered.

"Hey, man, I don't know what this is about but I'm not my father," Russo Jr. began, holding his hands up.

"Is it true you're on the outs with your father?" I questioned, arms folded over my chest.

Russo paused, giving me a sideways glance. His dark eyes narrowed as he examined me. "How the hell do you know that?"

"I know people. Is it true?"

"What the fuck is it to you?" he questioned defensively.

I wasn't perturbed. I'd be defensive, too, if someone I just met started asking questions about my father.

I stepped closer. "I don't like your father either."

He grunted. "Get in line. There's a whole list of people who can't stand him."

"I'm at the top of that list."

He shook his head. "No one hates that fucker more than me. No one."

I stared into Mike Russo Jr.'s dark eyes and saw the pure hatred that sizzled there. He was telling the unmitigated truth. This man hated his father. I could use that.

"I've been trying to figure out the best way to get back at him for years now. Ruining his real estate deals hasn't been enough. He's weakened but still in business."

Russo's eyes widened. "That was you? I've been trying to figure out who's behind his real estate business tanking."

"Why?"

"Why?"

I nodded. "Why have you been trying to figure that out?"

He glanced around the empty changing room.

"What you say won't leave this room."

"How the fuck am I supposed to know that?"

I narrowed my eyes on him. "You don't, but you also wouldn't be here if you weren't the type of man who took risks, either."

He grunted and nodded. "I've been trying to get my father put away for years. I became an accountant just so I could learn the ins and outs of money laundering and racketeering to pass what I knew about my father's organization to the FBI."

I paused with a raised eyebrow. He was dead serious.

"Money laundering?"

Russo nodded. "He's too good at covering his tracks with murder and selling drugs but the money never lies."

I knew that. It had been what held me back all of these years. Russo Sr. had too many ties with the local law enforcement.

"What if I told you I knew someone on the inside who worked for him and was ready to pass some information to you that could help put him away?"

"I'd tell you I need a fucking name and number."

I smirked. "You seem anxious."

"I've been waiting to do this my whole fucking life. Anxious isn't the word."

I nodded. "Cool. Here's my card." I moved, picking up my gym bag from the floor and removing my business card, and then passing it to Russo. "Call me in two days and we'll make something happen."

He took the card, looking it over. "Two days."

I nodded. "Two days."

CHAPTER 13

*S*andra

I glanced over my shoulder as Damon came up behind me. We'd just exited the town car that dropped us off in front of one of Williamsport's most popular lounges. The lounge turned into more of a nightclub after ten p.m., which is what the time was. We'd gone out for dinner and now were meeting some of Damon's friends.

"Did I tell you how sexy your ass looks in that skirt and with those heels?"

I lowered my head, giggling, only for Damon to lift my head from under my chin with his finger. I was starting to realize how much he liked watching my facial expressions. I tried to remember, but sometimes my shyness still consumed me.

I'd worn a black, leather skirt with a black, sleeveless silk top, and paired it with my favorite leopard print six-inch heels. I'd bought both the skirt and heels over a year ago but hadn't had the nerve to wear them outside of my apartment until that night.

"Yes, but I don't mind hearing it again," I answered, surprising even myself with how flirtatious I sounded.

Damon growled in my ear, biting my earlobe, causing another round of giggles.

172

I jumped a little in surprise when he slapped my ass, before raising his hand to the small of my back.

"Keep that same energy once we leave this damn club and I get you all alone."

I was half tempted to tell him we could skip the club but I bit my tongue. Instead, I asked, "Who're we meeting here tonight?"

Damon shook hands with the bouncer, who nodded and stepped aside, letting us easily bypass the long line out front.

"My boy, Xavier Grant, and his wife, Chanel."

I wrinkled my forehead, knowing the name sounded familiar. "Xavier Grant, the restaurateur?"

Damon glanced down at me. "You've heard of him?"

I nodded. "He's from Houston, right? I think I read an article on him in *Black Enterprise* magazine a while back."

Damon nodded just before we got to the bar. Reaching across, he shook hands with the bartender. He seemed to know everyone in here, but his left hand never left the small of my back.

"Yeah, that was him. I read that same article."

"How long have you known him?"

"We're up here." He tilted his head in the direction of the stairs that lead to the VIP section. "Almost eight years now."

I didn't respond, simply followed as Damon took my hand and led me up the stairs.

"There he is!" a deep voice sounded as we entered the VIP section. It was much quieter up here, though the music could still be heard from the first floor of the club.

I glanced up as I stepped on the top step, Damon stepping to the side so I could have a clear view of the section. I swallowed as a man with chestnut-colored skin, a solid build of just over six-feet, and dark, coffee-colored eyes moved closer to Damon with his hand outstretched. Damon slapped fives with the man I knew to be Xavier Grant. They did the half-handshake, half hug thing most men did as greeting.

"X, this is my lady, Sandra," Damon introduced, pulling me into his side.

The butterflies that moved through my belly hearing Damon refer to me as his were slightly overwhelming. I swallowed before letting my gaze trail up to Xavier's eyes.

"Pleasure to meet you, Sandra," he stated, holding out his hand to me.

I shook his. "Pleasure, Xavier."

"Call me X. Most of my friends do."

"Will do, X."

He smirked. "My wife's around here somewhere. Probably giving someone legal advice some damn where." He glanced over his shoulder. "Have a seat. I'll be right back."

Damon and I moved farther into the VIP section as Xavier sauntered off, apparently going to retrieve his wife.

"His wife's a lawyer, right?" I questioned Damon as we sat. I thought I remembered reading that in the magazine article. He'd recently gotten married but that was nearly two years ago.

"Pssh," Damon made an exasperated sound with his mouth, as he sat back, wrapping an arm around my shoulder. "Dude had the nerve to marry a damn divorce attorney. And a pretty good one, too. He's crazy as hell." Damon shook his head, laughing.

"Why's that make him crazy?"

Damon lifted an eyebrow my way. "'Cause he married her without a prenup. He has no choice but to stay with her for the long haul. She'll clean him out."

I frowned. "So the only reason he should stay with his wife is because she could take him to the cleaners?"

Damon gave me an amused look. "Look at you getting all in your feelings. I didn't say all that. I was just teasing. Calm your pretty ass down. And like I told you, keep that same energy for later." He moved closer, brushing his lips against mine.

"I will if you will," I responded against his lips. Yeah, clearly my inhibitions had been lowered when it came to Damon.

His beard tickled my chin as he grinned, lowering his face to press a kiss to the corner of my lips.

My eyelids fluttered and I nearly shut them entirely when I heard, "My bad, didn't mean to interrupt."

I turned to the deep voice that'd just spoken to find a smirking Xavier Grant staring down at Damon and I. To his right was a shorter, curvy woman, who he had his arm wrapped around. She smiled down at us.

Damon and I stood.

"Chanel." Damon moved forward to press a kiss to the woman's cheek.

"Don't get too close to my lady," Xavier ordered, giving Damon a hard glare.

"Cut it out," Chanel stated, waving her hand toward her husband.

"Sandra, this is Chanel, my wife," Xavier introduced.

"Pleasure to meet you," she said, extending her hand.

Smiling, I reached for her outstretched hand. "Likewise. I love that jumpsuit you're wearing," I complimented without even thinking. The jumpsuit appeared to be a dark blue silk material with cuffed sleeves that stopped just above the elbow. One side of the jumpsuit left her shoulder exposed and the waist was secured by a wide belt that was the same color as the rest of the outfit. While Chanel couldn't be described as thin, she definitely was in shape, and well put together. The outfit screamed confidence and style. Her hair fell in big barrel curls around her shoulders. Chanel appeared to be around five foot five or six inches with the four-inch heels she was wearing.

She smiled widely. "Thank you. I'm loving that leather skirt."

"Here the women go talking fashion."

I gave Damon a sideways glare to which he responded with a chuckle.

"Don't let your mouth get your ass in trouble," Xavier warned Damon, laughing.

"Anyway, Damon," Chanel interrupted, "it's nice to see you. What've you been up to?"

"You know me, constantly working."

"Not always, apparently." Chanel turned brown eyes on me.

I felt Damon's hand wrap around my waist, pulling me closer to the warmth of his body. Instinctively, I melted into his frame, almost as if I was supposed to be there all along.

I swallowed down the feeling that that thought evoked in me.

"Not always." He gazed down at me.

"This one is working at all times. She was just trying to give the damn waitress legal advice," Xavier added, side-eyeing his wife.

I giggled at the look she gave him.

"I was just trying to be friendly. She's separated and has two kids. She took on waitressing as her second job just to be able to afford her kids' extracurricular activities because apparently her husband refuses to pay until she takes him back." Chanel rolled her eyes. "Men," she sucked her teeth, disgusted.

"Daaamn. We're standing right here," Damon spoke up.

Xavier laughed. "She doesn't mean it. She's just hormonal. The baby and all."

My eyes widened and my gaze bounced from Damon to Xavier, then to Chanel to see her glaring a hole into the side of her husband's head. Xavier appeared unbothered and quite cocky as he grinned at the two of us.

"Another one? You don't miss, do you?" Damon cheered, slapping fives with Xavier.

"Whatever." Chanel waved them off.

"Congratulations," I told the couple, before dipping my eyes to stare at Chanel's stomach, on instinct. From what I could tell she wasn't quite showing.

"Thank you," they both stated at the same time.

"How you got your ol' lady in a club while she's with child?" Damon teased as the four of us sat down in two of the white leather lounge loveseats that sat opposite one another, with a low sitting black table in between.

"You think I'ma let her out of my sight? Dudes don't know how to act when they see a pregnant woman."

Chanel rolled her eyes. "The truth is, I've been in the house so much being sick from this pregnancy that once my medications had me feeling better, I made your boy take me out."

"Morning sickness?" I questioned.

"Hyperemesis gravidarum," Chanel responded, grimacing.

I frowned. I'd heard of it but thank god I hadn't experienced that level of sickness while pregnant with Monique.

"Sick, pregnant and all, some of these clowns don't know how to act. So, I keep my lady close," Xavier added.

I raised an eyebrow. Xavier did have a point, from what I could remember. When I was pregnant with Monique, I received noticeably more male attention. I wasn't too thrilled with the extra attention.

"Why is that?" I asked without thinking. I clamped my mouth shut when I found three pairs of eyes staring back at me.

"Why is what?"

I homed in on Damon's distinctive eyes since I felt safest staring into his, and answered his question.

"Men and pregnancy. Why are men more …"

"Attentive," Chanel intervened.

I nodded in her direction, pointing. "Yes, attentive. Why are men, strangers no less, more attentive to pregnant women?"

I felt Damon's hand move to the back of my neck, cupping it gently. I had to fight hard not to lower my head and arch my back into his hold. *We're in public and that would be embarrassing*, I reasoned.

"You have experience in this, I take it?"

I shrugged. "When I was pregnant with Monique …" I paused, glimpsing at the couple across from us. "I have a nine year old—"

"Ten. She just turned ten," Damon corrected.

I laughed, turning back to Xavier and Chanel. "Her birthday was two weeks ago. I'm so used to calling her nine. Anyway." I glanced back at Damon. "Yes, I did experience more attention when I was pregnant." Unwanted attention but attention no less.

"Shit. It's in our DNA," Xavier began. "I was all over Chanel when she was pregnant with the twins."

My eyes ballooned. "Twins?"

"Right?" Chanel spoke up, side-eyeing her husband. "I gave this man not one but *two* babies for the price of one. Babies that look *just* like his ass, I might add. And he still had the nerve to beg me for more."

"Beg?" Xavier gave her an incredulous expression. "It didn't take much begging once I put—"

"Anyway," Chanel stated loudly, turning to me, cutting her husband off.

Both Damon and Xavier began laughing loudly. I covered my mouth, giggling also.

"I need to go down to the bar. Sandra, would you like to come with me?" Chanel asked.

Before I could even answer, Chanel's husband intervened. "What do you need to go to the bar for? You're not drinking, and anything you want, I can have the waitress bring up."

Chanel pressed a kiss to Xavier's lips before standing. "I need to stretch my legs. I'll just be a few minutes. You can see the bar from where you're sitting. Calm down," she insisted.

I stood. "I'll go," I added, hoping that might calm Xavier down. Anyone could see he obviously had a protective side when it came to his wife.

I turned to Damon who was giving me an inquisitive look. I hadn't realized his hold at the back of my neck had tightened until I went to move away. It wasn't a painful hold but possessive.

"What you need at the bar?"

I grinned and leaned in, pressing a kiss to his lips, much the same way Chanel had done to her husband when confronted with his possessiveness.

"Walking Chanel. We'll only be a minute, I'm sure."

His hand loosened but the frown on his face didn't let up. I reached up on tiptoes and pressed another kiss to the corner of his mouth.

"Aren't they pains in the asses?" Chanel questioned low in my ear, as we made our way to the stairs.

I gave her a look, laughing.

"I know, I know. Can't live with them, can't live without them."

To that, I nodded and continued following her to the bar.

* * *

DAMON

I stared after Chanel and Sandra as they headed down the stairs that led from the VIP section of the club to the main dancefloor. While I was well aware that the club had all types of safety precautions and Sandra was safe in here, I still didn't like the distance between us. Shit, that was becoming more and more commonplace. My chest would ache a little more each time I had to drop her off at her apartment, or she had to leave my place to get back home to hers.

"You look like you got some shit on your mind."

I turned from the women who were now making their way through the crowd toward the bar, to look at Xavier. His dark eyes were pinned on me, just waiting for me to say whatever was on my mind. He took a sip of the glass of dark brown liquor he'd been sipping on, but his eyes never left mine.

"Let me ask you something." I motioned with my head before inching closer and planting my elbows on my thighs, leaning into him.

His lips spread, as if to say he'd been waiting for this. He leaned closer as well, setting his glass on the napkin on the table.

"What's up?"

"How did you know you'd fallen for Chanel?" It wasn't a question that I'd even been thinking of asking until that very moment.

"You think you've fallen in l—"

I held up my hand. "I didn't say all that."

Xavier lowered his head, chuckling.

"The fuck is so funny?"

He laughed harder. "Man, by the time you ask that question, you're already gone." He shook his head. "It just takes time for your head to catch up to that muscle at the center of your chest."

I frowned. "The fuck are you talking about?" This fool done went and got all Shakespeare or Rumi or some shit.

He laughed some more. "Don't even worry about it. But listen, I'll answer your first question. I knew my wife was the one for me when I was ready to take her ex's damn head off his shoulders for what he'd done to her."

I frowned, squinting. I remembered some time ago there'd been an article in some off brand gossip blog about Chanel and her ex-fiancé who was the son of a senator or some big time dude in Washington. Apparently, her ex had beat her up when they were together.

I swallowed as my hands tightened into fists at the thought of Sandra's ex doing something like that to her. From what I knew, she'd never been engaged to the man who'd gotten her pregnant. She was always tight-lipped about him. But the look in her eyes whenever I questioned her about him …

"Yeah."

I glanced up to see Xavier pointing at me, glass in hand.

"See how you're feeling right now?" He gestured to my tightened fists. "That's how I felt. It's also how I knew. Still took me some time to get clear on it all though."

Sighing, I sat back, loosening my hands. I shook my head, shaking off my previous thoughts. "I need a drink."

Xavier chuckled again. "Shit, I do, too." He held up his hand and waved for the waitress to bring a glass of whatever he was having over for me. "I don't understand what the hell my wife needed to go all the way to the bar for when we have a waitress right here."

That reminded me that Sandra and Chanel were still over at the bar. I turned my head, eyes searching for the two women, or rather, the one woman I'd come with. I'm sure Xavier was looking for his own woman.

I pushed out a breath of air when I spotted Sandra from behind. I licked my lips as my eyes roamed down the back of her petite frame. The off-the-shoulder, loose fitting top was neatly tucked into the leather skirt that stopped a couple of inches above her knees. I was stunned into silence when she opened the door and I got a look at the outfit for the first time. She'd told me she had the skirt for months but hadn't worn it. I was glad she'd chosen that night to put it on. And I'd be even more happy when I could peel it the fuck off her body.

Just as I was imagining all of the things I'd do once that skirt was laying on my bedroom floor, a tall figure obstructed my view of the woman I'd been fantasizing about. My eyes narrowed and a possessive heat coursed through my abdomen. I didn't even realize I was on my feet until I brusquely pushed past a waiter who was bounding up the stairs to the VIP section.

"The fuck?" I heard curse behind me. I assumed it was Xavier but didn't take the time to look or slow down long enough to find out. As I rounded the area from the stairs, my view of Sandra at the bar as she'd been standing next to Chanel, talking, was obstructed. I pushed past people on the dance floor, and as my view of Sandra cleared, I watched the clown I'd observed from the VIP section reach out and grab a handful of her ass in that leather skirt.

Oh hell no!

Just as I moved past the last couple that stood in between me and my intended target, I reached out to lay hands on this fool, but by the time I'd gotten there his ass was already laid out on the floor. I blinked, staring at the pile of shit that lay crumpled on the floor directly in front of me, holding his crotch in his hands as he writhed in pain.

I lifted my gaze, raising my eyebrows in surprise to see an angry looking Sandra standing over the dude. She took one last look at the man on the ground before blinking and staring up at me. Within a few heartbeats, her anger subsided and she bit her bottom lip in that sexy ass way that she didn't even know was sexy as all hell to me.

I swallowed and lowered my head remembering that jackass on the floor had had the nerve to put his hands on her ass, and I managed to send a kick to his knee, before two of the bouncers were lifting him up to carry him outside.

"What the fuck was that?" I growled angrily at Sandra. I wasn't pissed at her. At least, I didn't think so. She was obviously just defending herself.

"Your girl obviously has better hands than you," Xavier joked beside me.

I glared at his ass before turning back to Sandra.

She shrugged. "He needed to learn how to take no for an answer."

"She showed his ass exactly how," Chanel laughed.

"This is why your ass doesn't need to be out here wandering around this damn club," Xavier stated sternly, looking down at his wife.

"What? I wasn't even the one in trouble."

That had me glancing back at Sandra, who was staring to me confused, as if what just happened wasn't a big deal.

"It's time for us to go."

"Same here," Xavier added.

"But … are you sure?" Sandra questioned.

I couldn't even answer her. I was pissed. And the motherfucker I wanted to take my anger out on had already been handled by my woman and carried out by security.

Cupping her arm at the elbow with my right hand, I reached in my pocket for my cell phone to text the driver of the town car we'd ridden in. I tossed Xavier and Chanel my good-byes over my shoulder and was escorting Sandra out of that damn club seconds later.

It was a silent and tense twenty minute ride back to my place.

CHAPTER 14

*S*andra

"Did I do something wrong?" I questioned as we entered his condo. The question was barely out of my mouth, the door hardly closed all of the way, before my back was pressed up against it, Damon's big body hovering over mine, his hands bracketing me in, and eyes barreling down on me.

"What the hell was that?"

My eyes widened. He wasn't angry. He was pissed. His body was rigid with it.

And still, I wasn't afraid of him. He wouldn't hurt me. I knew that instinctively by now.

I put my hand to his chest, still confused as to exactly *what* he was angry over.

"What was what? Me defending myself?"

He closed his eyes briefly, shaking his head, before pinning me with his gaze again.

"You shouldn't have had to defend yourself. And what the hell did you do to take him down so quickly? I didn't even see it."

I smiled, feeling proud. "I elbowed him in the ribs before kneeing his dick." Just saying the words had me reliving the moment and feeling powerful.

"Where'd you learn that? They don't teach that shit in Pilates."

I giggled. "I've taken self-defense classes off and on for years."

"Why?"

I furrowed my eyebrows. "Why? Isn't it obvious?"

"Say the words out loud," he demanded. He had a thing about me saying what he wanted to hear.

"I was eighteen when my grandmother kicked me out, alone and pregnant. I worked at a place where it was common for women to be groped and touched without permission. I didn't always live in the best places when Monique was young so I figured self-defense classes would be helpful. I take a renewal class at least once a year," I explained.

His jaw clenched, a muscle jumping just beneath the beard. He lowered his forehead to mine.

"You should've let me handle his stupid ass."

I blinked; the anger vibrating throughout his voice had my nipples pushing through the lace bra I was wearing. Never had I had a man so angry on my behalf before. Who knew it was such a turn on?

Reaching up, I cupped his cheek, running my fingers through his beard. "I can take care of myself," I responded.

I gasped in surprise when he grabbed the hand that had been stroking his beard and pinned it to the door behind me. He lowered his face to mine.

"You shouldn't have to," he growled before capturing my lips in a searing kiss.

I lifted my face, giving him better access to my mouth. All of the anger he'd been feeling he poured into that kiss, his hand tightening around my wrist. I arched my back, pressing my front into his body as a puddle began to form in my panties, between my legs. He kissed me with a passion I'd never felt before, and caused all of the nerve endings in my body to catch fire. At least that's what it felt like.

"Damon," I whispered, breathless as he moved from my lips to my neck, licking the vein that was beating erratically there.

"Don't move," he commanded, sternly in my ear.

I worked to remain as still as possible, fearing that if I budged even an inch he'd pull away and end this web of passion he'd begun weaving around the two of us.

I felt his free hand move down my thigh and begin to trail upwards, underneath my skirt, until he reached the lace panties I wore.

"Spread your legs," he ordered, with one hand on my panties and his other hand holding my left arm above my head, against the door.

On shaky legs, I separated my feet, moving my legs a few inches apart.

Slowly, he began pulling my underwear down my legs, keeping his eyes on me.

"Keep your arm where it is." He waited for my agreeance.

I nodded, and he released my left arm as he lowered his body to his knees while he pulled my panties to the floor.

"Step out of them."

I did so, leaving him to pick my discarded underwear up, bringing it to his nose and inhaling. My eyes bulged. He actually sniffed my damn underwear.

But before I could continue questioning his sanity, he stored the panties in the back pocket of his pants, lifted his head, and said, "Place both of your hands over your head. Against the door."

I hesitated, wondering what he was going to do next.

"Now," he growled.

My right hand shot up, meeting my left over my head.

Satisfied, Damon lowered his head, pushing it between my thighs until his entire head was underneath my skirt. My heart began beating erratically. Before I could question how the hell he could even breathe like that, his two large hands went to the backs of my thighs, slowly moving my skirt upwards, exposing the entire bottom half of my body. As soon as my skirt reached my waist, bunched up, Damon moved, tossing my right leg over his left shoulder and took the first swipe of my pussy with his tongue.

A thud sounded but I barely acknowledged the pain of my head hitting the wooden door behind me. All I felt was ecstasy as Damon consumed me from the inside out. At least, that's what it felt like. He used one of his hands to spread my lips, giving his tongue better access to the sensitive button at my center. I swore he put every ounce of anger and passion he'd been feeling earlier into delivering pleasure.

I moaned and writhed against the door—arching into this seeking mouth, trying to wring out every bit of what he was giving.

"Damon, don't stop!" I panted, begging, feeling myself reach for my orgasm.

He moaned something against my body but I was too far gone to understand what he was saying. The only thing I knew for sure, in that moment, was that if he stopped, I wouldn't survive. I just would not make it.

"Shiiit!" I cursed, as my legs began quivering and the orgasm slammed into me. My hips bucked wildly. If I had been cognizant enough, I would've feared hurting Damon with my jerky movements. But again, I was not in my right state of mind. My body had taken over and demanded more.

As I came down from that first orgasm, Damon slowly moved his head from between my legs, lowered my foot back to the floor, and ran a hand down his now glistening beard.

Did I do that? I questioned myself, blinking, as I looked at the moist hairs of his beard.

"Don't look like that. This shit is better than beard oil." He chuckled, rubbing his hand through his beard again.

"You're nasty," I whispered against his lips as he moved in for a kiss.

He chuckled. "I'm not the only one, little one," he reminded me, squeezing my ass in his hand.

I moaned into his mouth as we kissed before he pulled back.

"Don't think I forgot about these," he stated, stepping back and pulling my panties from his back pocket.

I tilted my head, wondering what he had planned for those.

He shook his head. "Not yet. Come here, little one," he growled, kissing me again and lifting me so my legs circled his waist.

I felt us moving as he carried me down the hall, our lips still locked together. Once we arrived at his bedroom, I expected him to lower me to his bed, but he lowered me to my feet by the door.

"These need to go," he stated as his hands went to my shirt, pulling it over my head.

My arms raised, willingly exposing myself to him. Shyness be damned, my body was still humming from that last orgasm and wanted … no, *needed* more.

He spun me around, reaching for the back clasp of my bra, pushing it down and off my body once he'd undone it.

Within less than a minute he was eyeing me as I stood before him completely nude and unashamed.

That was when he lifted the panties of mine that he still had in his hands. "Lift your wrists."

My head shot backwards, surprised. "What?"

"Your wrists. Hold them out to me."

I lifted my wrists, holding them together out in front of me. I watched, breath leaving my body, as Damon used some sort of intricate knotting method to bind my wrists with my own underwear. But before I could even fully grasp what he'd done, he was leading me over to the bed by my bound wrists. However, instead of laying me down first, he stripped down to his boxer briefs and laid down.

"I promised you a seat on my beard tonight. I'm a man of my word."

To be honest, I hadn't fully comprehended what he'd meant when he said I'd be using his beard as a seat. But when he took me by the hips and helped me position my body so that my hips hovered above his mouth, I got it.

"Hands on the headboard," he ordered.

I sighed, feeling lewd while the evidence of how turned on I was seeped out of me, coating the tops of my inner thighs.

My shaky hands went to the shiny wood of the headboard, cupping it. Damon pulled my hips lower, and the contact of his warm tongue sent a shiver through my entire body. It didn't matter that he'd just performed this same act on me out in his living room. My nerve endings responded even quicker to the feel of his hairs against my inner thighs, the hold of his strong hands on my hips and buttocks, and of course, his probing tongue against the most sensitive part of my entire body.

I began moving my hips, essentially riding his face. I stopped when I grew concerned over how my movements might be hurting him.

"Oh!" I gasped when a smack to my ass caught me off guard.

"Don't stop!" he demanded, and even though it was muffled due to his positioning, I understood completely. He liked it when I rode his face. I tightened my hold on the headboard and began moving my hips back and forth before swirling them around, angling my body to get everything out of his mouth and this positioning.

All it took was a few more swipes of the tongue from Damon and my eyes were squeezing shut, head lolling backwards, and the orgasm came crashing through my entire body.

By the time I came down from it, my throat was scratchy from the yelling. Ordinarily, such actions would've had me clamming up in my shyness, but the turned on look in Damon's eyes had me feeling anything but shy.

He moved quickly, and before I even realized it, he'd not only removed his boxer briefs but had also sheathed himself with a condom.

"You rode my face now I want you to ride this dick."

He was so damn nasty.

My nipples pebbled as I nervously bit my bottom lip. This position was a first for me. Holding up my hands, which were still bound by the wrists, I told him, "I need my hands," as I straddled his waist.

He shook his head. "No you don't."

Before I could even ask him how that was possible, his own hands began lifting my hips to position me over his straining muscle.

Lifting my tied hands, I reached out to grasp him.

"No hands," he said sternly. "Put them behind your head."

I glared at him. He only returned my glare with a mischievous grin.

Damn, why did that make me ache even more to have him inside of me? Slowly, I lowered my hips, Damon's hands now at my waist, helping me onto his member. As the tip of his cock breached me, I let out a small moan.

"Damon," I whispered his name, and was surprised when I felt him twitch inside of me.

Our eyes connected. Both of his had darkened. He became incredibly turned on whenever I said his name during sex. I swallowed against the feeling of power that sent coursing through me. I let out all of the air I'd been holding in once he was fully seated inside of my body.

I started to feel awkward, not sure what to do or how to make this pleasurable for him, but the look in his eyes directed me. It told me he had all of the confidence in the world in me, and that somehow convinced me I couldn't let him down. I sat up straighter, causing my breasts to stand out.

His hands moved, covering my breasts and pinching my nipples. I bit my bottom lip from the pleasure of his hands on me and the sensations moving down through my body down to my core. Instinctively, I rose and then dropped my hips, sliding up and down on Damon's appendage. I let out a deep sigh at the feeling of his fullness inside of me. I rose and came down again.

"Ride it," he growled, spurring me on.

Again, I lifted, this time squeezing my pelvic muscles as I lowered.

"Shit!" he cursed, obviously feeling what I'd done.

I did the same movement again and again, ramping up the passion coursing between both of our bodies. I sent a silent thank you out to the man who invented Pilates for the core strength I'd developed over the previous six months. The next time I lowered, instead of rising, I swiveled my hips, allowing him to hit each of the four corners of my insides. My head fell backwards as a deep tremor moved through my entire body, starting at the tips of my toes.

Damon's hands moved from my breasts to my hips, squeezing as his own hips began rising and falling with my movements. My hands remained in place, at the back of my head, as I surrendered to all of the feelings flowing between the two of us. My hesitation had been replaced by need and something else.

I looked down to see Damon staring intently at me. He always watched me as we made love. It made me feel even more wanted, and possibly *needed.* Within minutes, my lips were parting and my eyes tightened as my third orgasm of the night ripped through my body so violently my shoulders shuddered. Without opening my eyes, I heard Damon's breathing increase and he cursed, his own body giving into the orgasm that it demanded.

We came together, loudly and aggressively.

It was perfect.

* * *

Sighing, I stretched out my arms as I prepared to step onto the treadmill at work. For days I'd been walking around feeling as if I was floating on air. I'd heard people say things like that. I'd read that feeling so many times in the many romance novels I'd devoured over the years. I'd spent much of my free time, once Monique was tucked into bed, diving in between the pages of one of my favorite authors, searching for that feeling. But nothing compared to actually having it in real life. Certainly, it was too early to call what Damon and I had love. Wasn't it?

If it was, I knew I wasn't too far from it, but I'd decided to keep those feelings to myself. From what I knew, most men were intimidated by such admissions.

I stepped onto the treadmill to do my usual two to three mile walk while on my lunch break. I'd grabbed a pair of five pound hand weights to utilize for a few arm exercises while walking.

"Daydreaming again?"

I blinked and glanced to my right just as the belt on the treadmill started. I smiled at Emma, the main lawyer I'd been working with as of late. "I didn't see you there."

She nodded, staring down at her treadmill's screen, pressing buttons to turn it on. "I know. Someone's had her head in the clouds lately."

I giggled before looking away. Emma and I weren't particularly friends outside of work, but we had a nice rapport. Apparently, my happiness hadn't managed to slip past her. Suddenly, another thought crossed my mind and I frowned.

"I haven't been making mistakes, have I?" While I was happy in my personal life, I certainly didn't want that to derail my career due to my lack of attention to detail or anything.

Emma shook her head as she pressed the button to increase the speed on her treadmill. She was a runner, where I was typically a walker.

"No, not all," she replied, panting a little as her pace increased. "Your work has been great as usual. It's good to see you happy." Turning her head to face me, she winked. "You used to wear an almost forlorn expression when you first started."

I looked away from Emma, toward the screen of my treadmill, upping the speed by two notches. I didn't want to think about the reason I'd come to work for Mansfield, Duvall & Mason in the first place. While the transition had been a great move career wise, it wasn't a happy reason that'd prompted me to leave my previous employer in the first place.

I was happy when Emma didn't say much else after that, in an attempt to goad me for information. She continued her run while I increased the incline of my treadmill and lifted the weights I'd brought over doing a few shoulder presses and other moves. The location of our building's gym looked out on the Williamsport bridge which traversed the Williamsport River. It was moving into mid-April and spring had made its full appearance. The sun was shining brightly and the leaves on the trees were in their full bloom. Spring was my favorite season because it spoke to new life.

Sighing, I let myself take in the beautiful views as I worked the kinks out of my body. Thankfully, I wasn't someone who sweated too much while working out. That was the only reason I felt comfortable working out in the middle of the day. By the time my thirty minute cardio session ended, I was still feeling good, though slightly winded from having pushed the intensity a little more.

"I'm going to go change and pick up the lunch I ordered," I told Emma as we headed into the changing room of the gym.

She nodded. "See you back in the office. Oh, an attorney from Wittaker & Wittaker is stopping by over the Steve's Diner case."

I squinted. "That wasn't on the schedule."

She nodded and swallowed the water she'd just taken a sip of from the plastic bottle in her hand. "They called this morning while you were in the meeting for Mason's case. It's just an introduction thing, or maybe they're looking to settle. Either way, we'll find out. Wittaker is your old firm, right?"

"It is."

"Oh, maybe it'll be someone you know. I can't remember his name."

I paused, my heart squeezing in my chest, and not in a good way. Thankfully, Emma strolled off and I took a minute to remind myself I was likely being irrational. There was no way *he* could be the one working this case. None at all.

I kept repeating that assurance to myself as I changed back into the black pants I'd worn to work with a matching bow belt at the front, and a maroon silk blouse that I tucked in at the waist. I chose to slip my feet into the black ballet flats I kept in my desk for when I needed to run errands and didn't feel like wearing my heels, to go and retrieve my lunch.

Since I'd been feeling so good lately, I'd opted to treat myself to the diner next to our office building. I'd ordered a tuna melt with a tomato bisque soup. As I exited the deli with my food in hand, I was thinking about how I'd only eat half of the tuna melt and save the other half for Monique since she enjoyed them as much as I did, when out of the corner of my eye a male figure entering into my office building had me freezing in place. I blinked and he was gone, passed through the doors of the building.

"It's not him. It can't be him," I mumbled to myself, reassuringly. I strained to think back to the last days at my previous firm. Trying to remember what type of law he'd practiced. I hoped to hell it wasn't employment law.

"What are the chances?" I reasoned out loud, standing in the middle of the sidewalk. I quickly clamped my mouth shut and proceeded into my office building.

I forced myself to think about the mountain of files on my desk that I needed to get through and that I would definitely be eating while working. But the entire time I tried to think about something else, my mind was screaming at me that something wasn't right.

I made it back up to the firm's office and my desk, my eyes darting around the office for any trace of the man I thought I'd seen entering the building. I pushed out another breath, and again, forced myself to think about the work at hand.

Placing my food on my desk, I changed from my flats back into the black pumps. Sitting down, I put in my password to reboot my computer and reached for a file that was at the top of my pile. I was in the middle of researching old sexual harassment cases involving waitresses around the country.

Before I could even open the file, I startled when the phone on my desk rang. I glanced up to see Emma's extension.

"Yes, Emma?"

"Sandra, could you come in to take notes for this meeting?"

I swallowed. "S-sure thing." I hung up the phone, not even knowing why my body was trembling. After grabbing my tablet, I headed for Emma's office which was only across the hall and down a few feet from where my desk sat.

I knocked before entering as the door was partially shut.

"Come in," Emma called on the other side.

I pushed the door open and my eyes first landed on Emma, who raised an eyebrow. "Sandra, please meet Mr. Jameson," she stated before I was even able to fully enter her office.

I began shaking my head from side to side before even seeing him. When I finally did, I nearly dropped the tablet I'd been holding.

"Oh God!" I blurted out. "E-excuse me." I glanced down at the tablet that I'd caught right at my knees before it hit the floor. When I looked up again, there he was.

Randy Jameson.

Tall. Almond-colored skin, and dark brown eyes. He'd grown a goatee since I'd known him in high school. I'd seen that the one day he'd been introduced as the new attorney at Wittaker & Wittaker. The one day I also happened to be away from my desk when he was being walked around introduced. That same day I caught a glimpse of him just in time to duck behind one of the empty office doors until he passed by so he wouldn't see me.

It was that same day that I'd gone to meet Kayla in the Williamsport Park nearly in hysterics on how I couldn't continue working at the same place he worked at.

"Sandra and I don't need introductions," he stated.

My throat filled with bile and I had to internally beg my body not to deceive me by throwing up right there and then.

"We're old friends. Right, Sandra?" Randy's voice was sickeningly sweet.

I wanted to scream at him to never say my name again, but what came out was, "Y-you wanted me to take notes?" I directed my gaze at Emma, ignoring Randy's words entirely. It was the only thing I could do to keep it together.

Emma gave me an odd expression. Typically, I'd apologize for my rudeness, but I couldn't. Not then. And not to him.

"Yes," she nodded, "that would be great. Mr. Jameson." She held out her hand, gesturing to the office chair in front of her desk.

I moved to the corner of the room where the leather chair that was placed by the window sat. I could've sat in the other chair, next to Randy, but that wasn't happening. Thankfully, Emma didn't question me about it. With shaky fingers I did the best I could to type out notes from that meeting. Though my stomach roiled with nausea throughout the meeting upon learning that Wittaker & Wittaker had assigned Randy Jameson as the lead attorney on this particular case.

That would mean running into him, God only knew how many more times, before this case wrapped up—which could take months, or possibly years.

I sighed in relief once the meeting was over.

"I'll go type these up and send them to you," I told Emma as I brushed past her and out of the office. I didn't bother to look at her, certain she'd have another odd expression on her face. The notes were already typed up, seeing as how I'd been working on my tablet to take them, but I couldn't stop to explain to her that being in the same room as him for one second longer would cause me to crawl out of my own skin.

I made it back to my desk, sighing as I placed the tablet down. I pushed the lunch that remained untouched into the top drawer of my desk. My hunger had long since disappeared. Instead of sitting down, I opted to head to the restroom to gather myself. Hopefully, by the time I emerged Randy Jameson would be long gone.

I made it to the restroom and just stared in the mirror for I don't know how long. I reminded myself that I was not that naïve, eighteen-year-old girl anymore.

"This can't be happening," I pushed out, while reaching down to wash my hands, simply because I needed something to do. I felt dirty just being in the same room as him.

Drying my hands, I figured enough time had passed and that he would have left the office by now.

Apparently, my luck had run out for the day because as soon as I exited the bathroom and took three steps toward the main entrance of my office, I slammed into a hard body. Revulsion surged through every cell in my body and I jumped back, out of the hands that held me by the arms.

"Don't touch me!"

"Whoa!" Randy held his hands up in a mock surrender as if he was harmless.

That movement pissed me off even more. I took another step backwards.

"What's all that about?"

My fists tightened at my sides and my jaw dropped. How dare he even ask me a question like that.

"Sandra, it's been a long time. Whatever happened in the past we—"

"Whatever happened … Are you serious right now?" I squeezed my eyes shut before opening them and inhaling deeply. I had to force myself to remember I was at work. I needed to get out of there. "Just stay the hell away from me," I growled before spinning around and walking back into the women's restroom just so I wouldn't have to brush past him on my way back to the office. Again, I perched over one of the sinks, closed my eyes, and steadied my breathing. However, the anxiety, fear, and shame refused to quit pulsing through my entire body. I needed to get out of there or else I would explode.

After peeking my head out of the bathroom door to ensure that Randy was no longer in the hallway, I stepped out and hightailed it to my desk. By then, it was nearing two o'clock but there was no way I could remain in that office for three more hours.

"Emma, I need to uh, go. I need to pick up some medicine for Monique."

Emma's head popped up from her desk, surprised. Her eyebrows raised as she stood. "Is she okay? Did she get sick again?" she questioned, worry lines creasing her forehead.

A pang of guilt moved through my chest. I shook my head. "No, she's okay. But I forgot to pick up her insulin and she will need it." I swallowed down the shame I felt for lying and using my daughter's illness to do it. "I'll take my laptop home with me so that I can get some work done later."

Waving her hand, Emma nodded. "Go do whatever you need to do."

My shoulders slumped as I sighed in relief. She was so understanding. "Thank you." I didn't give her or anyone around a second look as I gathered my belongings and practically fled the office. I needed to be out of there, but I also didn't want to be alone at the moment, either. There was only one person who would understand what I was feeling, so as I pulled out of the parking garage from my office building, I made a right onto the street that would take me directly to Kayla's office.

CHAPTER 15

*S*andra

"I need to talk to you," I stated, bursting into Kayla's office. Thankfully, she was alone, and once I'd told the receptionist in the outer office I was looking for her, she let me go right in.

Kayla's auburn curls bounced as her head shot backwards at the abrupt manner in which I'd entered her office. She stood, her left hand going to cover her belly as she rose.

Again, guilt rose in my belly and I felt embarrassed and ridiculous bothering my heavily pregnant friend while she was at work no less.

"What's wrong?" Kayla questioned, coming over to me.

I shook my head. "You know what, this was stupid. I was totally overreacting. You don't need me bothering you." I started to leave but Kayla wasn't having it.

"If you take one more step, I will pick up this phone and call Damon and tell him to get his ass down here immediately."

I spun around, eyes enlarged, mouth ajar, staring at her. "You wouldn't."

"I absolutely would. Try me."

She was serious as a heart attack. Sighing, I relented, shutting her door all of the way, and ambled my way over to the chair across from her desk. I slumped down in my seat, watching as Kayla eyed me before sitting down.

"Now tell me what has you so upset."

"Kayla, really, if you have patients—"

"I am free for the rest of the afternoon. I was only doing paperwork which I hate anyway so I'm available. Start talking."

Pushing out a heavy breath, I glanced up toward the ceiling. "I saw him." That was all I could say at first.

The room became silent for a few heartbeats. I raised my head to look up at Kayla. She wore an empathetic expression as she leaned back in her high-back leather chair.

"By *him* you mean—"

I began nodding. "*Him.* The reason I left my last job, *him.* The man who—" I couldn't say it. I shook my head, biting my lower lip and turning to look out of the window to my far right. "I was feeling so happy this morning." I turned back to Kayla. "I was in a good place. Damon and I are … perfect. Well, maybe not *perfect,* but closer than I'd ever expected to be. Monique is doing great. She hasn't had an incident in weeks. The pump is working well. I enjoy the work I'm doing." I was even talking with my grandmother regularly. I'd let Monique sleep over her house a handful of times, and she'd loved it every single time. Monique would come back singing my grandmother's praises.

And then this happened.

"Maybe it's a sign."

Raising my gaze, I met Kayla's eyes. Slowly she stood and moved around her desk, her belly leading the way.

"Perhaps this happened for a reason."

"And what reason would that be?" I questioned, feeling defensive all of a sudden.

She shrugged. "I don't know. Maybe that's what you're supposed to be finding out here."

I stood, shaking my head, pacing back and forth in Kayla's office.

"Sandra, listen to me," she began, but paused long enough for me to turn my attention on her again. "You never confronted what happened to you. I'm the only person you've ever told. It's been long enough. Maybe it's time you tell someone. Seek therapy or some help."

I shook my head. "No. I don't need to do any of that."

"And if you don't you'll always be running from it. Just like I was."

"I'm not like you Kayla. I'm not brave—"

"Bullshit!"

My eyes widened at how adamant she'd become.

"You happen to be one of the bravest people I know. You look at your daughter every day and love her just as much, if not more, than any other caring mother I've seen. You've taken care of her, diabetes and all, by yourself for the last ten years. If that's not bravery what is it?"

Snorting, I turned my head, my hair brushing the tops of my shoulders.

"You've been running from this for a long time. It's not easy to confront the truth about what happened and how Monique was conceived but it'll be worth it."

My vision became blurry as my eyes glassed over. I began trembling at the idea of talking about this with anyone else. With Kayla it had been difficult, but something had propelled me to share my secret with her. Once I'd learned what happened to her, I'd realized why it'd been easier sharing with her. She had experienced something similar. Not quite the same but close enough I could open up to her about it.

"Here," she said as she moved back around her desk, as quickly as her belly would let her. Opening one of the top drawers, she pulled out a business card. "I got this for you a while ago."

Taking the card, I eyed the pink, purple, and blue colors speculatively. I squinted even more once I read the name on the card. It was a support group for women who'd been sexually assaulted.

"I went there myself."

I looked up at Kayla. "When?"

"Right after I found out I was pregnant." She rubbed her belly, cradling her baby in the only way she could for now. "I thought I'd worked through everything that happened to me, you know? We went to trial, he was convicted. I was married and in love. Then I found out

I was pregnant. And while we still don't know for sure the sex, the thought of having a daughter …" She trailed off.

I swallowed, remembering the days of my pregnancy.

"The thought of something like this happening to her—" She shook her head, her words breaking off. "So I went and I talked and I listened."

"Did it help?"

She nodded.

"Does Josh know you went?"

She gave me a little smile. "He drove me to the meeting, and waited outside the whole time. And each time I've gone since that first time."

Swallowing, I closed my eyes. *I wonder if Damon—*

No. I wouldn't even think about that. I opened my eyes. "I'm not you, Kayla. Thank you for listening to me but I'm better now. I need to go." I grabbed my pocket book, stuffed the card she'd given me inside, and made a beeline for the door, shutting it behind me. Thankfully, that time she didn't try to stop me.

I made it all of the way to my car in the parking lot before I felt the urge to cry. I cursed myself for feeling so weak. It'd been more than a decade. I'd taken self-defense classes for years. Hell, I'd taken down a guy twice my size in a nightclub just two weeks earlier. I should be over it by now. Seeing Randy after all this time shouldn't bring me right back to the spot I was when I was eighteen years old. Without thinking, I pulled out my cell phone and pressed the number for the one person who always made me feel strong, whether he realized it or not.

"I was just thinking about you."

His deep voice had a calming effect on me with just those six words.

"Yeah? What about?"

"I've got something for you."

"What is it?"

"I'll show you when I see you tomorrow night."

A small smile touched my lips.

"Everything cool? You sound … not like yourself."

I sat up in my car and tried to straighten myself out even though he couldn't see me. He obviously had a sixth sense. "I'm okay just a rough day at work."

"Case kickin' your butt, huh?"

I worried my bottom lip. "Something like that. What were you working on?" I questioned.

"Just got out of a meeting about buying one of the abandoned buildings on Lakefront."

I nodded, remembering that he'd told me about that meeting the previous night when we'd talked on the phone. I smiled as I remembered how he'd Facetimed with Monique and I so we could read her a story together before she went to bed.

"How'd it go?"

"It went well, I guess. I've been eyeing this property for a long time. For years. It's taught me to be patient, but we're close to owning it. I can feel it."

He was so sure of himself, his ability. I sometimes wondered what a man like him could possibly see in someone like me.

"You sure you're all right?"

I perked up. "Yeah. I'm fine. I was just taking a break from work and wanted to hear your voice. No big deal. Listen, I've got to go. I'll talk to you later."

"Allright—" I don't know what else he'd been getting ready to say since I hung up the phone so quickly.

Glancing at the clock, I noticed it was getting close to three. I figured I'd call Ms. Oralia, Monique's sitter, and let her know she could take the afternoon off. I'd pick up my daughter from school and we could spend the afternoon and evening cuddled up on the couch, watching movies and eating popcorn or something. That was all I had the energy for at that moment. And knowing my baby girl was okay, was the only assurance I truly needed, or so I tried to convince myself.

* * *

DAMON

"He sounds like he's trying to sell you a bag of dreams," Sean stated coming up behind me as I stared at my phone. I was still caught off-guard by how quickly Sandra had ended the phone conversation. She didn't say it but, in my gut, something felt off with her.

Pushing those thoughts out of my mind for the moment, I turned and glanced up at Sean. We were still in the boardroom of my office, having just completed a meeting with members from the city council. I was yet again making a play for the abandoned brick building that was in the Lakefront section of Williamsport. Business and professional matters weren't the only reasons why I was so interested in this particular venture.

"Russo Sr. already lost his bid for the building."

I nodded, already knowing that information. "Jr. comes in real handy," I commented. Since that night at the Underground, I'd been working with Mike Russo Jr. to take out Russo Sr. in more ways than one. Turns out, Sr. wasn't just a murderer and drug dealer but a shitty father as well. The guy I had on the inside of Russo Sr.'s business had passed Jr. some private files that shed light on the inner workings of his business. As far as I knew, Sr. was being heavily investigated by the FBI and this file was one more nail in his coffin. He might not go to jail for my father's murder but he'd be put in a cell someday soon, and I already had a few of my old connects waiting for him once he was.

"His business is drying up," Sean added.

I didn't say anything.

"You sure about working with the feds?" my cousin questioned.

It was a question I'd asked myself, more than once. I wasn't exactly keen on the idea of getting into bed with the feds, but then again, I wasn't the one working directly with them, either. Russo Jr. was. He really was on the straight and narrow, as far as I could tell. His one venture somewhat outside of the law or proper society was joining the Underground. He'd rebelled against everything his father had tried to raise him to be.

"It's cool. Jr. has gotten what he needs. Russo should be arrested soon, and when he is, I'll pay him a little visit."

Sean lifted an eyebrow at me.

"He won't die by my hands but he won't live much longer either. I'm good with that," I told Sean.

"You sure?"

I nodded slowly, running my hand through my beard. "I'm sure. I'm ready for this shit to be over."

"For what it's worth, I'm glad I didn't need to convince you not to take him out yourself."

I glanced over at my cousin. He'd never been involved in the drug game with me. He'd hated that life. Apparently, that was one of the reasons his mother had chosen to pick their family up and move to the West Coast. To ensure her son wasn't raised in that life. Being older and thinking about my own future, I could understand that. I'd be shot dead before one of my kids ever ended up working on the streets.

"Kids?"

Shit.

I glanced up, realizing I'd said my thoughts out loud.

"She's got you thinking about kids, huh?"

I rolled my eyes. "Mind your damn business, man."

"You are my business, fool," he chuckled.

I laughed, too. "Whatever, I need to head out."

"Me too."

We slapped fives and parted ways. I watched Sean as he exited the conference room. A few minutes later, I shut the light off in my own office.

"Charlotte, I'm heading out." My sister looked up from whatever she'd been typing on her computer.

"Okay. You're still coming over to Mama's for dinner this weekend, right?"

I side-eyed my sister. "When did I ever agree to that?"

She frowned at me. "See, Damon." She shook her head. "Mama hasn't seen you in a month of Sundays. And neither one of us has met this woman you're seeing. What's her name, Sondra?"

"Sandra," I corrected sternly.

She lifted a perfectly arched eyebrow. "See. Just that tone alone tells me its serious and we haven't met her. Last time I knew anything you were dating a woman named Scarlet or something."

"Scarlet's old news and she was never my girlfriend." I refused to go into detail to my little sister that Scarlet had been one of a few women I was dating. While Sandra … there was no one else. She was it.

"See? I didn't know that."

"You didn't need to know all of that. You don't tell me who you're seeing."

"That's because I'm not seeing anyone. I'm taking time out for me," she answered with her head raised high as if trying to prove something to herself.

I lifted an eyebrow wondering what was going on there. However, I shrugged it off and picked up the stack of office mail that was sitting in the basket she kept it in. I began thumbing through the envelopes. "The one time she came to the office, you happened to have called in sick that day." I frowned at her. I swear, if it wasn't low work ethic, my sister wouldn't have a work ethic at all. That was probably my damn fault. I'd spoiled her as a kid. I wanted to give her all of the things my father would've given her.

"Well, I won't be sick this Saturday. Mama wants to see you. Dinner with all of us would be perfect."

I gave her a look.

"I'm serious, Damon. Bring her."

"She has a ten-year-old daughter."

"Bring her, too," she quickly added.

I rubbed my lips together while running my hand through my beard. "I'll think about it and let you know."

"Today's Wednesday."

"I know what damn day of the week it is."

Charlotte held up her hands. "Just making sure. You only have a few days to decide."

"Whatever, sis. I'm heading out."

I glanced at my watch. It was just after five o'clock. I had a business dinner that night at seven but decided I needed to make a stop before heading to the restaurant. I tucked the gift-wrapped box I'd taken from my desk inside my briefcase.

I hadn't planned on stopping by to see Sandra that night but when I thought back to the tone she'd used while we were on the phone, an urge to lay eyes on her and make sure she was okay overtook me.

CHAPTER 16

*D*amon

"Hi," she greeted, smiling but looking surprised to see me as she opened the door.

"Hey."

"Hi, Mr. Damon!" Monique stated excitedly from behind her mother, before pushing past her legs and rushing me, throwing her arms around my waist. I look down at the little girl hugging me, and without even realizing I had, my arms had surrounded her, hugging her back with the same energy she was giving me. I looked up at Sandra whose gaze was pinned on the both of us. Something stirred in her eyes.

"You want to watch Netflix with us?"

I grinned down at Monique. "Having a Netflix and chill night, huh?" I noticed the cream-colored silk pajama shorts and top Sandra wore that matched the same long sleeve and pants pajamas Monique had on.

Sandra shrugged.

"If this is a bad time I can—"

"No, come in," Sandra stated, stepping back making room for me to enter.

"I'll go grab Mr. Damon some popcorn," Monique said before rushing off in the direction of the kitchen.

"I know it's not always cool to drop in on people unexpected like this, but—"

"You were in the area?" She smiled up at me, questioning.

I shook my head. "Nah, I wasn't. But I needed to see you," I answered honestly because I did. Reaching out, I cupped her cheek, stroking it with my thumb. "I didn't like the way you sounded on the phone earlier."

She sighed and her eyelids floated closed as she nuzzled her cheek against my palm. My arms went around her body as she stepped closer. She wrapped her arms around my waist, pulling me in tighter, and laid her head on my chest. She was holding on for something more than just gratefulness to see me. It was strength she needed. Strength for what, I didn't know, but I was bound and determined to find out.

"Here, Mr. Damon. Mommy got us caramel corn. I can't eat too much but that's okay because I like sharing," Monique insisted, getting in the middle of Sandra and I to hand me a bowl of the caramel corn. I didn't have the heart to tell her I was supposed to have dinner else-where in an hour. Which was why—as she led me by the hand to the living room couch, directly across from the television where they'd been watching a new Netflix show—I pulled out my cell phone. I scrolled through my contacts and sent Sean a text asking if he'd be up for going to the dinner meeting in my stead.

Within a few minutes he responded that he would. And I set my phone down on the coffee table, face down, ready to watch whatever the hell it was they'd been watching.

Monique tucked herself into my right side, underneath my arm, while I drew Sandra into my left. She laid her head against my shoulder and hit the play button, taking the freeze frame off the screen.

I frowned, not familiar with the show. "What is this?"

"It's called *Tidying Up*," Monique answered, her eyes planted on the flat screen that was mounted on the wall.

Sandra glanced up at me, obviously taking in that I still had no idea what the hell this show was or was about. "Marie Kondo is an expert in decluttering and helping people organize their spaces. She developed a unique approach to helping others figure out what belongs in their life and what doesn't. Sounds simple but it's compelling to watch."

I lowered my head and brushed my lips against hers. I didn't give a damn about watching people get rid of their shit, but she looked taken in by it, so whatever. I had no problem watching.

We spent the next hour and a half just like that, on the couch. When seven o'clock rolled round, I ended up ordering from a nearby Thai restaurant because the idea of moving from the couch to do anything more than retrieve food from a delivery guy didn't sit well with any of us.

After dinner, we watched another episode before Sandra finally put an end to the binge watching and made Monique brush her teeth and start getting ready for bed. Reluctantly, I got up to leave, but Sandra took ahold of my wrist, silently asking me to stay. Again, the look in her eye told me something was up with her.

I nodded in agreement, which was how some twenty minutes later, I found myself perched on my knee at the side of Monique's bed while Sandra sat on the other side, reading her a story.

"Thanks for doing that with us. I keep thinking today's the day she's finally had enough of me reading to her at night. But I'm always pleasantly surprised when she insists on reading before bed. I know it'll end one day," Sandra stated forlornly, as she glanced back at Monique's now closed bedroom door.

"She'll outgrow it, but she'll never forget it," I responded, looking at Monique's door as well. I remembered every time my father took time out of his busy schedule to do stuff with just me. He might not have gone the legal route in terms of career, but he always wanted more for Charlotte and I. As a result, he had us involved in tons of activities and he made sure he showed up for them all.

Sandra smiled up at me. We moved up the hall into the living room. It was around eight-thirty.

"Hey, I know I said I'd give this to you tomorrow when we went out, but since I've got it now …" I reached for the briefcase I'd placed on the floor by the door when I first enter and pulled out the gift-wrapped box.

Sandra looked from me to the box and up at me again.

"It's not going to open itself."

She smiled. "Why are you getting me a gift?" she asked, taking it from me.

"Because I want to. Open it."

She took one last look at me before slowly removing the top from the box. She gasped once she got a glimpse of the rose gold timepiece with floating diamonds in the face.

"What's this?" she asked through trembling lips.

"It's our second mockup." I took the watch from the box, fully holding it up for her to see before I moved it to wrap around her wrist. "I knew it would look amazing on you," I stated, holding her arm with the watch up.

"Damon, it's gorgeous."

"Nah, it's just a watch." I moved my gaze from the watch to her eyes. "But on your arm it comes alive." I lowered my lips to hers, cupping her face and kissing her deeply. She stepped closer, wrapping her arms around me, and I ran my tongue along her bottom lip, causing a shudder to move throughout her body. When I felt that pulsating in my groin begin to happen, I took a step back.

"I should go."

Sandra's eyes widened. "No. Stay," she requested.

I gave her a look. "I can't sleep in your bed." I couldn't stay in her bed and not have my hands all over her. And with her bedroom right next to her daughter's room … it didn't feel right.

Her eyes wandered over to the couch we'd just been sitting on watching television. "You can stay for a few hours longer. If you want," she quickly added.

If I wanted? I don't know when it happened but damn near overnight wherever she was is where I wanted to be.

I nodded and took her by the hand, leading her to the couch. I kicked my shoes off and stretched out, feeling grateful that the couch was long enough for my six-foot-three length. Sandra laid down, half on top of me and half next to me. It was a tight fight, but when I wrapped my arm around her it felt right.

"What are you doing Saturday?"

She lifted her head to look down at me. "What am I doing every Saturday? Either spending it with you or with Monique," she giggled.

"How about you spend it with the both of us?"

She raised her eyebrows, questioningly.

"And with my mom and sister."

"You want me to meet your family?"

I nodded. "Why not? I've met yours."

"I know but that's different."

"How?"

She shrugged awkwardly due to the position she was laying in. "Because it was just me and Monique for so long. She was my entire family. And, well, my grandmother just came back into my life but that's it."

"My mom and sister are my only family, too. Well, them and Sean, but you've met him."

She'd met Sean two weeks earlier when we double dated with a woman he was seeing.

She pursed her lips, thinking about it. "Okay. Wait, you said me and Monique?"

"Yeah. If you're okay with it, I'd like to bring you both to dinner at my mother's." I ignored the wave of hesitation that question caused me. Hell, I didn't even spend a great deal of time with my own mother. But now I wanted Sandra to meet her. Truthfully, in the back of my mind, I wanted Sandra to see what she was getting into with me. I may not be all that close with my mom but she was my family and I'd provide and take care of her until the day she left this earth. That's the only way I knew how to take care of the people I loved.

"We'll go," she finally agreed.

I laid my head back against the couch pillow, feeling thoroughly satisfied with her answer.

"Thanks for staying with me tonight."

I opened my eyes to find her staring up at me, her chin resting on my chest. And there was that look again. The look that had me wanting to declare to the whole damn world that this woman and her child were off limits to fuck with.

Reaching up, I brushed one of her stray curls out of her face. "You know you can tell me anything, right?"

She folded in her lips, rubbing together as if thinking over something. "I know. It was a rough day at work. Listening to the women speak about what they endured while just trying to earn a living." She laid her head back on my chest.

My hand continued to stroke her hair. Perhaps that was the truth. Maybe it got to her to hear instance after instance of women being harassed at work. Especially, when, from what she'd told me, she'd experienced something similar.

That may have been the truth.

Or, she was just holding something back that she didn't want to tell me.

We laid in silence, watching some random shows on Netflix for a while longer until we both fell asleep.

* * *

"Hey, Ma," I greeted as she opened the door.

My mother's eyes widened as they always did when I showed up at her door, as if she was completely thrown off by seeing me. Even when I'd spoken with her to let her know I'd be over. Her light brown eyes traveled from me, to the woman next to me, and then down to the little woman in front of me.

"Ma, this is Sandra and her daughter, Monique," I introduced.

"Hi, Mrs. Richmond," Sandra greeted, holding out her hand.

"Hi, Mrs. Richmond. Are you really Mr. Damon's mommy?" Monique asked.

I chuckled and lowered to Monique. "Short stuff, I already told you we were meeting my mother."

"I know but I just wanted to make sure. You don't look alike. Everyone says me and my mommy look alike."

"Monique," Sandra called, slightly embarrassed.

My head popped up when I heard the unfamiliar sounds of laughter. My eyes widened when I saw a genuine smile on my mother's face as she laughed.

"You are too cute. Come in, come in." My mother waved us inside as she moved to the side.

"We brought some homemade banana pudding. Damon said it was your favorite." Sandra held up the glass bowl she'd meticulously layered the pudding in with Vanilla Wafers and slices of banana.

"As long as you used Vanilla Wafers it's my favorite."

Sandra giggled. "I'd never even think to use anything else."

My mother laughed again, and I found myself speechless. I could maybe count on one hand the number of times I'd seen my mother laugh or crack a genuine smile within the last ten years.

"I'll set this in the fridge until we're ready to eat it. Charlotte should be here in a few."

"That damn girl is always running late."

Sandra lightly slapped my chest with the back of her hand.

"What?"

"Don't talk about your sister like that."

I snorted. "Nah, I'll talk about her ass. That girl acts like she doesn't know the difference between eight a.m. and eight p.m. Always coming in the office late, talking about, *'my bad, there was traffic on the highway.'* Yeah, it's called rush hour. Folks are trying to get to work, which she should've been doing."

Sandra giggled. "Not everyone gets into the office at five a.m. like you do."

"Right?" my mother interjected as she re-entered the living room area. "That's what I keep telling him."

Sandra laughed some more.

"I don't get into the office at five in the morning. That's my workout time," I corrected.

Sandra rolled her eyes and my mother tutted.

"Who the hell wants to get up that early just to run on a treadmill?"

"I do," I responded to my mother more defensively than I'd intended. "It helps me think."

Sandra placed her hand at the center of my chest. "Hey, you know we're just teasing, right? I love how dedicated you are and how hard you work."

Her words and touch soothed any anger that'd been starting to form, from just being in the presence of my mother. Grasping her hand, I lifted it to my lips.

"Mommy, look!" Monique called from the dining area of my mother's condo.

We looked over and found Monique pointing out the floor-to-ceiling glass window at the sun setting.

"My mommy says sunsets are magic. Right, Mommy?" Monique said to my mother who'd moved closer to her.

"Right," Sandra answered, walking over.

I followed and listened to Monique say that Sandra had explained to her that if she'd made a wish while staring at the sunset, it would come true. I glanced down at Sandra who had a far off expression. She looked to me and gave me a half smile.

"Hey, hey!" a female voice interrupted.

I glanced over my shoulder to see my sister entering my mother's condo with the spare key I'd had made for her.

"About time," I stated by way of greeting.

"Good to see you, too, big brother."

I frowned. "We just saw each other yesterday."

"And how wonderful to see each other *today.*" She rolled her eyes. "Anyway," she stated, pivoting her gaze to Sandra. She smiled. "You must be Sandra. I'm Charlotte, Damon's sister and top notch administrative assistant, office manager, and design specialist."

I frowned. "If you were all of that my company would be in danger."

Sandra squeezed my hand in warning, giving me a side-eye before turning back to Charlotte.

"Hi, Charlotte, pleasure to meet you. This is my daughter, Monique," Sandra introduced as Monique moved to stand beside her.

"You're pretty," Monique added.

"Please don't tell her that," I groaned, shaking my head.

"He's such a hater. Hey, Mama!" Charlotte greeted before stooping down in front of Monique.

"You're pretty, too, little bit."

Monique giggled. "Mr. Damon calls me short stuff."

Charlotte glanced up at me then back down to Monique. "That's a cool nickname. We'll stick with that, short stuff."

"Mommy, I need a snack," Monique stated, looking up at Sandra.

"Oh." Sandra began digging in her bag.

Monique turned back to Charlotte. "I have diabetes, and sometimes when my blood sugar gets too low, I need to eat. Mommy says I shouldn't be embarrassed of having diabetes but then she also says I don't have to tell everybody, but since your Mr. Damon's family it's okay that you know. Right, Mommy?" Monique looked up at Sandra, her large eyes blinking innocently.

"Yes, Monique. Here." Sandra handed her one of the homemade granola bars she often carried with her to keep on hand for times when Monique needed something to eat.

"Well, we're about to have dinner. You all sit down at the table. Charlotte will help me serve."

I listened as Charlotte mumbled about not coming over here to be put to work. I had half a mind to tell her that since she lived in the same damn building and still had the nerve to be late, the least she could do was help serve, but I kept my mouth shut.

"You feeling better, short stuff?" I stooped low, asking Monique as she chewed on her granola bar.

She nodded and swallowed before answering. "Yes. Your sister's pretty. She looks like your mom."

I grinned. "Yeah, I looked more like my dad."

"Oh, but you don't have a dad anymore, right?"

"Monique—"

I held up my hand, cutting Sandra off. "That's right. He died a long time ago. I wasn't much older than you when he did."

Monique's expression softened, and before I knew it she moved into my arms and threw hers around my neck. I glanced up at Sandra who wore an uncertain expression on her face. I hugged Monique back.

"Thank you," I stated when she pulled back.

"I know what it's like not to have a dad."

Sandra gasped, but before either one of us could respond my mother and sister were entering the dining area carrying plates full of chicken parmesan, spaghetti, and a large bowl of salad.

As we ate, my mother asked Sandra what she did for work. She seemed genuinely interested. And to be completely honest, it was the first time in years that I could remember being around my mother and not wanting to be anywhere but there. Regardless, I still felt tense in her presence. It was hard not to. The woman had spent the past eighteen years either seemingly incapable of doing anything but laying in bed all day, depressed, or being bitter over what life had done to her. I used to be more patient with her, but after years of the same thing over and over, I'd grown tired of it.

"Excuse me," I said as my phone buzzed toward the end of our meal. I stood, glancing at the number, and seeing that it was Mike Russo Jr., I pressed the answer button.

"Yeah," I greeted into the phone as I moved down the hall, stepping into one of my mother's spare bedrooms and closing the door.

"I heard some news I thought you'd want to hear."

"Go ahead," I urged.

"The files I got from your guy on the inside were exactly what the FBI needed to nail the bastard. They're finally able to bring him up on charges for racketeering, embezzlement, and money laundering. When convicted the fucker will never see the outside of a jail cell again."

The excitement in Russo Jr.'s voice was undeniable. He really hated his father. From the little he'd told me, I could see why. The scars I recalled seeing on Russo's back and chest the night of our fight, weren't from Jr's previous bouts but from his own father, growing up.

"How long before an arrest?" I questioned.

"Shouldn't be longer than a week, I'm told. I'll keep you posted."

"Make sure you do."

I hung up the phone and pulled open the door to my mother's guestroom just as Charlotte was passing by, heading to the bathroom.

"Hey, was that work?"

I shook my head. "Personal."

She squinted those almond-shaped eyes at me. "What kind of personal?"

My head shot back, and I looked at her like she'd lost her damn mind because evidently, she had.

"I'm just asking because I happen to like Sandra, even though I just met her. And I'm half in love with that little girl of hers already. And they both are over the moon about your brooding ass. Though don't ask me why. Anyway, if you're playing her—"

I held up my hand. "I'm not," I stated sternly. I knew I was just as far gone over Sandra and Monique as my sister believed they were over me, but she didn't need to know all of that.

"Good. Don't mess up a good thing."

I squinted. "Like you and your job."

She gave me a sly grin. "Whatever, big bro. You wouldn't fire me." She waved me off as she confidently strolled passed me to enter the rest room.

I rolled my eyes. Little did she know. I'd fire Charlotte in a heartbeat if I could find someone competent enough to take her position in my company. The problem was, I didn't trust many people. And pain in the ass that she was, I trusted my sister. But it was probably time to start looking for her replacement. For my own damn sanity. I'd always take care of her, but she needed to find a career that she really wanted and I needed an assistant who was in it for the long haul.

I made my way back to the dining area, ready to make my apologies for having to take a call during dinner, when I found my mother and Monique staring up at the sky. The sun had set and it was dark, which was when the stars shone their brightest. Surprisingly, my mother listened intently as Monique pointed to and named the various stars in the sky.

"Hey, we waited for you before we started with dessert," Sandra stated, wrapping an arm around my waist. "Everything okay?"

I looked at her.

"With your phone call, I mean?"

Leaning down, I kissed the tip of her nose. "Yeah, just some old business I need to get squared away. And you all didn't have to wait. I don't really like banana pudding anyway."

Sandra blinked. "Why didn't you tell me that? I could've made something for you to have."

I shrugged. "It's cool." I dipped low so that my lips were next to her ear. "I plan on having my dessert later anyway."

She gasped when I bit her earlobe and then pressed a kiss to just below her ear, quickly before my mother and Monique turned around. And for good measure I reached behind her and squeezed her ass just so she knew that *she* was on my menu for dessert.

"Umhm, I saw that," came from behind us.

I glared at my sister over my shoulder. "Stay out of grown folks' business."

Charlotte sucked her teeth as she walked past. "Whatever. And I forgot to tell you, your invite for that cancer fundraiser hosted at the hospital came in today."

I frowned, looking at my sister as she passed. "The annual fundraiser hosted by Williamsport General?" I questioned.

"Yeah, that one," she responded flippantly over her shoulder.

Shaking my head, I rolled my eyes heavenward. "I need a new damn assistant," I growled. I lowered my head when I heard Sandra's giggles.

"She's not that bad."

"She's fucking terrible. You want a new job? I'll double your salary." I wiggled my eyebrows.

She gave me a frown. "I couldn't work for you."

I tilted my head. "Why not? I'm a hell of a boss."

Sandra glanced over her shoulder before turning back to me, inching closer so only I could hear her. "I know you look damn good in a suit. I'd be too preoccupied with … other things besides getting work done," she whispered.

A slow grin spread across my face. "Now *that* I can't seem to find a problem with."

Sandra laughed and lowered her face.

I moved my finger below her chin, raising her face again. "While you consider the job offer, you should also think about what dress you want to wear to this fundraiser."

She gave me a funny look. "The one you go to every year? That Josh is a big donator for?"

I nodded. "Kayla told you about it?"

She nodded. "She told me she went last year, and it was the first time she'd seen Joshua since she'd left Williamsport seven or eight years earlier."

I nodded. "That's the story I heard, too. Anyway, I think you'd look perfect in something shimmery."

"I'd have to start looking for something."

"You've got a couple of weeks."

"What are y'all talking about over there?" my mother called from the dining room area. "We were getting hungry for dessert."

I frowned.

Sandra laughed and pulled me by the hand toward the dining room table where Monique was watching something with Charlotte on her phone.

"Can she have pudding or is it too sweet for her sugar?" my mother asked Sandra, referring to Monique.

Sandra nodded. "She can have a little."

My mother nodded and moved to the kitchen to take out some bowls.

"Thanks for finally getting my boy over here," my mother said to Sandra as we began to leave.

I raised an eyebrow but didn't say anything.

Sandra looked back at me. "We'll try to get him to see you more often."

Frowning, I glanced down at her. She gave me a questioning look. "I see you plenty."

My mother looked at me, eyes wide. "Before tonight I hadn't seen or heard from you in weeks."

Here we go. "Ma …" I paused, refraining from calling my mother a liar. "I called you last week."

"And when was the last time I actually saw your face?"

I clenched my teeth, again stopping myself from telling her that the last time I was there she'd stormed out of the room like a little damn kid, leaving me to clean up and leave without her saying a word. She may have been somewhat of a pleasure to be around tonight but that didn't erase years of her bitter or reclusive behavior.

"Damon's really busy with work but he loves you deeply," Sandra added while slipping her hand into mine.

"Mr. Damon's really nice. You did a good job as his mommy," Monique stated as Charlotte helped her put on the light jacket she'd worn over.

In spite of my frustration with my mother, I smiled and winked down at Monique.

"We'll see you later, Ma. Thanks for dinner." I leaned down and pressed a kiss to her cheek. "Char, I'll see you on Monday."

"Oh, I might have to—"

"Don't play with me. Have your as—" I glanced down, remembering I was in the presence of a child when Sandra squeezed my hand. "*Behind* at work on Monday. Eight-thirty," I added for emphasis to which my sister simply rolled her eyes.

"See, now you've met my family," I stated as the door to my mother's condo shut behind us.

"They were nice," Sandra replied as Monique moved in between the two of us. On instinct, I took her left hand in my right while Sandra took Monique's right hand in her left. We strolled down the hallway toward the elevator just like that, as if we'd done so hundreds of times before.

CHAPTER 17

*S*andra

"You brought us back to your place," I stated the obvious as I glanced around the parking garage we'd pulled into only seconds before.

"I did. It's another twenty minute drive to your place which isn't that long but I wanted you two to stay with me tonight."

I blinked at the vulnerability in his voice. My heart actually felt like it skipped a beat.

"You have a spare bedroom," I responded, not a question. I'd been to his place several times and was well aware of the layout.

"Does she have enough medication for the night? I can go to the store if you need to get her snacks or anything."

I turned to look at a sleeping Monique and smiled. "We have enough. The only trouble will be getting her from the car to the bed without waking her." I frowned.

"I got it covered," he announced just before exiting the car, and lightly shutting his driver's side door and pulling the back door on his side open.

I got out of the car, and by the time I stood upright I was surprised to see he had Monique cradled in his arms.

Frowning, I wrinkled my forehead. "She isn't too heavy?" I whispered. My baby wasn't such a baby anymore at ten years old. I'd long since stopped carrying her but Damon stood there are if she weighed little more than five pounds.

"Light as a feather." He motioned with his head for me to walk ahead of him toward the elevators.

I took one last look at him as Monique's arms had tightened around his neck but she remained asleep. We made it up to his place within a few minutes and Damon moved swiftly, carrying Monique to the spare bedroom that was on the opposite end of the hallway from his own bedroom. I watched from the doorway as he gingerly laid her down, removed her shoes and jacket, and then neatly tucked her beneath the light blanket. Again, my heart nearly fell out of my chest when he leaned over and pressed a kiss to her forehead.

"G'night, Mr. Damon," Monique mumbled.

I lifted an eyebrow, surprised that she was semi-awake. Damon froze also but Monique simply turned over and took a deep sigh, eyelids tightly sealed. Her breathing steadied and we both realized she was fully asleep once again.

Damon sauntered over to the door, wrapping a hand around my waist and pressing a kiss to my lips, which I willingly lifted my face to allow.

He motioned with his head and we exited, shutting the door behind us. Instead of heading to his bedroom, which I'd expected, we made our way toward his living room. Damon surprised me again by sliding the glass door leading to his balcony open and reaching for my hand, pulling us out into the night air. It was toward the end of April and the weather was warming up, though it was still a bit chilly at this time of night. Damon fixed that problem when he placed a light jacket over my shoulders.

I glanced down, then back up at him. "I thought you didn't wear jackets."

He chuckled as he pulled me down into his lap on the wooden lounge chair that was set up on his balcony. "I don't. But they come in handy when I want to keep you warm. Is it too cold out here for you?"

My eyes fluttered shut as I leaned back against his strong chest and his arms came around my body.

"It might be too hot," I mumbled.

He laughed again and pressed a kiss to the space between my neck and shoulder. I shivered and then stared up at the sky. It was dark but I could still make out a few clouds as they hovered around the moon.

"It's a full moon tonight," I told him as I watched the huge light in the sky.

"That must've been the reason my mom was acting so damn odd tonight."

I glanced over my shoulder. "Odd? She was very welcoming and friendly."

"Exactly," he stated. "That is not how she is on a regular basis, at least, not when I'm around."

"Which isn't too often according to her."

He snorted. "She's always exaggerating."

Hearing the tension in his voice, I reached down for his hands and brought them to my lips.

"How come you don't like her?" I asked.

"It's not that I don't like her—"

"You don't. You love her. I know that. You've taken care of her all of these years, but you don't *like* her. I could sense it almost as soon as she opened the door. You seemed on edge every time she opened her mouth."

Sighing, he lifted his right hand. I didn't need to turn around to face him to know that he was rubbing his hand through his beard—a move he often did when frustrated or thinking seriously about something.

I laid my head back against his chest and waited for him to respond to my question.

"I had to take care of her. I was thirteen when my father died ... was killed," he corrected, his voice taking on an edge I'd never heard before. "And she ... gave up. I get that she was in mourning. I fully understand that. But she still had two children to look after. Charlotte was only seven years old, and instead of our mother taking her to and from school, that job was left to me. That wasn't even the bad part. I had no problem helping with Char. But when the bill collectors started calling and the bank began foreclosing on the house, she still did nothing. That was when I knew taking care of everything was up to me. I went out and did the only thing I could do at thirteen. And it was the one thing my father had lost his life to keep me out of."

That was when I turned to face Damon. His gaze was focused on the sky behind me.

"That's why you're still upset with her?"

Shaking his head, he snorted. "What kind of a mother just gives up on her kids like that?"

I worried my bottom lip, my gaze lowering. I inhaled deeply. "It's not that easy," I stated, my voice low. "I had no intentions of becoming a young mom … but things didn't work out as I had planned."

"Yeah, but you didn't give up."

I pushed out a deep breath. "But I spent every night of my pregnancy praying and hoping that I could find the strength to love the baby growing inside of my womb."

That was when his eyes met mine again. He tilted his head.

"Remember when Monique said I'd taught her to make wishes as she watched the sunset?"

He nodded.

"It's because that's what I did every evening as I walked back to my tiny, dingy apartment from work, while I was pregnant. I worked the mid-day shift and always seemed to leave around the time the sun went down. I'd look up, my hand would go to my belly, and I'd wish that I could be strong enough to love her as deeply as she deserved." I clamped my mouth shut, just shy of telling him exactly *why* I feared I couldn't love my daughter.

"And it worked."

I nodded. "As soon as she was put into my arms in the hospital all of those fears disappeared." Of course, new fears reemerged, like how I was going to actually take care of her, but I had fallen instantly in love with her.

"My mother isn't you."

I shook my head. "No, she isn't, but she is your mother and it might be time to cut her some slack."

He slowly nodded. "I'll think about it."

Moving in, I pressed a kiss to his soft lips, running my hand through the hairs of his beard. Damn I loved that thing.

"I was there when my father was murdered."

My hand stilled; I stared at him. My mouth dropped open, but no words formed.

"I didn't see it. But I heard it."

"H-how?"

The Adam's apple in his throat bobbed up and down, and again his dark gaze went to something over my shoulder.

"A few weeks after I turned thirteen, I accidentally overheard a conversation between my father and one of my uncles. He wasn't a blood uncle but one of my father's closest confidantes, or so I thought. He spent a lot of days and nights at our home. Anyway, my father was in his private office, the one he never let me, my mother, or my sister inside of. The door was slightly opened and I heard him raising his voice with my uncle as I walked past. I stopped because I rarely heard my father raise his voice like that. He was telling my uncle that he was done with that life. Drugs weren't for him and he was going into real estate with the money he'd saved over the years."

He paused, clenching his jaw.

"What happened?"

His eyes came back to me and my breath caught in my throat. They were so raw and filled with emotion. I instinctively knew I was the first person he was telling this story to.

"I pushed the door open. My father and uncle looked at me, stunned, but I was pissed. I looked up to my father. Saw him as super-human almost. He'd spent my entire life telling me he was in business. Never stating what kind of business, and I had to find out like that. My uncle left shortly afterwards, and my father and I had a huge fight. I called him a liar and a criminal. I went to school with kids whose parents were doctors, lawyers, ran companies because that was the environment *he* wanted me raised in. And all along he was selling drugs. I stormed out of his office and locked myself in my room for hours.

"Later that night I heard him saying something to my mom about going out. Again, I heard agitation in his voice and he *never* spoke to my mother like that. And while I was still pissed at him, something in my gut told me to follow him. He'd said he was going to see someone. I was familiar with the name. And since I didn't have a car, I waited until my pops left and then snuck out of the house. I had called a cab and told it the address I believed where the man lived. We arrived and I watched my father get into another car parked outside of the house and pull off. I begged the cab driver to follow him. He did and we followed him to a dark alley that I wasn't familiar with. I paid and got out of the cab. He drove off. I ran to the alley where my father was, calling after him. The fear on his face when he saw me standing there —" He broke off, shaking his head.

"He demanded I get behind a dumpster and make sure I was hidden. I tried to apologize for what I'd said in anger but he brushed it aside and told me to hide and not come out until he came and got me. I did, and within seconds, it felt like, I heard some familiar voices. My father told the man he was done with that life. I heard the fear in his voice, but it held determination as well. I felt both proud of and scared as hell for my dad. I don't even know how it happened, but within minutes there were gunshots. I covered my mouth to keep from yelling out, remembering what my father had told me about remaining unseen. A long while passed and then there was silence. I dared to look out from behind the dumpster and there was no one. My father was gone along with the other men whose voices I'd heard. I saw streams of blood running down the alley but they led nowhere. It was raining that night so eventually it all got washed away. Two days later, police knocked on my door and told my mother my father's body had been found in an abandoned building on the other side of the city."

It was silent for a long time between us. I had to take in everything he'd just revealed. I couldn't imagine hearing the murder of your own father and being powerless to do anything to stop it.

"Did you ever go to the police?"

Damon gave me an expression that said *yeah right.* "The police hated my father. They'd long since known what he did for a living but were unable to actually do anything about it for one reason or another. His death didn't garner any sympathy from the Williamsport Police Department."

"Yeah, but you were there. You knew who did it." I knew I was sounding like that innocent, naïve girl again but I couldn't help it.

He shook his head. "My father was just another dead black drug dealer to those cops. They didn't give a shit, and the man who'd killed him … he had connections. Nah, I didn't say anything." His hands tightened into fists.

I covered them with my own hands and felt the rigidity in his body. He pulsed with the anger and emotion of that night so many years ago. He'd carried so many burdens in his young life. I leaned in closer.

"I love you," I whispered against his lips. I pulled back to see his reaction to those three words.

His eyes widened.

"I know it's way too early for that, but … I couldn't help it."

My heart rate increased, fearing that he would reject me because I was too clingy. I'd always worn my heart on my sleeve. It was what had gotten me into trouble in the past but I was learning that I was who I was.

Without saying anything, Damon leaned down, capturing my lips in his. I moaned into his mouth because that was my body's natural response whenever he put his lips on mine.

"Is Monique a hard sleeper?" he questioned just after pulling back.

I wrinkled my forehead in confusion. "What?"

"Is she a hard sleeper? She won't hear us?"

Grinning, I shook my head. "She's been sleeping well throughout the night since she got her pump."

After taking my lips again in a kiss, he stood, and lifted me to wrap my legs around his waist as he moved us from the balcony to his bedroom, farther down the darkened hall. Damon closed the door behind us and casually strolled over to his bed, all the while peppering my lips with kisses.

I released my legs from around his waist and went to kiss him but he pulled back. I stared at him, startled.

He stared down at me, hard, as if trying to figure something out. "You know you can tell me anything, right?"

I gave him a confused look. "I know."

He stared at me for a long while as if waiting for me to share something. The one thing I'd been holding back, I didn't have the heart to share in that moment. I just couldn't. Even after he'd shared with me about the murder of his father. I was too much of a coward and I knew it.

Instead of spilling my guts I rose to my tiptoes and pressed a kiss to his mouth. His lips held firm for a few seconds but eventually his entire body softened and he welcomed the kiss, his arms moved around my waist, going to the button of my jeans.

Once his hands made contact with the skin underneath my shirt, neither one of us was thinking anymore about secrets from our past.

* * *

Damon

"You sure you want to go in there?"

I glanced over toward the driver's seat where Sean sat. He stared straight ahead at the metal fences that served to separate the huge brick building of the jail from the surrounding area. We were two hours outside of Williamsport at a maximum security jail. The same one where Mike Russo Sr. had finally been carted off to, nearly a week earlier. It'd taken some finagling, but through Josh I was able to get in for a visit with Russo

"Hell yeah," I finally responded. "Been waiting a long time for this one."

"Don't do anything stupid. You've got companies to run and a lady to look out for."

"Two ladies," I corrected.

Sean glanced over at me, eyebrow lifted.

"She has a ten-year-old daughter, remember?"

He grinned. "Two ladies. They don't need your ass getting locked up in a place like this." He tilted his head toward the prison.

"Never gonna happen. I'm just going in to talk to the man."

Sean snorted.

I didn't say anything. Didn't need to because Sean and I both knew that while I was just planning on talking with Russo, this would be one of the last conversations of his life.

"I won't be too long."

With that, I got out of Sean's Lexus SUV, shutting the door behind me and heading over toward the gate to the visitor's entrance. This wasn't my first time in this particular prison. I'd visited one or two of my past business associates here, and I hated it every single time. But this visit was different. As I gazed up at the cloudy sky, I noted the feeling of anticipation that flowed through my veins at this particular moment.

I had to go through the entire process showing my I.D., getting searched, and answering way too many questions for my liking. If I wasn't sure that Joshua's connections would help to erase any trace of my being here, I would've thought twice about showing up. But I needed this meeting just as much as I needed my next breath. To get it over with.

"Fifth window down on your right," the guard gruffly ordered, jutting his head in the direction of the long succession of windows and metal stools for me to walk down.

I didn't glance backwards as I started for the fifth window on the right. I sat down on the hard, metal chair, staring at the door where I knew prisoners entered in, opposite me. A handful of seconds later, the door opened, a guard stepped forward then moved to the side, allowing the man I'd only seen in pictures and from far away all of these years to emerge.

Mike Russo Sr.

He was about five-eleven and the orange jumpsuit looked like it added twenty years to his fifty-five-year-old body. His dark hair was greying at the edges, his eyes held huge circles beneath them as if he hadn't slept in a week, and his pot belly protruded as he turned to the side, holding out his hands for the guard to remove his cuffs. When he looked over in my direction to see who his visitor was his eyes narrowed. He didn't recognize me.

Casually, he shuffled toward the window and took his time picking up the phone on his end. I slowly reached for my phone, bringing it to my ear.

"You my lawyer's assistant? Law clerk or something?"

I chuckled. "I look like a fucking law clerk to you?"

His eyes narrowed even farther and he stared at me as if trying to figure out who I was.

"Confused?"

He glanced around briefly, ensuring that the guard was still standing at the door, before leaning in close to the window.

"Who the fuck are you?"

"The reason you're sitting where you are."

His eyes widened for half a second.

"I don't have much time, and unlike you, once this conversation is over, I can get up and walk out of this place. Just know, I've waited almost two decades to see you like this. You were tough shit that night in the alleyway, eighteen year ago."

A deep V settled in his forehead as he tried to pin down exactly what I was referring to.

"See, the man who you killed and used your connections with local PD to make it look like he was somewhere else he wasn't supposed to be, wasn't alone that night. It might've taken this long to get shit squared away but it was worth it." I paused and leaned in closer. "Lamar Richmond."

Russo's eyes widened.

"You're his—"

"His son. And I never forgot that night. The police covered it up for you but it's all good. Your own son helped put you in here." I pointedly glanced around the four walls of the prison we were in. "Must suck to know your own seed did this to you. But don't fret.

This isn't the worst of it. I've got eyes and ears all over this place. You don't have too many friends anymore, especially not in here. Remember that when you lay your head down to sleep at night."

With that said, I stood and hung up the phone, staring down at Russo whose eyes had taken on a ghosted look. His mouth widened and closed and few times. I straightened the jacket of my suit, smoothing it down before glancing over at the guard, noting his attention was on another inmate. I made a gun with my thumb, pointer, and middle fingers, aiming it at Russo's forehead, before mock pulling the trigger.

I watched as his skin went pale.

I took a step back, granting him one last look before I turned and walked out of the room and out of that prison for good.

Two weeks later, the city of Williamsport was shocked to learn about the beating death of one Mike Russo Sr., though no one was particularly surprised. And unfortunately, because it'd happened in the middle of the night, and his body had been found in the laundry room of the prison, no one was certain who had done it, or exactly how he'd ended up down there after hours.

And while it'd taken eighteen years to get that resolution, I realized that people who said payback wasn't worth it, were fucking liars. Knowing the piece of shit who'd taken my father from me and my family was resting in hell, helped to put an end to my nightmares.

CHAPTER 18

*S*andra

I swallowed nervously, looking down at the blank screen of my phone. I had just abruptly ended a call with Damon because I couldn't keep it together with him on the line while knowing I would have to see Randy again. Damon had called right as I was finishing up my lunch time workout. Emma had already been in the changing room and informed me that there had been an impromptu meeting scheduled with the opposing attorney in the Steve's Diner case. That meant Randy Jameson would be in the office.

Ever since that first encounter, I'd managed to avoid seeing him; he hadn't come to the office again. However, I had seen his name on the legal documents for the case, and my stomach roiled with nausea every time.

My hands shook as I changed back into the pastel pink and white tweed skirt I'd worn that day with a white, long sleeve turtleneck, lightweight sweater. I made my way back to my desk and tried to busy myself by organizing the files I needed to have arranged for Emma during the meeting. However, the entire time I tried to figure out some way to get out of the meeting. But it was useless. I needed to be there and this was my job. I just couldn't run out every time he showed up. No matter how much I wanted to.

I became lost in my thoughts, but when I heard voices behind me I was quickly pulled from my reverie.

"Here's Sandra," Emma stated.

I dropped the pen I'd been holding as I turned to see her moving toward my desk, Randy Jameson a half a step behind her. I had to work at it, but I kept my face completely neutral instead of the scornful look I wanted to give him.

"Sandra, can you show Mr. Jameson into the conference room? And bring all of the files. I'll be there in a moment."

I opened my mouth to tell her I absolutely could not do that but she was too fast. Emma turned and headed to her own office, apparently needing to retrieve something.

I swallowed, holding back a curse before slowly lifting my gaze to Randy, who had the audacity to step closer. I gave him a scathing look, to which he halted his forward movement.

Those brown eyes of his moved from me to my desk, glancing around.

Without a word I turned and grabbed my tablet and the papers that I figured I'd be needing for the meeting. When I looked back to Randy, I saw his gaze was transfixed on something behind me. Curious, I glanced over my shoulder to see what he was staring at and my heart plummeted.

Moving quickly, I lowered the picture that I kept of Monique and I so that it was face down. I turned back to Randy who's eyes had squinted as he glared at me.

"How old is she?"

"None of your business," I responded through gritted teeth but kept my voice low enough so that only he could hear. "The conference room is down the hall to the left." I moved to the side and held my arm out for him to move ahead of me. I didn't trust him standing behind me. I didn't trust him anywhere near me, to be honest, but I was forced to work with him for now.

"You can say more than two words to me. It would be the professional thing to do," he had the nerve to say once we entered the conference room.

I glared at him from the opposite side of the long, shiny, wooden table. "Keeping my commentary to as few words as possible *is* the most professional thing I can do right now. Trust me."

"Sandra, we have a history together. No matter how things turned out between us, we—"

"Just don't talk to me. Don't say my name. Don't even *look* at me. I am not who you're here to meet with anyway. Emma will be in shortly." God, I hoped she hurried up. I did not want to be alone with him for one more second.

"She looks just like you. Your daughter."

His eyes got wide when I slammed the files I'd been holding down on the table. "You don't *ever* mention her." I parted my lips to tell him I'd stand over his dead body before I let him speak any further about my daughter, but Emma entered the room, effectively ending that confrontation.

"My apologies, Mr. Jameson. I trust that Sandra was able to keep you company while you waited. I was on the line with another client. So, from our earlier correspondence, I gather you're here to make an offer to my clients," Emma began as soon as she entered the room.

I settled in a chair on the opposite side and farther from where Randy sat. That was the only way I could keep enough distance between the two of us so that I wouldn't try to reach across the table and throttle him. He easily towered over me by nearly a foot and he likely outweighed me by more than fifty pounds, but when he'd talked about Monique, my size no longer mattered. I wanted to rip his throat out just because.

"I'm sure you're aware that I need to discuss all of this with my clients, right, Mr. Jameson?" Emma asked once the meeting began winding down.

Though I'd typed notes throughout it all, I hadn't taken in anything that was said. I kept having visions on how I could take someone's life and get away with it.

"Sandra will be able to send over the notes from this meeting. And once I speak with my clients and they make a decision we will get back to you." Emma stood, holding her hand out to Randy.

More bile filled my stomach when he took her hand in his then looked across the table as if he was expecting me to reach out my hand for him to shake.

Fuck him.

That was the one reigning thought in my head, but I managed to keep the curse from flying out of my mouth.

"Sandra, can you show Mr. Jameson out?"

I opened my mouth to refuse but it was cut off by Randy's reply.

"That's fine, Ms. Leslie," he said to Emma. "I know the way." He nodded in my direction, which I didn't even acknowledge, and then sauntered out of the room.

"What are you thinking?"

I blinked and turned my attention to Emma. "What was that?"

"About the case? What are your thoughts on the meeting? The offer they gave."

I rolled my eyes upward, trying hard to remember what was even said during the meeting. Apparently, the diner was ready to make an offer to stay out of court.

I shrugged. "It's a decent offer I guess," I hedged.

"Decent, yes. Enough? Considering what those women have been through for years? I'm not sure." She shrugged. "We'll have to take it to them and see what they think. Send me and Jameson those notes as soon as possible, please?" she requested just before exiting the conference room.

I nodded but didn't verbally respond. I followed behind Emma and passed her as she entered her office. Going back to my desk, I placed everything I had in my hands down and moved to reboot my computer when something out of the corner of my eye caught my attention. I turned to glance over at the right side of my computer where I kept the picture of Monique and I. I distinctly remembered lowering the picture facedown so that Randy couldn't see it. I'd left it like that as I'd walked off to the conference room. However, as I stood there, the frame was staring me in the face, in its upright position.

I turned to see nobody around, save for the usual paralegals in this section of the office, and they all were engrossed in their own work. An uneasy feeling of dread that'd been with me for so long that it had begun to feel as if it were a part of my being started to well up in my stomach.

* * *

DAMON

"How did you know something was wrong with Kayla when she came back?" I questioned as I paced back and forth in Joshua's office. I couldn't even stand still long enough to look at him as he stood behind his desk. Joshua's office was located inside of the Townsend Industries building since he ran the real estate division of the company.

"What happened?" he questioned, his tone sharp.

"I don't fucking know. I knew for a long time that she was hiding something. She was skittish and shy and ..." I paused, not willing to tell Josh that in the beginning of our sexual relationship she was too damn shy for a woman that'd carried and birthed her own child. That hadn't ever sat right with me, but I chalked it up to the fact that Monique's father, whoever he was, had impregnated her and left her alone to raise a kid. I'd imagine that'd make a woman at least some-what hesitant about becoming sexually involved with another man. But hell, that didn't make sense either seeing as how Monique was ten. The idea that a woman as attractive and put together as Sandra was hadn't had any relationships over the past ten years led me to conclude that something was off. Because it's not like Sandra didn't have a sexual side. That fear had long since been dismissed after our first night together.

"Look, Kay hasn't told me anything, but—"

"But what?" I questioned anxiously, pausing for the first time since I'd entered his office.

"Last year. One day I came home from work and found Kay in the kitchen cooking and she was upset. So pissed that she cut herself with a knife due to negligence. I asked her what was wrong, but she said she couldn't say."

I squinted, wondering what this had to do with Sandra.

"She wouldn't say but she did ask if I knew of any law firms that were in need of a paralegal."

I angled my head at Josh who stared at me, waiting for me to put the pieces together.

"You helped Sandra get the job at Mansfield, Duvall & Mason," I stated, remembering the conversation from the day of the baby shower.

Josh nodded. "Kay passed me her resume and said that it was important she find another job quickly. She remained tight lipped about why, and I didn't ask seeing as how I didn't know her at all back then. Her resume checked out, and soon after I passed it along to one of the partners at the firm she was hired."

I clenched my teeth. "And you don't know why she was in such a rush to leave her old job?"

"Not at all. I'd ask Kay, but—"

I waved my hand. "That won't be necessary."

"Look, I don't know what happened or *if* something happened to Sandra …" Josh paused when I gave him a hard glare. "Okay, probably something did happen to her. Trust your gut. What I know is that when my instincts were telling me what yours seems to be telling you, I trusted them. I used everything at my disposal to root out the piece of shit who hurt her." Josh's eyes narrowed, and I could tell he was taken back to thinking about the ex-police officer that'd assaulted his wife.

A muscle in my jaw jumped. It wasn't the same thing. Kayla had been living in Portland, Oregon at the time of her assault, and only moved back to Williamsport after it happened. I knew Sandra and Kayla had only met once Kayla moved back to her home city. But maybe …

"Whatever you're thinking, go with that feeling," Joshua stated.

I glanced up at him.

"What I've learned is that if she's keeping something from you, it's not because she doesn't trust you enough. It's because she's ashamed of whatever went down."

Shame was a powerful and ugly emotion. I knew it well. I knew the shame of a thirteen-year-old boy who'd listened and did nothing while his own father was murdered.

"Let her know she's not alone in whatever it is. If you're serious about her."

"I'm fucking serious," I growled.

"Then make sure she knows that."

I didn't respond verbally to Joshua's words. I didn't need to. Actions spoke louder than words. It was a concept we both understood.

"You feel like getting into a fight tonight?" he questioned after a brief period of silence.

I rubbed my hand through my beard. "More than you fucking know. But not with the Underground." I needed to take this fight to the source. And to do that, I needed to find out exactly who or what the source was. That required I talked to one person and one person alone. Getting her to answer questions wouldn't be an easy feat, however.

"I may need some of your connections to help with this one," I told him.

Joshua lifted an eyebrow. "Which connections?"

I pondered the question for a moment. "Not sure yet, but when I find out whoever has kept that ghosted look in Sandra's eyes for so long, I may need you to call on every connection you have. The bastard won't get off as easy as Russo did."

Joshua let out a low whistle. "Just say the word."

I nodded. "Bet."

CHAPTER 19

*S*andra

"This isn't too much?" I questioned, turning to the side again in my full-length mirror, eyeing my body in the sparkling, long, black gown I wore. The dress was sleeveless, displaying my toned arms, pulled in waistline, and the expansion of my hips.

"You look beautiful," my grandmother stated from behind me as she stared at me in the mirror.

"You look perfect, Mommy. Almost like Princess Tiana when she got dressed up. You just need a tiara," Monique added.

I giggled before turning back to the mirror. I could admit that I looked damn good in the dress. I'd pulled my hair up into a high topknot with a few curls hanging to give myself that alluring look I thought it provided. I'd even opted to wear red lipstick which was something I never did, because as a child my grandmother had taught me that red lipstick was for *loose* women and girls, as she called them. But now, watching her smile at me through the mirror, I couldn't help but feel a little vindicated somehow.

"That's him," I stated hearing the telltale knock on the door. I could always tell when it was him.

"I'll get it! Coming, Mr. Damon!" Monique called as she hopped off my bed, running out of the room for the door.

I didn't even have time to reprimand her for running before she was out of the door. I looked toward my grandmother, who was babysitting her for the night.

"I'll go. A lady should always make an entrance. Wait a few minutes and then come out," my grandmother suggested.

I nodded and smiled as she hugged me from behind and made her way out of the room to catch up with Monique. If someone would have told me even a year ago that not only would I have a second chance at a relationship with my grandmother, but also be completely in love with an amazing man, I would've had no problem calling that person a liar and a cheater. But here I was, my grandmother seeing me off on a date as if she were sending me off to my high school prom.

That thought had me shuddering just thinking about the person I went to my actual high school prom with. I began to bite my bottom lip as my stomach sank, realizing that unfortunately that same person was back in my life due to my job.

"I'll get Mommy!" I heard Monique yell. Her little footsteps were soon halted.

"Your Mommy's probably still getting ready, short stuff," his deep voice moved down the hall and sent chills down my spine—in a good way. Thoughts of any other man were replaced instantly.

I fixed one of the hanging tendrils of hair and then smoothed the sides of my dress, giving myself one final look over. Thankfully, I'd worn no smear lipstick so I didn't need to re-apply any. I grabbed the small, black clutch I'd chosen for the occasion and went out to meet my date.

I rounded the corner and stopped short, just staring at Damon's back in the black and white tuxedo he wore. Even from behind he was the stuff that fairytales were made of.

"I promise next time I'll bring some more brownies, short stuff. But that's *if* you promise to keep your room clean like your mommy asked you to. She told me someone was having trouble keeping her clothes off the floor," he lightly scolded in that deep yet sensitive tone he always took with Monique.

"But—" Monique started, but was interrupted by my grandmother.

"And speaking of your mother …"

Slowly Damon turned around and his eyes widened. "Goddamn," he stated airily.

"Ohhh, Mr. Damon cursed!"

"Shit!" he cursed again. "My bad. Does she have to hear every curse?" he questioned, looking at me.

I giggled as he moved closer, pressing a kiss to my lips. "You …" he lifted my hand to his lips, "look …" another kiss to the corner of my lips, "amazing. This is that no smear lipstick, right?"

I smiled and said, "Yes."

"Good. Otherwise you'd have this red all over your face when I'm done with you. And I can't promise I'm going to wait until *after* this damn fundraiser to get my hands on you." That was said low in my ear so that only I could hear him before he pulled back to stare down at me, taking me in.

I went to push a stray curl behind my ear but found my hand was wrapped up in his hold. He obviously had no intention of letting it go either, as evidenced by the fact that he continued to hang onto it even as he spun around to face my grandmother and Monique again.

"Doesn't she look beautiful, Mr. Damon?"

My heart melted at my daughter's words.

"She absolutely does, short stuff." He stooped low to get eye level with Monique, though still clutching my hand in his. "And thank you for letting me spend time with your mama tonight. I promise I'll take good care of her."

Monique nodded. "Diego says that it's a man's job to protect women and children."

Damon's lips quirked up. "Lucky for that little boy he was actually right about that. Maybe his daddy is teaching him something after all."

I laughed and swatted Damon's shoulder with our conjoined hands. "Leave Diego alone."

Damon stood. "I'm not worried about that little boy. As long as he does right by my short stuff, he's cool."

I gave Damon a look. "He's ten."

He lifted his eyebrows. "You don't want to know what I was doing at ten."

I laughed. "You know what? You're right. I don't. How about we head out instead?"

He nodded. "Sounds good to me. But short stuff better not be up late facetiming that little boy tonight either."

I laughed, shaking my head. He was dead serious. I couldn't tell who he was more protective over. Me or Monique.

We hugged and kissed Monique goodnight, as she'd be long asleep by the time we got back. I would've stayed the night at Damon's but my grandmother had an early morning appointment the next day, so I'd chosen to be brought home instead of having to leave his place extremely early.

We said our good-byes and Damon escorted me to the front entrance of my apartment building. I was surprised to find that he'd chosen to have us driven to the fundraiser, which was held at the Williamsport Museum of Natural History instead of the hospital as it had been in previous years.

He waved the driver off and held the door open for me while I entered, climbing in behind me. As the driver went back around to the driver seat, I asked, "Why did you choose to have a driver tonight?"

Damon gave me a mischievous grin as his hand slid over to the door and he pressed the button to raise the partition. The Beyoncé song immediately came to mind as I watched his eyes glow with mischief. He slid closer.

"So I could do this instead of driving." He reached behind me with one hand, cupping the back of my head and pulling me closer to him.

I willingly moved in and let his lips capture mine. He slipped his tongue into my mouth, and my entire body grew heated. The feel of the hairs of his beard also turned me on, as they always did. I rose my left hand to cup his beard and run my fingers through it. He pulled back, chuckling.

"There you go. You're going to fuck around and have me make a seat out of this thing before we even get out of this car."

I laughed, lowering my head to his shoulder. "You started it," I retorted, moving closer to wrap my arms around him. I inhaled deeply and closed my eyes, bathing myself in the feeling of safety that his strength afforded me.

It'd been over a week since my last face-to-face encounter with Randy Jameson, and that haunted feeling I had once I'd seen that the picture of Monique and I had been turned over on my desk, had stuck with me. I hadn't told anyone about it. There was only one person I could tell, but I feared Kayla would try and push me to go to that counseling group she'd given me a card for. I didn't want that. I'd endured this thing on my own for so long, I just needed to figure out a way to make it through this particular case at work and I'd be fine.

Those were the thoughts I filled my mind with as I squeezed my arms around Damon's waist, pressing my body to his, trying to seek out his warmth. If only I could hide inside of his warmth until all this blew over. I sighed.

"Hey," he pulled back, tipping my chin to raise my face to his, "you ready to talk about what's going on with you?"

I began shaking my head. "What? There's nothing—"

I stopped short when he began shaking his head. "Don't." His voice was stern and full of warning. "Don't even finish that sentence because it'll just mean you're lying to my face. And we both know the truth, which is there is something you haven't been telling me. I've been patient because I am a patient man. I've been patient for as long as I could. But there's a time for patience and a time for action."

I pulled back. "I don't know what you're saying."

"I'll spell it out for you then. You've been putting off whatever you're not telling me for long enough. And I'm tired of waiting for you to let me in. So, once this fundraiser is over, we're going to discuss whatever it is you obviously don't want me to know. Because, if you haven't figured out by now, I'm in this with you for the long haul. I want you and Monique to move in with me, eventually. Someday soon. You know I'm not bullshitting when I say that. That's not who the fuck I am."

"I know that."

"Good. Then you should know that who is bothering you, or whatever it is that has you so scared that it puts that ghosted look in your eyes, is in a world of trouble once I find out the truth. Just know that."

My mouth dropped. I was dumbfounded, speechless because what the hell are you supposed to say when someone makes a declaration like that?

Thankfully, I didn't need to find any words at that moment because the driver pulled into the parking lot of the museum. A minute later we stopped out front of the main entrance while the driver held the door open for us to exit.

Damon held my hand, helping me out of the car. I dared to look into his eyes and saw again the searing seriousness they held. I didn't even want to think about what he'd said in the car. I didn't want to think about forcing myself to tell him the words that were so difficult for me to say.

When he reached around and lowered his hand to the small of my back, I straightened my shoulders, held my head up, and pushed all of those ugly thoughts to the back of my mind. I'd figure out what to say later that night. Right then, I would focus on taking part in a fundraiser in which Joshua and Kayla were big contributors to and organizers of.

"You know Joshua started this as a tribute to an old friend of his and Kayla's that died of ovarian cancer," I remarked, glancing over at Damon as we made our way up the stairs to the main entrance. I was trying hard to push past the uncomfortable moment.

Damon nodded but kept his gaze straight ahead. "Chelsea. Joshua's ex and Kayla's former best friend," he replied, obviously knowing the same story I did.

"It's kind of them to remember her in this way."

Damon nodded but didn't say anything.

We made it up to the entrance where he gave the security staff our names, after which we were quickly let inside. I glanced around the entrance and found a number of people dressed up in their gowns and tuxedos as well.

"Joshua and Kayla are already here," Damon stated as he looked at his phone. He stuck it back in the pocket of his pants. "You want a glass of champagne?"

I nodded, not really wanting a drink but feeling like I needed to fill my hands with something. Not only had our impromptu conversation in the car rattled me but I'd never been to an event such as this one. I may have grown up around some of the well-to-do in Williamsport thanks to my grandmother's connections, but it'd been a long time since I was in these circles. The actual mayor of the city was present, along with the police commissioner, state senators, top business leaders, high-ranking hospital staff, and more.

And then there was the man I came with.

I glanced up at his profile. Even with the awkwardness between us, I still couldn't keep my eyes off him for too long, nor did I want to. He was a true specimen. He also must've noticed me staring at him out of the corner of his eye, because he soon peered down at me and gave me a quick wink before lowering to grant me a small peck on the lips.

I pushed out the breath I'd been holding. Just that quickly he'd reassured me. Perhaps everything would be all right. Maybe I could share with him my deepest, darkest secret. Lord knew I was tired of holding it in.

"Damon."

I glanced up and my eyes widened, stunned to see the youngest of the Townsend brothers smiling as he approached Damon and I, his obviously pregnant wife on his arm.

"What's up, Ty, Destiny?" Damon greeted, shaking his hand before leaning down to press a kiss to Destiny's cheek.

"Hey, Sandra," Destiny greeted. I smiled at her. She and I were close to the same height, while the men on both our arms towered over us at six-foot-three inches. However, when Tyler glanced down at his wife, his hazel-green eyes softening, it was evident who really held the power in that relationship.

I looked up to find Damon staring at me in much the same way. My knees grew wobbly at that realization.

"Are you enjoying your off-season, Mr. MVP?" Damon asked.

Tyler chuckled. "Hell yeah," he answered, pulling Destiny—who cupped her baby bump—into his side. "Running errands all day for this one."

Grinning, Destiny shrugged. "The babies want what they want."

"Yeah, and last night they wanted chocolate chip cookie dough ice cream at one in the morning." Tyler frowned.

"I remember those cravings. I had them with Monique," I added.

Destiny looked up to her husband and pointed at me. "See? I'm not making these things up." She turned back to me. "Thank you for letting my husband know that I'm not faking these cravings. I don't even like sweets all that much. It's the babies," she insisted.

I laughed. Destiny was pregnant with triplets. If Tyler knew what was good for him, he'd just comply and get her whatever she wanted.

We talked and laughed for a few more minutes before Damon and I parted from Tyler and Destiny. Damon grabbed two glasses of champagne from a passing waiter, one for each of us.

"Did you really have those types of cravings when you were pregnant?"

I looked at him with raised eyebrows. "Absolutely. But it wasn't ice cream. For me it was bananas with doughnuts. Glazed doughnuts only." I shook my head, shuddering at the memory. It was a snack I devoured while pregnant but hadn't eaten since.

"Bananas and doughnuts," he reiterated, pulling a face.

I shrugged. "I think it was also because I had access to both working at the diner while pregnant. Thank god the cravings subsided once I had her."

He laughed and I stared at his perfect smile.

"You know a part of me believed that was the reason why she got sick with diabetes."

He paused, his champagne flute halfway to his mouth. "Really?"

I nodded and shrugged, eyes moving around the room of people before looking back up at him. "It's common. At least, that's what the doctors told me. Parents often blame themselves when a child ends up sick. I thought because I'd eaten so unhealthily and had been stressed while pregnant that maybe that was why she was diabetic. She was only five when she was diagnosed. But they reassured me this wasn't something I caused."

"But you still didn't believe them," he stated, not questioned.

I smiled. "You know me too well. It took a while. I still have guilt sometimes but not nearly as much as I used to."

"Good. From what I've read on type 1 diabetes, there was nothing you could or couldn't have done to prevent it."

It was my turn to pause and look at him. "You've been reading about Monique's illness?"

He nodded. "Of course."

My shoulders slumped a little as I took in what he'd said. A lump formed in my throat and I had to blink rapidly to keep the tears at bay. It was one thing to know that Damon cared for me. In my past life, before Monique, that would've been enough. But to know he took the time to learn what he could about my daughter's illness …

Just as I opened my mouth to tell him again that I'd fallen head over heels in love with him, a female voice sounded behind him.

When Damon stepped to the side to reveal the couple standing behind him, all of the air left my body.

"Angie," Damon greeted, apparently knowing the woman.

"Damon, this is my date, Randy Jameson."

I nearly cried out as I watched Damon's hand extend and Randy took it, shaking it.

"This is my girlfriend, Sandra," he stated, moving his hand around the small of my back.

"I-I, pleasure," I said to the tall woman who stood next to Randy.

Reluctantly, my eyes moved to Randy's and I hoped to hell he wouldn't let on that we knew each other. I couldn't bear that right now.

"Sandra." He nodded, extending his hand. "How are you?" he had the nerve to inquire with his hand out.

I felt Damon look down at me, but I couldn't meet his gaze. "You two know each other?"

I couldn't reply but Randy did.

"Yes. I'm an attorney at Wittaker & Wittaker. Sandra works for opposing counsel on a case I'm lead on."

I cleared my throat. "Y-yes. The diner case I told you about," I added, trying to sound as normal as possible.

"Well, Angie said she knew you from some work you'd done together, and she wanted to introduce us."

I silently watched as it was explained that Angie was a real estate agent who'd worked with Damon on a couple of projects before.

"I don't do individual properties anymore," Damon explained. "However, I have just purchased the building on Lakefront. We're looking to turn that into loft-style condos. They'll be ready in about a year and a half to two years, so if you're still looking then, let me know." Damon pulled out a business card. He paused when I began coughing, choking on nothing but air.

"You all right?" he questioned, concerned.

I nodded, sucking in air. "I need to go to the restroom. Excuse me," I lied and darted off before I even finished my statement. I hightailed it through the expansive space of the museum's entranceway, that was being used for the fundraiser, pushing through people in pretty dresses and tuxedos until I arrived at the hallway that led to the women's room. Glad to see there was no line, I pushed through the heavy, wooden door, and locating the first empty stall I could, I burst inside.

Thankfully, the stall itself was large enough that it contained a sink and I moved to it, grabbing a paper towel and dampening it with warm water. I patted my forehead, neck, and cheeks with the wet towel, hoping that would help bring me back to myself. I tried to steady my breathing and I cursed myself for having this reaction every time I saw him. But it wasn't just seeing him that had brought this on. It was seeing him so close that he actually shook hands with

Damon. He chatted him up, talking about apartments. The thought of Randy living in one of Damon's buildings sickened me.

But I needed to pull it together. I couldn't cower in a bathroom all night, and I needed to prove to myself that Randy Jameson no longer had that kind of power over me. The sick bastard that I knew he was.

After tossing the used paper towel in the trash, I opened my clutch and reapplied my pressed powder to smooth over my makeup. Even though I didn't need it, I recoated my lipstick for good measure. With my hand to my stomach, I inhaled and prepared to go back out there. I came up with the excuse that I had an upset stomach to tell Damon but that I was fine.

Unfortunately, I didn't even have time to properly construct the lie in my head, because as soon as I pulled open the door to the women's room, there stood Randy Jameson. I inched backwards, backing myself farther down the hall simply because I didn't want to be within ten feet of him. I looked up at his face to find him glaring down on me as if I'd stolen something from him.

"What are you doing?" I demanded, trying to sound intimidating. I tried to remember all of the self-defense moves I'd learned over the years, but my mind was drawing a blank. I might be capable of taking down a stranger in a nightclub, but staring at my real life monster under the bed was a different story entirely.

"Your daughter ..."

My eyes widened. "She's none of your—"

"How old is she?" he demanded through clenched teeth, stepping closer.

"I will never tell you anything about her."

"I bet you fucking will. Is she mine?"

"Get the hell away from me," I warned.

"I wo—" Randy's response was cut off from behind when a large hand cupped the back of his neck, pulling him backwards.

"She fucking told you to get the hell away from her, right?" Damon growled, pulling Randy away from me, and moving so he was in between us.

"I was just asking her a question."

"No fucking reason to be asking her a question when I'm not around."

Randy attempted to look at me over Damon's shoulder, which was a stupid move on his part because before I knew what was happening, Damon had his left elbow in Randy's throat, pinning him against the wall.

"Maybe you didn't hear me the first time. I said there's no reason you ever need to confront my woman."

"Damon," a male voice shouted.

I groaned inwardly when I looked over and saw Joshua Townsend rushing toward Damon and Randy. I felt even more terrible when a heavily, nine-months-pregnant Kayla rushed over as well.

Joshua separated Damon and Randy.

"Are you okay?" Kayla asked me, staring in worry.

I nodded. "I'm fine. I'm so sorry."

"Was he—"

"No," I shook my head, not even wanting to hear what she was going to ask with that question.

"I don't know what the hell you did to get him that upset, and I don't give a shit either." Joshua stared at Randy. "But you need to go. We'll give you back your check," Joshua swiftly cut off any protestations from Randy and had security escorting him out. He and Damon exchanged a few words before Joshua wrapped his arm around Kayla's waist and left, leaving Damon and I alone in the hallway.

I took a chance and glanced up at him. I wanted to avert my eyes, but I was tired of being a coward.

"Let's go," was all he said.

Within seconds, his hand was at my back as we made our way through the crowd once again, only this time there was no mingling. No stopping to talk to any of the who's who of Williamsport. We exited through the same way we entered, and a half a minute later our town car was pulling up. Damon waved the driver off and held the door open for me to enter before entering and shutting the door himself. He hadn't said a word to me.

My eyes went to the partition as it was rolled up.

"That motherfucker is Monique's father?" His question broke the tense silence that had surrounded us in the car.

I looked away, unable to answer his question.

"So now you don't hear me?"

I tightened my fists in my lap, feeling all sorts of emotions. Pissed at Randy, not only for tonight but for the way his actions had disrupted my entire life. Pissed at myself for being so naïve back then and so cowardly now. And ashamed at the idea of having to open my mouth and actually give Damon an answer.

"Sandra, is that motherfucker Monique's fath—"

"I don't know!" I blurted out, finally turning to look at him. "I don't know who Monique's father is!" I shouted.

CHAPTER 20

*D*amon

I blinked, feeling like I'd just been knocked the hell over, and not in a good way. Sandra had moved as far away from me in the back of the town car as she could after yelling out her response to my question. I was too stunned and angered to even respond. I didn't say anything else until the car stopped moving and the driver got out to hold the door open.

It wasn't until that moment, that I realized he had brought us back to Sandra's place instead of mine. This wasn't a conversation I wanted to have in the vicinity of her family, but we were there now. Monique was likely asleep anyway and I was much too anxious to get some answers than to wait until he drove all of the way across town to the building where I lived.

I held out my hand for Sandra to help her out of the car, but she refused it, helping herself out instead. I didn't have time to give the driver instructions before Sandra was rushing into her building. I caught up quickly.

"Where the hell are you going?" I asked like a damn fool, as if I couldn't figure it out.

"Home," she responded, tersely. "You have your answer, okay?"

"The hell I do." I took her by the arm, cupping it, but not tightly. Thankfully, she didn't pull away. I reached for the key she held, and used it to unlock her apartment door, once we arrived in front of it.

I moved inside with her arm still in my grasp. Her grandmother, who by the looks of it, had been laying on the couch, reading, stood. However, her smile dropped when she caught the expressions on either one of our faces.

"We need to talk privately," I told her without waiting for an answer. I moved down the hallway, behind Sandra.

She entered her bedroom and I closed the door behind us.

"Explain." That was what I needed, explanations. Because none of this shit made any sense. Sandra wasn't the type of person to not know who the hell the father of her child was. I could surmise that about her from the first moment we met. And I didn't *not* believe what she'd blurted out in the back of the town car, so something wasn't adding up.

She held out her arms, shrugging. "What's to explain? I don't know who the father of my child is." She shrugged again, trying to appear casual about it all. "Just think of me as one of those thots or whatever this generation is calling it. My grandmother used to call them *loose* women. Whatever. I'm one of them."

"Bullshit." She was trying way too hard to come across nonchalant. But the tears that were forming in her eyes gave it away. "You're trying really hard to avoid telling me the whole truth." I moved closer, taking her by the upper arms, stilling her movements. "Just say the words."

Her eyes closed but her mouth began moving. "I don't know who my daughter's father is because I was unconscious when she was conceived ..." She pushed out a breath. "Roofied."

I loosened my hold on her arms until my hands fell to my sides. Not because I didn't want to touch her but because of the anger that pushed through my entire body, vibrated through every pore. I didn't want it to spill over onto her. I took a step back as she raised those maple syrup pupils to meet mine.

I watched as she inhaled a shaky breath and her lips parted. I didn't want to hear anymore, but I kept my mouth shut, letting her continue.

"Randy was my boyfriend, or so I thought. He was the star football player in my high school. We'd gone to school together for years and I knew him because his father was a city official. His mother and my grandmother were close. Anyway, our senior year, I started tutoring Randy in pre-calculus. We became close friends. Then in early spring he asked me out on a date. I was excited and agreed. But he told me not to tell anyone. I didn't realize then it was because he already had a girlfriend at another school. I didn't have many friends in high school and kept to myself. Anyway, when he tried to have sex with me, I told him that I wanted to wait until I was married to give my virginity to my husband. It was how my grandmother raised me. He balked a little but eventually let it go."

Her words were coming out hurried now. As if she needed to finally get this all out. It was obvious she hadn't shared all of this with anyone. And in spite of myself, I made my body stand there and listen to every word. To take in every syllable she said.

"We went to our prom together. Turns out, his actual girlfriend was out of town that weekend. I later found that out through the grapevine. Anyway, prom was terrible because he again ramped up the pressuring me for sex. I almost gave in but felt so disgusted by his behavior. He was drunk. I made him take me home. I was disappointed but he apologized, and I tried to let it go. We kept dating, and when I asked what we would do the following year when he was away playing football and I was still in Williamsport on my full ride, he shrugged and said we would figure it out. I thought I loved him. So when a couple of weeks after graduation he invited me to a party at his father's place outside of the city, I trusted him enough to go. I already told him I wouldn't have sex with him, and he said it was fine. It was the one time I lied to my grandmother. I told her I was staying with a girlfriend of mine for the night."

Sandra shook her head as if she, out of everything, she blamed herself for that little white lie the most.

"When we got there two of his friends from the football team were already there. No one else. Randy said more people would be showing up later. I was uneasy, naturally, but I trusted him. He was my boyfriend and our families had known each other's for years. When he passed me my first drink of alcohol I hesitated. I did recognize that I was the only girl in a home by herself with three guys, but again, I trusted Randy. And the two other guys weren't paying me any attention aside from a few words here and there. I thought they were waiting for the girls they had invited to show up. It was all a lie.

"Something felt off within a few minutes of taking my first couple of sips of the beer. I started feeling lightheaded and dizzy. But it was my first time drinking and I just assumed it was from the alcohol. I only remember flashes from the rest of that night …" Her voice trailed off and she stared toward the corner of her bedroom. "The next morning I woke up bloody and in pain. When I asked Randy what he did, all he said was that I kept saying I wanted it. I felt terrible and my body hurt all over but he made me take a shower. I did and then he drove me home. I was sick all that day and tried to discern what was real from what felt like a dream from the night before. Two days later Randy, who'd been ignoring my calls, sent me a text saying that he was breaking up with me because he couldn't trust a girl who would do what I did with his friends." She shook her head.

"The worst part was a month and a half later, finding out I was pregnant. That was when I knew without a doubt what had happened. I went to a local clinic to schedule an abortion. I was certain I wouldn't go through with the pregnancy. But when I got there, and the nurse started talking, I just couldn't. I had no idea what I was going to do but I knew I couldn't abort my baby no matter how she came about."

She moved to the bed, sitting down, her shoulders slumping.

"That was why you wished every night to love her," I stated, staring at the wall, putting two and two together. "Not because it was an unplanned pregnancy but because of the way …"

"Yes. I was terrified that whenever I looked at her I'd see … them and that night."

"You never told your grandmother the truth?"

"I never told *anyone.* Kayla was the first person I told, and that was just last year. I never told her all of the details."

"Kayla …" I turned to face Sandra. "And she helped you get your new job?"

Sandra lifted her head, blinking away the tears, nodding. "I worked at Wittaker & Wittaker for six years. Last year, one day, out of the blue, I saw Randy being walked around by one of the partners of the firm. He was introduced to the staff as the newest attorney in the office. I hid behind a corner until they passed, and then I called Kayla. I told her what happened and that I couldn't work at that firm any longer." Shrugging, she cast her gaze toward the floor. "She asked me to send her my resume and she'd pass it along to Joshua to see what he could do. A few days later I had a call from Emma saying her firm was looking for a new paralegal and I'd come highly recommended. She had my resume in hand. I gave Wittaker & Wittaker my two weeks and worked from home for the remainder of my time with the company. Not until he walked into Mansfield, Duvall & Mason did I see Randy again."

Once she finally stopped talking was when I realized that my teeth were clenched so tightly that my jaw ached. I wanted to ask more questions, but I could tell she was drained. And at that moment, I wasn't in my right mind. I didn't want to scare her with the intensity of my anger.

"I need to go," I stated low, my voice hard.

Her head popped up. "Go?"

I turned back to her and knew I couldn't leave this way, but I was too full of fury to explain exactly what I was thinking. Hell, I didn't even know myself. I just knew somebody was going to fucking hurt.

Moving closer to her, I pulled her up from her seated position by her arms and pressed a kiss to her forehead.

"I'll be back soon." I released her and quickly moved to the door, my fingers itching to put my fist through somebody's face.

"Where are you—" She stopped when I yanked the door open, and on the other side stood her grandmother, tears streaming down her face.

"Oh my God," she cried, lips quivering, hands going to cover her mouth. "I didn't know."

I glanced back at Sandra who couldn't hold the tears back any longer. Yeah, it was time for me to go. Instead of saying anything, I moved past her grandmother and down the hall. I glanced across the hall at the closed door that lead to Monique's bedroom. I hoped to God she was sleeping and didn't hear any of what her mother had just revealed to me.

Moving through the rest of the apartment, I exited, shutting the door tightly behind me before pulling out my cell phone. I punched in the name at the top of my contact list.

"I need a favor," I said into the phone as soon as he picked up.

"Been waiting for this call. Especially after tonight. What's up?" Joshua questioned.

I strolled down the hallway, taking the stairs to the front entrance of Sandra's apartment building as I explained to Joshua exactly what I would need.

* * *

Sandra

I stared at Damon's retreating back until it disappeared around the corner into the hallway. I didn't have the strength to get up and ask him where he was going. And I honestly didn't want to know what he was thinking. I couldn't bear it if he thought less of me because of what I revealed.

My gaze moved to my grandmother who stood just outside of my bedroom door, shaking, tears streaming down her face as she covered her mouth with her hand. She shook her head and slowly moved into my bedroom, shutting the door behind her.

"Sandra," she called, her voice barely above a whisper as she moved toward me. "Oh my God," she repeated for at least the second or third time.

I pushed out a breath. Obviously, she'd heard everything. I could see it in her eyes. The door to my bedroom hadn't been closed all of the way.

"Why didn't you tell me?"

I shook my head and sighed, moving to sit on my bed again.

She followed, taking my hands into hers.

In the past, I might've rejected her touch, but I'd forgiven my grandmother for her actions. She was a different person now than she was back then. I could see that.

"I was ashamed, embarrassed. And you were so angry. So adamant about me getting an abortion. And when I tried to explain ..."

"I wouldn't let you."

I nodded. "But I couldn't find the words back then. It took me more than nine years to admit that I had been raped."

My grandmother let out a wail so deep it startled me. "I did it again," she cried, her hands going to her chest as she let the tears fall. "I was so strict with your mother after your grandfather passed away that she rebelled. She wants nothing to do with me. And you. I was even harder on you, doing everything I could to ensure you wouldn't end up like her that I pushed you both away. And I put you in a position to be hurt, and then kicked you out ..." She broke off, her voice trembling as she cried.

Before I could do anything to console her, she quickly wiped her eyes and shook her head. "No. I'm sorry. This isn't about me. I won't make this about me. Please, Sandra," she demanded, sitting down again and taking my hands into hers, "tell me what you need from me."

I stopped and looked around the room but not seeing anything. What did I need? It'd been so long since someone asked me something like that. Especially, my grandmother. But a second later the thought came to me.

"Now that you know, you need to promise me you will *never* treat Monique any differently. She is the best thing that has ever happened to me conceived out of the worst thing that has ever happened to me. It took me a lot of years to reconcile those two facts of my life. But I have, and if you have *any* reservations about whether or not you could love her the same, then—"

My grandmother shook her head vehemently. "I love that little girl with my whole heart. I could never … you have my word."

Exhaling, I nodded. "Okay." I stood and paced back and forth. It was only then that I realized my entire body was shaking. "Where do you think he went?"

My grandmother stood, coming in front of me. "Damon?"

I nodded.

"I don't know."

"Do you … do you think he sees me differently now?"

"What?" My grandmother seemed shocked by my question. She shook her head. "Absolutely not."

"Then why did he leave?"

"Sandra, men like Damon … they're protectors. They're not always the most talkative but more about action. Especially when it involves someone they love."

My eyebrows shot upward. "You think he loves me?"

"Of course."

"He's never said it back." It hadn't bothered me that he hadn't said it back until that moment.

"Actions, not words. Let his actions speak for him. The words will come. He may have just needed some time to sort everything out in his head. But I realized he loved you when he told me the reason he didn't like me."

"What?"

"Don't get upset, but …" My grandmother explained the conversation she'd had with Damon the first time he'd met her, when they both came over for dinner. "He was protective over you then and he's even more so now. Give it a little time. That man isn't going anywhere."

I nodded, but in the back of my head I wondered if she was right. Maybe my past was too much for him to handle.

CHAPTER 21

*D*amon

"You like the view from up here?" I questioned with a grin on my face, turning to face Randy as we stood atop of my new Lakefront building. I frowned when he didn't answer.

"Cat got your fucking tongue?" I barked at him.

A satisfied sensation moved through me when he flinched, blinking with his swollen eye and moving backwards. When he took one step too many, he backed up into the brick wall that stood behind him. Not an actual brick wall, but one in the form of a huge six-foot-six, bulked up head of Townsend security who went by the name Brutus.

"The shit this job gets me into," Brutus mumbled, shaking his head.

I tossed him a grin. "But making sure rapists get what's coming to them is worth it, right?" I questioned.

Brutus nodded. "Touché."

I lowered my gaze to a petrified looking Randy and gestured to Brutus. "He speaks fucking French. Who knew?"

Randy began shaking his head looking from me, to Brutus, to Sean, and to a silent Joshua, who stood to my right.

"Look, I don't know what this is abo—"

260

I couldn't stand another fucking word out of his lying ass mouth, so I popped his ass, effectively silencing him, save for the scream of pain he let out.

I crouched low, since he'd buckled at the knees. "I'll tell you when to fucking speak, bitch. You don't get to say shit without being asked. 'Cause, see, you didn't ask Sandra what she wanted that night you fucking drugged and raped her. No wait, you *did* ask and she told you no. More than once, she told you sex was off the table, but like the bitch you are, you took the decision out of her hands. Then, ten years later you come back demanding to know who the father of her child is?"

My right hook landed in his jaw; a snapping sound I'd heard many times before while in the ring sounded. A bone breaking.

Good.

"Y-you can't d-do this to m-me," Randy managed to eek out through what I presumed was a broken jaw.

I chuckled. "But I am." At that point, I didn't give a shit whether I went to jail or not. The knowledge that this sick fuck had not only raped Sandra but gotten away with it for years and then tried to move back into town as if nothing had happened had driven me past the point of no return. But in the weeks since Sandra had told me the truth, Josh's security had done some background investigation on Randy Jameson. I wasn't surprised by what Brutus managed to dig up.

"See," I began, picking Randy's body up by the scruff of the collared shirt he wore, "I also know Sandra's not the only woman you've done this to."

"D-done what? I didn't do any—"

"Now is really not the fucking time to be lying," Joshua angrily said, cutting Randy off. "You see how fucking pissed he is?" Josh jutted his head to me. "I wouldn't play the denial game if I were you."

"Me either," Sean added, snorting.

I moved in closer to, tightening my hold on Randy's collar. "See, the only reason all three of them are here is to keep me from ending your life. Matter fact, you did say you wanted to see my building, right?"

Without waiting for Randy's response, I began dragging him toward the edge of the rooftop we stood on. It was well after midnight and we were the only people around for a few blocks, save for the other poor souls who were doing shit just as devious as we were. I didn't need to worry about being seen or heard.

"Wha-what? Help!!" Randy shouted as I bent him backwards over the edge of the rooftop.

I glanced upwards. "From up here, you can see all of the fucking stars. It'll be your last sight if you fucking lie to me again," I growled, pushing Randy a little farther over the edge of the roof. "You ready to meet your maker or you want to stop fucking lying?"

"Okay, okay," Randy protested.

I exhaled and took a step back, bringing him from over the edge of the building, but still crowding his space.

"Jack Murphy and Leon Walker. Those were your two teammates who you had over that night you raped Sandra, right?"

Randy visibly swallowed, staring wide-eyed at the three men behind me.

I snapped in his face. "Hey, don't look at them. I'm the one you need to be worried about. Jack Murphy and Leon Walker, they helped you assault her that night?"

Slowly Randy nodded.

"And Sandra wasn't the only woman you did this to, was she?"

Again, he hesitated, and I moved to push him over the edge again.

"Okay, no, no! She's not the only one," he finally responded.

"How many are there?"

"I-I don't know. Twenty maybe thirty."

I stood, moving back from him in disgust. "Fucking pathetic."

"You could just kill him."

That suggestion came from Joshua.

"*What?* No—"

"Shut the fuck up!" I growled.

"I mean, you said you don't want to put Sandra through a trial."

"I don't," I snapped at Josh. "But death is too quick for him." I turned back to Randy. "So here's what's going to happen. You're going to drain every penny of your inheritance. What's it like two point five million?" I asked as if I didn't already know. I was well aware of Randy's wealth, family history, and the devious shit he'd gotten away with over the years. "And you're going to track down every woman you assaulted and pay them. You're going to resign from the state bar because a piece of shit like you has no business practicing law. *Any* kind of law. Then, you're going to leave Williamsport." I stooped low, getting right in Randy's face. "Look at me when I say this, you're going to get the fuck out of here. Find someplace far from here. Hundreds of miles away, in a rinky dink little town, get a job as a bus driver or a busboy. I don't give a shit which one, but you're never to step foot in Williamsport again."

"That's too good for his bitch ass," Sean growled behind me.

I glanced over my shoulder at my cousin before returning my attention to Randy.

A smile crossed my face. "He's right. That *is* too good for you. But I'm feeling generous right now." I also knew something Sean didn't, but I wasn't about to say it right then. I wanted Randy to think I'd let him live out the rest of his days in peace.

"I-I don't know all of their names," Randy stated weakly. "I can't do what you want me to."

"We'll start with the ones you do know and work your way back. I have no doubt it'll come to you. I'll even send you some help to jog your memory. Isn't that right, Brutus?"

"Sure is," his deep voice answered from behind me.

"My friend Brutus, here, has been kind enough to offer up one of his employees to assist you in remembering every woman you've ever hurt and getting a portion of your inheritance to them."

I stood up, taking a step back.

"Well get the hell up!" I barked. "Your bitch ass doesn't have time to be sitting around. You've got shit to do. Unless you want to go over the roof."

"No! No!" Randy yelped, stumbling to rise to his feet.

I watched as he wobbled, unsteadily before Brutus grabbed him by the arm and walked him toward the door leading to the staircase to exit.

I waited a few heartbeats, glancing at both Joshua and Sean, who'd remained mostly silent, before starting in the same direction.

"I can't believe you're letting him walk away," Sean tutted.

I snorted. "Who the hell do you think I am? He won't be alive a year from now." I had already planned out his "suicide" with a letter explaining in detail how he'd assaulted numerous women over the years. I'd just opted to let Randy believe I'd leave him to live in peace once he'd done what I'd ordered.

"That's more like it," Sean replied.

"I think we're rubbing off you on," Josh stated, clapping me on the back.

I chuckled. "Shit. You must be," I replied, looking over at his grinning face. Everybody knew those Townsends were crazy as hell.

Silently, we exited the fifteen story building. Without thinking, I turned toward the right, moving closer to the alleyway that was created by the building my company now owned and the neighboring building. I'd spoken to the new owner of the building, who was converting it to boutique stores. It was dark out due to the time of night and I could barely make out the dumpster that still sat about halfway down the alleyway.

I glanced over my shoulder, hearing the footprints of Sean and Joshua behind me. I turned back.

"This is where my father was killed," I stated. I hadn't shared every detail with either men before. I nodded in the direction of the dumpster. "That was where I hid when it happened."

I opted not to say anything else. No more words were needed. Instead, I looked up at the building I now owned.

Sean moved in, clapping me on the shoulder. "You know you're crazy as shit, right? Almost throwing a man off a building into the alley where your pops was murdered. That's some crazy shit. You wannabe Suge Knight ass."

I chuckled.

"I've watched crazier things done in the name of protecting the woman you love," Joshua added.

"You would've," I grunted.

"Hey, your pops taught you the same thing mine taught me. Protecting the women in your life is the *only* thing that matters."

I nodded.

"What about the other two?" Sean questioned.

I didn't have to ask to know he was referring to Jack and Leon, the two players who also assaulted Sandra that night.

"You haven't heard?" I asked, raising an eyebrow toward Sean.

He shook his head.

"Former Williamsport High School star football player, Jack Murphy, died of an overdose," I stated as if reading a newspaper headline.

"While Leon Walker, formerly of Williamsport, is survived by his wife after a sudden heart attack," Josh added.

Sean glimpsed between the both of us and began shaking his head. "Crazy as hell."

I shrugged. "Whatever. I'm done with this. I need to go see my woman."

I gave one last look down that alleyway before turning my back and making my way to my car.

CHAPTER 22

Sandra

"Are you sure you want to go alone?" Kayla asked into the phone as I got out of my car and glanced across the parking lot to the three story brick building. From the outside the building looked like most others lining the street. Next to it was a church, and on the other side sat a building that housed a laundromat and a convenience store. A typical street in Williamsport, but the particular building I was going into housed a handful of businesses and organizations. Only one of them, however, was printed on the card that I held in my free hand. The same card Kayla had given me a couple of months prior, right before I ran out of her office because I was too much of a coward to confront my past.

"It's fine."

"I could meet you—"

"Kayla, you just had a baby three weeks ago. There is no way I'd ask you to come with me when you have a little girl at home who needs you."

Kayla sighed into the phone. She'd given birth twenty days ago to a beautiful baby girl she and Joshua named Victoria Chelsea Townsend. I went and visited her in the hospital the day after she was born, and then again a couple of days later, Monique and I taking a few meals over so she wouldn't have to worry about cooking for a while. Though, between Joshua's three brothers and their wives, his parents and Kayla's parents, they had enough food to last at least six months.

"But it wouldn't be any trouble to go—"

"No, I need to do this alone," I finally said, glancing up at the building again, noticing a couple of women walking in. Butterflies fluttered in my belly.

"I'm proud of you."

A small smile touched my lips. "Thanks."

"But I still wish someone was there with you. What about Damon? I think you should've told him."

I frowned. I'd told Kayla the entire story of what happened the night of the fundraiser, about three and a half weeks prior. Damon and I had talked often since that night. He called every night just as I was putting Monique to bed so we could read her a story together. But we'd rarely seen each other. He'd traveled to a couple of different places for work which was why I hadn't seen him. At least, that's what he'd told me.

"I'll tell him eventually." I wanted to wait until I saw him face-to-face and not through the phone. "I have to go. I'll call you afterwards."

"Okay. If you need to, you can come over after. I know those meetings can be emotionally draining sometimes. Or if you need me to take Monique for a little while so you can have some alone time, that's okay, too."

I smiled into the phone. I loved Kayla. I'd obviously hit the jackpot when I decided to open up to her.

"Thank you," was all I said before hanging up the phone. I wouldn't take her up on the offer. If it became too much, I'd just ask my grandmother to take Monique for a couple of hours once I got out of this meeting. My grandmother would bend over backwards to help me out with anything she could these days. But I tried hard not to take advantage of her guilt.

Inhaling, I took a step toward the front entrance, and then another and another, until my stride picked up and I was reaching for the door to enter. Glancing at the directory on the wall, I realized the office I wanted was on the second floor of the building. I opted to take the stairs and arrived at the glass doors that read "Helping Hands" within five minutes.

As I opened the door a young woman with brunette hair smiled warmly. "Welcome to Helping Hands, how can I assist you?"

I lifted my head, straightened my back, and said, "I'm here for the group meeting for sexual assault survivors." It took all of my energy to hold my confident stance and say those words but I had.

The woman nodded empathetically. "Is this your first time?"

"Yes. I registered on the website, Sandra Robinson."

She scrolled through a list of names on her computer screen. "Ah, there you are. Welcome, Sandra. The group meets in the room down the hall and to your left. There is coffee, water, tea, and some refreshments in the meeting room as well."

I nodded and gave her a small smile before heading off in the direction she'd told me.

My heart thundered in my chest as I grew closer and closer to the door. I couldn't believe I was finally doing this, but I also felt proud of myself. I should've confronted this a long time ago.

"Hi." A friendly looking older black woman waved.

I returned her smile.

She pushed the square-framed glasses she wore up her nose a little and tossed her long dreadlocks over her right shoulder.

"I'm Veronica. Nice to meet you." She moved closer to me, holding out her hand.

I took it, shaking it. "I'm Sandra."

"It's your first time here?"

I nodded.

"I'm the social worker who runs these groups."

"I saw your picture on the website," I noted.

Her smile widened. "Would you like some coffee or tea?"

"I'll have some of the herbal tea. If I drink coffee this time of day, I'll be up half the night."

She laughed. "Same with me. I'm incredibly sensitive to caffeine."

We talked for a few more minutes while more women trickled in. Soon, I made my way over to sit in one of the folding chairs that had been arranged in a circle of about twenty. I glanced around, noticing women of all ages, ethnicities, and races. That didn't surprise me. I'd read up on statistics of victims of sexual assault. Reading the numbers both saddened me and made me feel like I wasn't alone. Now, seeing some of the women in person, the stats were becoming more than just numbers read on the internet.

"Let's begin, ladies," Veronica stated as she took her seat in one of the chairs. "We start every meeting with introductions. Just your first name and where you're from, if you like."

We went around the circle and introduced ourselves to the group. Veronica began talking, explaining how the group meeting worked, I assumed for my benefit since I was the only one who'd shown up for the first time. The other twelve women, or so, had been coming for a period of a few months up to a couple of years. I listened intently as the women explained how they were better able to handle what'd happened to them as a result of coming to the group.

"Sandra, would you like to share?"

I blinked and looked over at Veronica. "I don't know what to say."

"Share whatever's on your mind. How you're feeling. What brought you here today. Whatever is on your heart, share it. Nothing we say leaves the walls of this room. Isn't that right, ladies?" Veronica questioned, glancing around.

The other women nodded emphatically in agreement.

Taking one last look around, I parted my lips and spoke the first words that came to mind. "I have a daughter."

I paused, glancing around. All eyes were on me but I didn't feel put on the spot. Each woman had shared a little about themselves, so it felt right to share myself. Also, since I'd told Damon the truth about that night a small weight had been lifted off of me. It'd freed me enough to actually show up to this group. The fear was diminishing.

"She's ten years old …" I glanced around before speaking again. "She's the result of that night. Most people who know me don't know that. Well, at least, they didn't. I've told the closest people in my life recently. But it's a secret I held onto for a decade."

"Why?" one of the women asked.

I lifted my gaze to meet hers. "I couldn't even admit to myself what'd happened to me. Then, I never wanted anyone to associate her with my assault. I didn't want that to be all anyone ever saw when they looked at her or to feel sorry for me because they believed I had to have her even if I didn't want to. I was raised in a very conservative home. Most people who knew me growing up would've likely assumed I felt obligated to keep her even though I didn't want her."

"And is that true?" Veronica asked.

I shook my head. "Not in the least. She's my everything."

"What made you finally tell?"

I looked at the young, blonde-haired woman who'd asked that. I estimated she couldn't be much older than I was at the time of my assault.

"He came back. The man who I thought I'd loved at one point in my life. The one who drugged and ... raped me along with two of his friends." I paused. "And because I fell in love. *Real* love. For the first time. And I didn't want my past holding me back anymore. I wanted to be all in."

"Speaking the truth is where the healing begins," Veronica stated, wisely.

I inhaled but didn't reply. I gave her a short smile, that hopefully conveyed the depths to which I understood her statement. She was right. Not saying my truth had kept me hostage for years. I had loved my daughter the best I could but had kept myself closed off from everyone else.

"Thanks for sharing your story," the same young, blonde woman who'd questioned me earlier stated as we all started folding up the chairs to line up against the wall to prepare to leave.

"Thanks for listening."

She nodded. "The same thing happened to me. A guy I was seeing decided he wanted to share me with his friends." Her eyes lowered to the ground. She shook her head, then peered back up at me. "I don't know if I could've made the decision you made," she remarked. "About your daughter, I mean."

I understood. "It honestly didn't feel like a decision. I tried to go through with the abortion and something in me just knew I couldn't do it."

She looked at me and nodded, ingesting my words. "What was the reaction of the guy you're seeing since you told him?"

I raised my eyebrows and glanced out the door. "Well, I could tell he was pissed."

"At you?"

I shook my head vehemently. I never got the impression Damon was pissed at me. Randy, yes. "No, at my ex, at the situation, but not at me. But … he's been a little distant." My chest ached admitting that out loud. I hated to think that speaking the truth would cause Damon to somehow think less of me or feel sorry for me, or whatever. I'd spent many nights wondering what he was thinking.

"He probably just needs some time," she reassured. She stuck out her hand. "I'm Catherine, by the way."

"I remembered from when you introduced yourself. I'm Sandra."

"Maybe I'll see you here again?"

"I think you will." I'd already made the decision to come back to the group again the week after next, when it was held. There was comfort in going someplace where I could talk about what had become the elephant in the room of the past decade of my life.

Catherine and I talked a little more as we passed through the doors of Helping Hands. She told me she was in her sophomore year at Williamsport University. Her assault had happened early on in her freshman year. In the few minutes we talked, I began to admire her bravery.

As we exited the building, I looked up to where my car was parked and my heartbeat increased. Leaned against my driver's side door was the man I'd wanted to hold onto for weeks.

"Is that him?" Catherine asked from next to me.

I smiled as I stared straight ahead at Damon whose eyes were glued to me.

"That's him."

"He's cute."

I smirked but never took my eyes off Damon. "He's mine too."

Catherine giggled right before leaving and walking toward her own car. I allowed my feet to carry me closer to my man. He wasn't smiling, but the look in his eyes was like a magnet, pulling me closer.

"Hi," I greeted as I approached.

He glanced over my head at the building I'd just exited before looking down at me.

"Kayla told me you'd be here."

"I figured." I had concluded as much on my own as soon as I saw him standing here.

"You should've told me. I would've brought you."

I looked back at the building and saw a few women from the group exiting. They waved. I waved back before turning to Damon. "I needed to do this on my own."

Frowning, he began shaking his head. He moved closer, cupping my face with his large hands. "You don't do anything alone. Not anymore. Not when you have me." His tone was so hard and sure, if he hadn't been holding me, I was certain I would've swayed a little bit from swooning.

I wrapped my hands around his wrists as his hands still cupped my face. "Are you sure about that?"

He lowered his forehead to mine. "As a fucking heart attack. I had to work out a few things, but you were always right here." He tapped his chest with his fist. "Both you and Monique."

I swallowed and briefly closed my eyes.

"You two are my world."

My eyes popped open. "It took you the last couple of weeks to come to that conclusion?"

He shook his head. "Nah. It took me the last couple of weeks to make sure anyone who tried to fuck with my world knew better."

I inhaled sharply, taken aback by the hardness of his tone. Then I remembered something.

"Randy abruptly quit Whittaker & Whittaker. We have a new

lawyer for the case he was working. He moved from Williamsport." I paused. "Did you have anything to do with that?"

Damon looked me straight in the eye and said, "Just know that anyone or anything that is a threat to my family will be handled."

"Why?" I asked, unable to stop myself.

"It's not obvious?"

Smiling, I shook my head. "I need to hear the words."

He smirked and placed a short kiss to my lips. "I've been in love before, but never, not once, like this."

"How?"

"With my whole entire soul."

I ducked my head, swooning, before lifting my gaze to meet his again. "I love you, too."

Rising on tiptoes, I brought my hands to his face and pulled his lips to mine. I kissed him with every ounce of emotion I had in me while I ran my fingers through the beard I enjoyed so much.

Damon pulled back, chuckling. "I don't even care that you only want me for my beard."

I giggled. "It does make a great seat."

His eyes widened prior to a huge grin covered his face. "Look what I started."

I laughed before pulling him in for another kiss.

EPILOGUE

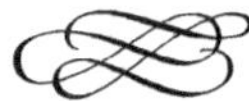

S *ix months later*
Damon

"All right, short stuff, you got the ring, right?"

Monique looked up at me with those same damn eyes as her mother and my actual chest tightened. She blinked just before nodding.

"Yes, I told you a hundred times already," she retorted, shaking her head as if *I* were the child instead of the other way around. I knew I should've told her to calm down or reminded her that she was only ten and not to be speaking to adults like that, but hell, I was wrapped around her pinky finger. I had no qualms admitting it.

"And do you remember your lines?" I questioned as we rounded the corner from my kitchen to my dining room area. I placed the salad I'd prepared at the center of my long, glass table.

"Yes. I am going to say that Mr. Damon and I had a long talk and we mutually decided that it's best for all of us to be a family. Like, under the same roof. And you're going to be my daddy from now on."

I paused, remaining completely still. We'd talked about this night for the last few weeks. I'd even showed Monique the ring I'd picked out for her mother. I was leery of doing so at first, but it turned out

274

she's great at keeping secrets. I'd keep that shit in mind for when she became a teenager. I'd have to watch her like a hawk during those rebellious years. My heart already tensed up just thinking about the shit she might get into. But hearing her call me her dad for the first time had stopped me in my tracks.

"Is that all right, Mr. Damon?" she questioned. I'd let her come up with her own lines. "When you and my mommy get married, you'll be my daddy, right?"

I swallowed and nodded, staring down at her. "That's right, short stuff."

Her smile made my heart leap into my throat. I was so far gone for this little girl and her mother. But I didn't have time to dwell. A few seconds later, there was a knock on my door. I knew it was Sandra. Although I'd given her a key months ago, I gave her grandmother specific instructions to tell her to knock tonight. I wanted to set the mood.

"Okay, it's showtime."

Monique's face brightened and she clapped, pressing down the sides of the fluffy, black and white polka dot dress she'd picked out to wear for the night. "Okay," she stated as she hurried off to the door, doing as we'd practiced.

I stood behind, a few feet away, straightening the edges of the tuxedo jacket I wore. Monique looked back at me and I nodded. She reached for the door handle, turning and pulling it open to reveal a stunning looking Sandra. She was dressed in a cream-colored, sparkly dress that stopped an inch above her knee but extended all of the way to the floor in the back.

I groaned inwardly when I saw that she'd worn her red lipstick for the evening. She thought we had plans to go out to the theater that night.

"Monique?" she questioned, confused, turning her gaze from her daughter up to me.

"Hi, Mommy!" Monique waved.

"What are you doing here?"

As far as Sandra knew, Monique's grandmother had taken her to spend the night after the trio had lunch together this afternoon. However, I'd had her grandmother drop Monique off over here so we could set everything up for the night.

"My great-grandma dropped me off. Mr. Damon and I have a surprise for your birthday."

"You do?" She glanced between us again.

"Yes. Come in." Monique took her mother's hand. "We hope you're not mad, but we won't be going to the theater until tomorrow. You look really pretty, by the way."

"Thank you, baby."

"She's right. You look stunning." Leaning down, I kissed her lips. "Hope you don't mind your outfit will be wasted on just the two of us tonight." I took the overnight bag Sandra had over her shoulder and placed it on the floor by the door.

"Wasted? On my two favorite people in the world? Bite your tongue."

I smiled. "Happy birthday, little one." I handed her a gift wrapped box.

"You're giving me my gift already?"

"That's gift number one. Open it."

Taking the box from my hands, she removed the light purple ribbon that held it closed and peeled it open. She gasped at the sight.

"That's our second timepiece for women. It's named the Sandra."

Her watery eyes moved up to meet mine. Pulling out the white gold band, I studied the face of the watch that was outlined in white diamonds. "These will only be sold as a limited edition. Can't have everyone wearing my woman on their arm."

She gave me a sweet smile. "I love it."

I placed the watch on her delicate wrist, securing it in place.

"Are you hungry, Mommy? We cooked dinner," Monique interjected.

"I am." Sandra nodded. I knew she would be. We had had plans to go out to dinner before the theater. "It smells great in here. What'd you two make?" Sandra asked as Monique led her to the dining area of my condo.

"Roasted duck, mashed sweet potatoes, and salad."

"Mmm, sounds delicious."

"Sit here, Mommy," Monique ordered as she started pulling out her mother's chair.

"I got it, short stuff." I moved behind the chair that faced the glass sliding door and window, giving us a perfect view of the sun that was getting ready to set. I'd timed this night out perfectly.

I then moved behind a second chair and had Monique sit down. I was going to be serving the ladies tonight.

"This looks great," Sandra stated as the food was placed in front of her. She grasped my hand. "Thank you for doing this."

Leaning in, I kissed her lips. "You haven't seen anything yet."

We ate dinner as Monique talked about her plans for the upcoming school week. I told Sandra about Sean and I finally signing with a major watch retailer and that we could expect our timepieces to be selling some time within the next year. She, of course, was more than elated.

"How was it being at the center today?" I questioned, looking across the table at Sandra. She had recently began working part-time with Kayla, Kayla's sisters-in-law, and their mother-in-law to create an organization for women who'd endured some type of abuse or trauma. Sandra had made the bold decision to continue working while going back to school part-time to get her degree in social work, to work as a counselor for young women and girls.

She smiled wide. "It was so great. Every one of us is dedicated to this project. I'm so happy they asked me to be a part of it."

"And speaking of," I began, "here's gift number two." I slid the envelop with her name on it across the table.

Her forehead wrinkled. "What's this?"

"Open it, Mommy!" Monique called.

Sandra looked from her daughter to me.

I nodded.

She opened the envelop and gasped when she pulled out the check. "What's this?"

"A blank check."

"I know but for wh—"

"Your tuition. You can go to school full-time while working at the center." The "center" wasn't the official name of the organization, but the women hadn't come up with one yet so we all just referred to it as "the center" for now.

"Damon, I can't—"

"You can and you will. But that's not all."

Sandra lowered the check and looked between Monique and I. "Now?"

I nodded at Monique. "Yes."

She sprang into action. Monique excused herself, moving down the hall to turn on the specialty lights I'd had set up.

"Don't move," I ordered as I got up and went into the kitchen to retrieve our dessert.

"What?" Sandra questioned as I walked back into the dining area with a slice of tiramisu with a lone lit candle inserted in the middle.

"Present number three," Monique answered at the same time the plug-in candles strategically placed around the room lit up. The candles led all of the way to the door which she opened, revealing the sunset behind us.

"Do you like the sunset, Mommy?" Monique asked.

Sandra nodded. "I do, sweetie." Sandra looked over at me.

"Good," Monique responded. "Mr. Damon and I worked really hard to have everything set up."

"I see that. It's perfect so far."

"And Mr. Damon and I have something to ask you."

"You do?"

Monique nodded, a serious expression covering her precious face. "We want to be a family." She looked up at me and I had to fight to keep it together.

"We are a family, sweetie," Sandra answered.

"Yeah, but we want to be one, for real. Right, Mr. Damon?"

"Yes, short stuff," I responded around the lump that'd formed in my throat.

"Mr. Damon wants to be my daddy and I want him to be my daddy, too, because I love him," she stated, taking my hand in hers.

Oh shit. My damn knees almost buckled. This little girl really was trying to rip my heart out of my chest before I could even get the question out.

"Oh," Sandra responded, looking over at me with watery eyes.

Monique reached out and opened the black, velvet ring box that held the three karat, princess cut diamond ring with a white gold band.

I decided to take over from there. Taking the ring from Monique's hand, I held it out to Sandra as I lowered to one knee.

"Short stuff is right. I want to be her father and I want to be your husband. And give her a sibling or two because I'm deeply in love with the both of you and I can't see my life without the either of you in it. Will you marry me?"

Sandra covered her mouth, eyes watering as she looked between the ring in my hand and my face as I knelt down in front of her.

"Say yes, Mommy!" Monique encouraged excitedly, after nearly a minute of silence.

My heart thundered in my chest. Not out of fear. I knew Sandra just needed a breather to take it all in. I was anxious to hear the word, though. My mind raced on what life would be like after that yes. I needed it to feel complete again. I'd thought my life was whole prior to meeting Sandra—I ran a successful company and was in the midst of starting up another, I had great friends, my family was doing okay, and I had fighting. But ever since this woman and her child entered my life, I realized I had just been bullshitting. All of that other stuff had been the foundation I needed to prepare to be man enough to make this woman my wife and Monique my daughter.

"Yes," she finally answered just above a whisper.

I immediately removed the ring from the box and placed it on her left ring finger before pulling her up from the chair to stand, kissing her with all of the passion and gratitude I had that she'd come into my life. I stopped myself before I got too carried away, however, remembering that Monique was watching us.

"Yay!" she shouted, slamming her body into the both of us, wrapping her arms around us.

I covered Sandra's hand that had went to Monique's back. I silently vowed to protect both of these women with my whole, entire heart.

"Thank you," I whispered.

Smiling, Sandra ran her free hand through my beard.

I grinned. "As soon as this little one goes to bed, I'm going to take you up on that offer," I whispered in her ear. She knew that her hands in my beard turned me on.

Sandra laughed, pulled back, looked me right in the eyes, and said, "Just say the word."

Oh, we were going to have a hell of a night ahead of us.

And a life.

We were going to have one hell of a life ahead of the three of us. I couldn't wait.

ABOUT THE AUTHOR

Looking for updates on future releases? I can be found around the web at the following locations:

FaceBook private group: Tiffany's Passions Between the Pages

Website: TiffanyPattersonWrites.com

FaceBook Page: Author Tiffany Patterson

Email: TiffanyPattersonWrites@gmail.com

More books by Tiffany Patterson

RESCUE FOUR SERIES

Carter's Flame

Non-Series Titles
    This is Where I Sleep
    My Storm
    Miles & Mistletoe
    The Townsend Brothers Series
    Aaron's Patience
    Meant to Be
    For Keeps

www.ingramcontent.com/pod-product-compliance
Lightning Source LLC
Chambersburg PA
CBHW051205220726

48293CB00014B/2033